S0-BJN-983

MRS. WIGGINS

Also by Mary Monroe

The Neighbors Series

One House Over

Over the Fence

Across the Way

The Lonely Heart, Deadly Heart Series

Can You Keep a Secret?

Every Woman's Dream

Never Trust a Stranger

The Devil You Know

The God Series

God Don't Like Ugly

God Still Don't Like Ugly

God Don't Play

God Ain't Blind

God Ain't Through Yet

God Don't Make No Mistakes

The Mama Ruby Series

Mama Ruby

The Upper Room

Lost Daughters

Stand-Alone Titles

Gonna Lay Down My Burdens

Red Light Wives

In Sheep's Clothing

Deliver Me From Evil

She Had It Coming

The Company We Keep

Family of Lies

Bad Blood

Remembrance

Right Beside You

The Gift of Family

"Nightmare in Paradise" in *Borrow Trouble*

Published by Kensington Publishing Corp.

MRS. WIGGINS

MARY MONROE

www.kensingtonbooks.com

This book is a work of fiction. Names, characters, businesses, organizations, places, events, and incidents either are the product of the author's imagination or are used fictitiously. Any resemblance to actual persons, living or dead, events, or locales is entirely coincidental.

To the extent that the image or images on the cover of this book depict a person or persons, such person or persons are merely models, and are not intended to portray any character or characters featured in the book.

DAFINA BOOKS are published by

Kensington Publishing Corp.
119 West 40th Street
New York, NY 10018

All Kensington titles, imprints, and distributed lines are available at special quantity discounts for bulk purchases for sales promotion, premiums, fund-raising, educational, or institutional use. Special book excerpts or customized printings can also be created to fit specific needs. For details, write or phone the office of the Kensington Special Sales Manager: Attn. Special Sales Department. Kensington Publishing Corp, 119 West 40th Street, New York, NY 10018. Phone: 1-800-221-2647.

Library of Congress Card Catalogue Number: 2020945314

ISBN-13: 978-1-4967-3258-3
ISBN-10: 1-4967-3258-8
First Kensington Hardcover Edition: April 2021

ISBN-13: 978-1-4967-3260-6 (e-book)
ISBN-10: 1-4967-3260-X (e-book)

10 9 8 7 6 5 4 3 2 1

Printed in the United States of America

This book is dedicated to my best friend, Maria Felice Sanchez.

Acknowledgments

It is such an honor to be a member of the Kensington Books family.

Esi Sogah is an awesome editor! Thank you, Esi. Thanks to Steven Zacharius, Adam Zacharius, Vida Engstrand, Lauren Jernigan, Michelle Addo, Norma Perez-Hernandez, Robin E. Cook, Susie Russenberger, Darla Freeman, the wonderful crew in the sales department, and everyone else at Kensington for working so hard for me.

Thanks to Lauretta Pierce for maintaining my website.

Thanks to the fabulous book clubs, bookstores, libraries, my readers, and the magazine and radio interviewers for supporting me for so many years.

To my incredible literary agent, Andrew Stuart, thank you for representing me with so much vigor.

Please continue to e-mail me at Authorauthor5409@aol.com and visit my website at www.Marymonroe.org. You can also communicate with me on Facebook at Facebook.com/MaryMonroe and Twitter @MaryMonroeBooks.

Peace and Blessings,

Mary Monroe

PART ONE

1917–1936

Chapter 1

1917

ME AND HUBERT HAD ONLY BEEN MARRIED A LITTLE OVER FOUR hours when he brought up the subject we'd been discussing quite a bit lately.

"Maggie, I can't wait for us to find a man to get you pregnant. Decide what fake name you want to use. Keep it simple so you won't forget and slip up and give him your real name, or a different fake name. Once we become parents, nobody will ever suspect we ain't normal."

My husband sounded so casual; you would have thought he was talking about the weather.

"I'll call myself Louise."

"Good! That's a perfect name. You look more like a Louise than a Maggie anyway."

I rolled my eyes and let out a loud breath. Just the thought of being in bed with a strange man—even one we'd handpicked—turned my stomach.

Hubert stared at me with his eyes narrowed. "Maggie, we will have to keep talking about it if we want our plan to work. You agreed that if we added a baby to the mix, this would look like a real marriage."

I was glad he sounded more serious now. But I was still tired of talking about this subject.

We occupied the bed we'd be sharing in the house he'd been renting for the past six months. He was stretched out on his back with his arms folded across his chest. I was lying on my side, gazing at the side of his face.

It had been fairly warm this afternoon when we got married. But now it was colder than usual for a January night. The wind had got so strong in the last couple of hours, it was rattling the windows and howling like a wolf. We had changed out of our wedding clothes into something warmer. Hubert had on beige flannel long underwear, buttoned all the way up to his neck. I had on a floor-length cotton gown that my mama had made out of flour sacks. My hair was in four plaits, covered in a thick scarf. Hubert had a stocking cap on his head, pulled all the way down over his ears. We both had on wool socks. We didn't look nothing like newlyweds was supposed to look on their wedding night.

"I been thinking. Maybe it won't be necessary for me to get involved with another man. Everybody in this town knows that me and you have been real close friends since we was little kids. They ain't never seen neither one of us on a 'date' with nobody else. So they ain't got no reason not to believe our marriage ain't for real. From now on, we will have to tell a heap of lies and act a certain way in public, and that won't be easy."

Hubert abruptly sat up and glared at me with his eyes blinking and his jaw twitching like he was having a spasm. "Just a doggone minute now! What are you trying to tell me? You having second thoughts *now* after we done come this far?"

"I ain't having 'second thoughts' about our marriage. I'm just making comments. I think getting married is the best thing in the world for messed-up people like you and me. But I'm skittish about us setting up a stranger to get me pregnant. That's the part of this hoax I hate the most. Just the thought of a man touching me that way makes my skin crawl."

"Look, girl. You want children as much as I do, right? As far as I know, the Virgin Mary was the only woman in history who got pregnant without having sex with a man."

"Don't be cute. You didn't have to come up with a example that extreme."

"Well, you know your Bible, so you know it's true."

"Yeah, I know. Praise the Lord. But making a baby is something we can do on our own . . ."

Hubert gasped. "That means we would have to have sex!" The last word shot out of his mouth like a bullet.

"I know what it means. It would be for a good reason, though, and there wouldn't be nary bit of pleasure involved. Shoot! I don't like sex any more than you do, but I'm willing to do it just enough times to make a baby. I'd love to have six or seven kids, but I know I couldn't stand to have that much sex. So I'll settle for just one."

Hubert gazed at me like I'd suddenly sprouted a beard. "Maggie, I ain't never said nothing about not liking sex. Making love is a wonderful activity and I enjoy it."

I let out another loud breath. "All right, then. Let me put it another way. *I* don't like sex, period. You don't like sex with *women.*"

"Exactly."

"You know for sure that's the direction you want to go in from now on, right?"

"I'd give up sex before I did it with a woman."

I reared back and looked at him with my mouth hanging open. "Well! That don't make me feel too good about being a woman. You hurt my feelings."

"Aw, stop pouting," he snapped, waving his hand. "Don't get too upset. You know I didn't mean no harm. I could have said it a better way, though."

"Okay, then. We'll find a man to get me pregnant." I sniffed and sat up. "When do you want to start hunting for one?" I had just turned seventeen a week ago and Hubert was twenty. We'd always been smarter and more mature than some of the other young folks our ages who lived in the same small country town of Lexington, Alabama. Even so, I couldn't believe we'd decided to go through with a fake marriage *and* the far-fetched scheme of me having another man's baby and pretending it was Hubert's. I'd thought it was a boneheaded notion when he first brought it up a week before our wedding.

"We'll start whenever you want to."

"Let's wait at least a couple of weeks, maybe even longer."

"I thought you had a itching to get this over with."

"I still got a itching to get it over with. But after thinking about it a little more, I'd like to get used to being a married woman first."

"That's fine by me, so long as we stick to the plan." Hubert sucked in his breath, stood up, and walked around to my side of the bed and stood in front of me with a serious expression on his face. "It'll have to be a man that lives out of town. Some joker looking for just a good time, not for a woman to get attached to. I'm sure we can find a good one in a town like Hartville."

"Hartville is only one town over. That's too close. A lot of folks here in Lexington got relatives there," I pointed out. "What about Birmingham or Huntsville?"

"Naw. Them places is too far away. That'd be too much wear and tear on that old auto of mine, not to mention a heap of money on gas. We might have to make a whole lot of trips."

A "whole lot of trips" meant a "whole lot of sex." My skin crawled again, and there was a nasty taste in my mouth.

"Setting up strangers for me to go to bed with, just so I can get pregnant, is starting to make me nervous."

"Why? Once the deed is done, you won't never have to see none of them strangers no more. Shoot!"

"Seeing them at all would be bad enough."

Hubert was looking so impatient and frustrated now, I felt guilty. I was starting to feel impatient and frustrated myself.

"Listen to me, Maggie. If you want a child as much as I do, you'll get them thoughts out of your mind and keep them out. We need help to get what we want. It'll be easier than you think. I know every one of them jokers we find would love to get their hands on a sweet young thing like you."

"Do me a favor and stop saying things like that. This is going to be hard enough on me."

"Okay. So, what about us starting in Mobile?"

"Uh-uh. I'd rather start at a bar in a small town like Toxey."

"All right, then. That's where we'll go on the first night."

"What if I can't keep one on the hook long enough to get me pregnant? Then what? If I have to be with a different man every week, I'd probably lose my mind."

"If you do crack up, don't you think you'd enjoy being crazy better if you had a sweet little baby to fuss over?"

I thought about Hubert's question for only a split second before I answered. "Uh-huh. I do believe I would."

Chapter 2

We stayed quiet for the next few moments. By now, the wind was so strong, branches on the pecan tree by the side of our house was hitting against the bedroom window. I had no idea what Hubert was thinking, but there was all kinds of thoughts spinning around in my head. If somebody had told me a few weeks ago that I'd be involved in such a outlandish situation, I would have told them they was crazy. But then again, maybe *me and Hubert* was crazy. Whether we was or not, I wasn't going to back out now. I needed this man, and I didn't want to do nothing to ruin our relationship. He was too important to me.

I knew a lot of people, but I didn't have no close friends. I had never even had a boyfriend or a close girlfriend. I had been living with my mama and daddy all my life, but there had been times when it seemed like I was the only one living in the house. I'd read magazines for hours on end to keep myself occupied and to stay on top of what was going on in the world.

Daddy was the town drunk and Mama was a used-to-be prostitute. She'd turned her life around before I was born, but folks never let her forget what she once was. They never let me forget it neither.

Now that Mama was a more righteous woman, she worked long hours doing everything that the wealthy white ladies didn't want to do for themselves. When she was at home, me and her talked about a lot of different things. Her main focus was me.

She wanted me to have a better life when I grew up, and she didn't think I could make that happen on my own.

"It's a heavy burden, but a woman's purpose is to find a good man and raise a family. That's what God made us for." She'd told me that more than once. And I believed her, even though she didn't seem too happy being married to Daddy.

I never asked a lot of questions. I just listened to my folks, other grown folks, and tried to get through life with as little discomfort as possible. Now that I had a husband, my burden was only half as heavy. With a baby, I wouldn't have no burden at all.

Hubert cleared his throat to get my attention. He rubbed the back of his head and gave me a woeful look. "Maggie, if we lucky, the first man you get with will get the job done." Hubert got a dreamy-eyed look on his face. "I always wanted to be a daddy and I can live with raising another man's baby. It could be ugly as hell, but that wouldn't matter to me. I'd still love him or her." He laughed.

"I'm glad to hear you say that. I'd hate for you to ignore or mistreat the child because of their looks."

"But it's important for us to find a man who favors me. Me and you got medium brown skin. So I doubt if we'd be able to convince anybody that a real light-skinned child or a real dark-skinned one with none of my features is ours. You know how folks talk in this town. They'll start spreading rumors that you fooled around with another man."

I snickered. "Hubert, I will be fooling around with 'another man.' That's the whole idea."

"I know. I'm just talking off the top of my head. But I'm serious about us needing a baby that got some of my features."

"I agree with you on that. And finding such a man shouldn't be too hard. You just a regular-looking colored man. There ain't nothing that stands out about your looks. I done seen quite a few who look enough like you to be your brother."

"I have too. Now that we done got that out of the way, let's move on."

"I just thought of something else we ain't considered. Something real serious."

"What?" Hubert looked frightened as he scooted a few inches away from me.

"Getting involved with a stranger could be risky."

"You think you might stumble into a maniac?"

I shook my head. "No, I wasn't thinking about that. But that is something we need to consider too. My mama told me she got with a man one night that tried to choke her for no reason. After she'd got away from him, she found out that the crazy house had just turned him loose."

"Well, we'll be taking risks, no matter what. There is oodles of crazy folks that ain't never been in the nuthouse. And some of the sane folks running around town do all kinds of crazy stuff."

"You got that right. But I was thinking about something else. It'll be hard for me to find a suitable man, and keep him interested long enough, if I can't tell him my real name and where I live. On top of that, having to find one that looks like you will make that part of the plan even harder."

"If you got some better ideas, I sure would like to hear them."

I sighed. "I ain't got none. It's just that this is really beginning to sound like more trouble than it'd be worth." I had to count to five in my head to keep myself composed so I could stay focused. "We need to have another plan in place. If we don't find the right man in the first few weeks, or if I can't stand to have sex long enough to get pregnant, let's find a couple."

Hubert gave me a confused look and hunched his shoulders. "A couple of what?"

"A man and a woman. We could pay them to have a baby for us. As soon as the woman gets pregnant, I'll start telling folks I'm pregnant. When it comes time for me to start showing, I can strap a pillow on my belly."

"Is that what you call a good idea?" Hubert laughed. But when he seen the serious look on my face, he stopped laughing and gave me a thoughtful look. "Hmmm. Maybe you done hit on something good, sugar. I'm sure there is a man and a woman out there in need of money who would be willing to help us out."

"All we'd need is for one of them to look like one of us. We shouldn't have no trouble finding a couple with a woman who looks like me. Everywhere I go, I see women with round faces, thin lips, and big brown eyes like mine. I get mistook for one of the Martin sisters all the time. And the Hardy girls."

"That's a fact." Hubert squinted as he gave my face the once-over. "I done seen men all over the place that favor me. But the couple would have to be from out of town too. And we couldn't tell them our real names and where we live at neither."

"I know that." My breath suddenly caught in my throat and a sharp pain shot through my chest. "I just thought of something else."

"Another good idea?"

"Not this time. What if we paid a couple to make us a baby and they decided to keep it . . . and the money? Then what?"

Hubert shook his head. "*Anything* could happen, sugar. They could even ask for more money after we done already paid them. Now is the time for us to decide exactly what we want to do. Other than us plucking a child from that colored children's orphan asylum, where your mama and daddy grew up—"

"No! Some are already in their teens. I ain't but seventeen. I ain't about to have somebody a year or two younger than me calling me Mama and giving me a hard time like most teenagers. I want a fresh, newborn baby."

"Okay. We'll stick to our original plan. But if we find a man and you think it's taking too long for him to get you pregnant, then we'll look for a couple. If that don't work, well . . ."

"In the meantime, we can still act like a regular married couple without children. If worse comes to worst, and we ain't got no baby after a year or two, we'll tell folks that a doctor told me, or you, that a physical condition is the reason we don't have no kids."

"Oh, well, if it comes to that, that's what we'll tell everybody. I guess we could still have a decent life with no children," Hubert said with his voice cracking. His last comment caused a lump to swell up in my throat.

"I hope to God it don't come to that," I whimpered. I couldn't even imagine never being a mother. But, if we didn't have no choice, I'd have to live with that. "Now, let's turn in and get some rest. We'll need a lot of that because we're going to be very busy in the next few weeks hunting up a daddy for our baby."

Chapter 3

I NEVER THOUGHT I'D HAVE A HUSBAND IN THE FIRST PLACE. AND the last man in the world I ever thought I'd marry was Hubert Wiggins. Even though we'd been raised in the same part of town, his family and mine was from two different worlds.

Daddy's mama had died giving birth to him, and none of his other relatives had wanted to take him in. Mama told me she was the child of the man who'd raped her mother when her mother was only thirteen, and her family had not wanted to raise a rapist's child or have anything to do with it. Once Mama was born, she never saw or heard from any of her family again, including her mother. That was why my parents had ended up in the asylum orphanage for colored kids. They'd been there at the same time, but had never interacted. When they left the asylum and went out on their own, they met at a bar one night. Their similar backgrounds attracted them to one another. At some point, Daddy dropped Mama for another woman. She couldn't make enough money cleaning houses and picking cotton to pay her rent by herself, so she got caught up in prostitution.

A few years later, Mama and Daddy bumped into each other again, realized they was still in love, and got married. I had never met none of my other blood relatives, so Mama and Daddy was all I had.

Even after they got married, life had been a struggle for

them. They'd lived on the outskirts of town in various shacks with tin roofs, outside toilets, and had to get water from a nearby spring. By the time I came along, they was doing better. Daddy didn't drink as often then, but being unemployed for such long periods of time eventually drove him to drink more. Full-time permanent work was hard to get, but Mama always managed to find enough part-time domestic jobs to keep a roof over our heads and food in our bellies. The house I'd been raised in was bigger and better than the ones Mama and Daddy lived in before. Life was okay for us, until Daddy started drinking almost every day and couldn't get and keep a job for more than a few days. Getting married and moving out was a huge advancement for me.

Hubert's family was as prominent as a colored family could be, and he had relatives all over the place. I used to wish that I had a family as wholesome and upstanding. His daddy, Reverend Leroy Wiggins, was the pastor at the First Baptist Church, and he also worked as a butler for our mayor's brother and his family. My father-in-law had several white friends in high places. They all loved him to death and even looked up to him—something most colored men would never experience. Hubert's mama, Clarice, was one of the most admired ladies in town. Being married to a preacher gave her a lot of status. And she was a hairdresser who could work straightening combs and marcel curlers like magic wands. She could make short brittle hair that looked like cockleburs look almost as heavenly as a halo. Women had been beating a wide path to her house to get their hair done ever since I could remember.

Hubert's uncle Roscoe was one of the two colored undertakers in Lexington. His wife had took off three years ago and their son had died in the military a month later. When Uncle Roscoe got over his grief, he took a shine to Hubert and treated him like gold ever since. He'd promised to leave him the house he'd inherited from his grandmother, so Hubert went out of his way to keep Uncle Roscoe happy. He even helped out at the funeral home because his uncle wanted him to take over the business someday. Other than selling homemade alcohol, being a undertaker was the best job for a colored man. Drinking and dying was two things that was always going to be profitable. We had a few colored doctors and lawyers in Lexington, but they didn't make much money. One of our lawyers made and sold alcohol on the side hisself.

Daddy had a lot of drinking buddies that used to come to the house on a regular basis when I was growing up. I was only seven when his best friend, a bald-headed, mule-faced old man named Mr. Royster, stopped giving me piggyback rides and started riding me.

He'd snuck into my bedroom one night and climbed on top of me while my mama and daddy was in the living room having a good time with some of their friends. From that night on, I had to let him do whatever he wanted to me. Each time he gave me a nickel and told me, "When you get better at it, I'll pay you half a dollar like I used to pay your mama when she was on the job." The few times I had tried to refuse to do what he wanted, he slapped me. He kept me from telling on him by threatening to kill my parents. He knew that I had no family, so if something happened to Mama and Daddy, I'd get sent to the dreaded asylum for colored orphans where they'd been raised.

That was my worst nightmare. I had heard so many stories from them about how bad they'd been treated in that hellhole; it was the last place on earth I wanted to end up. And since I didn't get no allowance from Mama and Daddy, them nickels that Mr. Royster paid me for my "services" (his word, not mine . . .) helped ease the pain of what I was going through with him.

Mr. Royster got me pregnant when I was eleven. When I told him, the first thing out of his mouth was "I got a family and I'm in the church. You ain't about to ruin my good name!" When he finished having his way with me that night, he made me drink the same quinine-and-whiskey concoction that the pregnant prostitutes used to get rid of babies they didn't want to have. Within a hour after I'd drunk that nasty stuff, my stomach cramped up so bad I could barely stand up. I made a beeline for our outside toilet. Other than the cramps, nothing else was happening, so a few minutes later, I wobbled up and stumbled back to my bedroom. I crawled into bed and went to sleep. When I woke up the next morning, there was a big clump of thick blood between my legs. I wasn't pregnant no more.

As soon as I was well, Mr. Royster started visiting my room again. The only difference was, he pulled out of me in time, so I never got pregnant by him again.

Despite what I was going through, I still did the usual things girls my age did. I played with some of the kids who lived close by, but they never let me forget who my parents was.

Me and Hubert first became friends in Sunday school when I was six and he was nine. I loved animals, so when he told me he had a pet squirrel he kept in a box behind his house, I liked spending time with him even more.

When Hubert's parents, or anybody else, low-rated my mama and daddy around me when he was present, he would always say something positive about them. He would say things like, "As long as we keep including your mama in our prayer chains, I know she'll stay on the straight and narrow."

Back then, Hubert lived in a house about half a mile from mine. The colored people who lived closer to his family occupied houses that was nicer and had indoor toilets, so people in my neck of the woods looked up to them. A few jealous folks talked trash about them, but I didn't. I was glad to see colored folks living good.

Hubert would come to my house almost every day after school and on weekends. On my twelfth birthday, I asked him why he didn't like to play ball or go fishing like the other boys we knew. He broke down and cried. And then he confessed, "I ain't normal. I like boys the way girls do."

* * *

When I was growing up, I only knew about one other colored man in Lexington who liked men. He was a older guy who used to work at the slaughterhouse, and he did women's hair on the side. He switched his hips like a woman when he walked, wore face powder, and even had a voice like a woman's. His whole family had disowned him. Other men called him names and beat him up. After somebody busted into his house one night and broke his arm, robbed him, and smeared lipstick all over his face, he finally left town. Nobody ever said what men he had been fooling around with. But whoever they was, they kept their secret hid. I could understand why Hubert wanted to.

I had suspected what he was for a long time, but it had never bothered me. If anything, I was relieved because it meant I'd never have to worry about him pestering me the way Mr. Royster had been doing. A few of the unruly boys I knew had attempted to do the same thing, but none of them had forced me like Mr. Royster.

I could see that Hubert's confession had made him uneasy so I was not about to say nothing that would make him feel worse. "Oh," I mumbled. "You told anybody else besides me?"

His jaw dropped. "What's wrong with you, girl? You the only one. And if you ever tell somebody, I'm as good as dead. You know how these people around here feel about folks like me."

"Then why come you telling me?" I asked.

"Because it's been a burden all my life. I'm tired of keeping such a heavy load inside. I been wanting to talk to somebody about it since I was a little bitty boy. You are the only person I know I can trust, right?"

"Right," I replied with a nod.

Hubert's eyes got wide and his lips formed one of the biggest smiles I'd ever seen on his face. "I declare, I feel better already. I knew I'd feel better if I let it out. Now, if you ever have a deep dark secret, you can tell me and I won't tell nobody."

It was good to know that I wasn't the only kid who had been suffering for years. Right after he stopped talking, I told him about Mr. Royster, including the part about him getting me pregnant. Hubert cussed under his breath.

"Maggie, from now on, we'll look out for one another," he told me before he gave me a quick brotherly hug. "I'm happy when I'm with you, so I guess we'll be friends even after we get grown."

"I sure hope so. There ain't no telling what the future got in store for us."

Chapter 4

After the Christmas Day celebration at church last month, Hubert had escorted me home. We'd laughed about some of the bizarre gifts a few folks had brought for the gift exchange. Then out of nowhere, just as we was walking past the colored cemetery, he asked me to marry him. I laughed at first. "Since when do sissy men get married?"

Hubert laughed too and then he got serious. "In the first place, some 'sissy men' do get married. Some even have kids. But you won't have to worry about having sex with me. The only reason I want to get married is to get my mama and daddy off my back. They done started asking me almost every day when I'm going to get married and settle down. If I had a wife, they wouldn't need to ask me that no more."

"You mean, we would have a pretend marriage?"

"You can call it whatever you want. We will be married in name only and it'll look like I'm as normal as every other man we know. It'll make me feel better about myself."

"That's good for you, Hubert. But what's in it for me?"

"Girl, if you was to marry me, people would stop looking down on you. I got a good job at the turpentine mill, I make extra money helping Uncle Roscoe at the funeral home, my family is about as upstanding as can be, and Uncle Roscoe is going to leave me his house and business in his will. We'll have everything a couple needs to be happily married. Except sex."

I shrugged. "All right. In that case, yeah, I'll marry you. Why not? I'm sure we'll be happy together for the rest of our lives."

We got up the morning after our wedding and went to church like it was any other Sunday. After spending most of the day listening to Pa Wiggins stand at the pulpit and babble on and on, we accompanied him and Ma Wiggins to their house for supper. I felt so blessed to be a member of the Wiggins family; I promised myself and God that I would never take this privilege for granted.

Monday after me and Hubert got off work, we went to the only secondhand store in town and picked out some new clothes for him. He had decided—and I had agreed—that he should stop wearing clothes that didn't look "manly" enough, especially them pastel-colored shirts and pointy-toed shoes. Since he needed a whole new wardrobe, it made more sense to pick up as much as we could secondhand. He wore the same kind of pants most men wore, so we didn't have to worry about getting no new ones. Since we'd save money by buying used clothes, we could afford to get him a pair of brogan boots to wear to work, some clodhoppers just for walking around, and a pair of dress shoes to wear to church.

It didn't take long for my new mother-in-law to take me under her wing. A week after the wedding, Ma Wiggins, came to the house and told me some of the nice things she and I would be doing from now on.

"Hubert told me how much you like blackberries when they are in season. When summer rolls around, whenever I go to pick a mess to make a pie, I'll take you with me," she told me.

"I'd love that, Ma Wiggins."

"There is a lot you can do around the church too, like helping me and the sisters with the bake sales, organize holiday programs, and whatnot. I want everybody to get to know you better real quick. They can enrich your life in so many ways. It's important to my family for you to be happy. We know that as long as you are, you'll make sure my son is happy too."

"You don't have to worry about nothing. Me and Hubert have been friends a long time. I know what it takes to make him happy."

Some of the same folks I had lived around and gone to church with all my life, and who had steered clear of me, immediately started treating me with more respect. Two weeks after my wedding, a popular woman I barely knew, showed up at my house that Saturday and invited me to go shopping and have lunch with her. Her name was Jessie Tucker. She was a cute, petite woman two years older than me. Since she'd never tried to be friends with me before, I was suspicious at first. But she was so sweet and charming, it didn't take me long to relax. We enjoyed each other's company so much that day, I knew it was the beginning of a great friendship.

Jessie lived in a little red-shingled house with her husband, Orville, only a few blocks from me and Hubert. We immediately started spending a lot of our free time together. I'd just been laid off from the housekeeping job I'd had for three months. Jessie helped me get hired at the rinky-dink restaurant where she worked, washing dishes and taking out the garbage. It was a miserable job and the pay was low, but I'd had worse. Last year I'd worked at the clinic emptying bedpans, wiping vomit and other body wastes off the floors and the patients, and disposing of used bandages. Things was so bad for colored folks when it came to work, I never looked a gift horse in the mouth. I was glad to be making a little more money and spending even more time with Jessie.

She had a heap of other friends. So she kept up with all the good gossip and didn't hesitate to share it. Even when it was about me. We had just made the mile-long walk to her house from the restaurant that Wednesday evening in February. We immediately kicked off our shoes, sat down on her front porch steps, and started rubbing our aching feet.

"Uh, Maggie, I don't like to stir up nothing, but I need to tell you something."

I gulped and looked at Jessie with my eyes narrowed.

She sucked in some air before she continued. "I heard that a few folks is already wondering how long it'll be before Hubert gets rid of you."

I inhaled with my mouth gaped open. "Huh? Why would folks be wondering something like that? Me and Hubert are in love," I said firmly.

"That don't mean nothing to them busybodies," Jessie said as she wiggled her toes and kept massaging her foot. "They can't understand what he sees in a girl like you."

"A girl like me? What's that supposed to mean? I ain't ugly and I ain't a bad person."

"Well, your daddy drinks like a big fish and your mama used to sell her body."

"So? I ain't never had no control over nothing my mama and daddy do! Daddy's going to drink, no matter what, but my mama really turned her life around when she got religion. Besides, what Hubert sees in me is nobody's damn business! The next time them busybodies say something about me, you can tell them I said they can all go to the devil." My lips was quivering, and blood was rising to my head. I cleared my throat and gave Jessie a hard look. "What do *you* think about Hubert marrying me?"

"Who, me? Praise the Lord. I think it's the best decision he ever made. Now that I've had time to get to know you, I can tell what a nice person you are. Every time I see Hubert now, he is smiling like he is the happiest man in the world. Before y'all got married, some days I'd see him walking around looking so gloomy, you would have thought somebody died. But since you married him, being around all them dead bodies at his uncle's funeral home don't even seem to bother him no more. A heap of folks been saying the same thing. I just hope that whatever you doing to keep him happy, you keep doing it."

"I will," I said shyly.

Jessie sniffed and leaned closer to me and whispered. "You been smiling a lot more yourself since you got married."

"I'm smiling more because I'm a happily married woman. Hubert is the best thing that ever happened to me."

Jessie scrunched up her lips and gave me a sly look. "Let me guess why. Is it because he . . . uh . . . knows his way around in the bedroom?"

"He ain't no dud when it comes to . . . uh . . . bedroom activity. But even if he was, I'd still be happy with him."

Jessie sighed. "You lucky heifer. I'm jealous. I figured he had something good going on in the bedroom. I seen him lift heavy things like they was as light as a feather, so I know he got a strong back. That's real important under the sheets." Jessie giggled as she nudged my arm with her elbow. "What else he got?"

I was getting annoyed with her questions and comments. But I liked Jessie so much, I was determined to stay on good terms with her. She was the first close female friend I ever had.

"Hubert got everything he needs to make me very happy in the bedroom," I said, almost choking on the words. I cringed when I thought about what gossipmongers like Jessie and all the others we knew would say if they knew what was really going on between me and Hubert behind closed doors. "And, before you ask me, I'll tell you another thing, I make him very happy in the bedroom too."

"I'm so pleased to hear that. I hope he don't take as long to put a bun in your oven as it's taking Orville to put one in mine. We been married a whole year and he been mounting me like a dog almost every night. I still ain't got pregnant. He was born with a bad heart, so maybe some of his other body parts is defective too. But if he don't succeed in his job in the bedroom soon, I might find me somebody who can help me become a mother."

I couldn't believe the smug look on Jessie's face. "You'd cheat on Orville?" I asked.

"Pffftt! You crazy or what? You know I love the Lord too much to stoop that low. My vows mean the world to me. I'm talking about getting help from a hoodoo. I hear that they make potions for just about anything."

"I done heard that too. But I think getting help from a hoodoo ain't just too extreme, it's dangerous. I also heard that if you get on a hoodoo's bad side, they could make your life hell.

I'd hate for you to get involved with any of them folks and end up regretting it. So I hope Orville finally gets his job done. I'll be praying for y'all."

"You right about them hoodoos, Maggie. I don't know what I was thinking. I don't even have enough nerve or money to make a deal with no hoodoo, so you ain't gotta worry about that. In the meantime, I'll just keep praying for God to bless me and Orville with some children. And I'll be praying for you and Hubert too, not that y'all will need it!" Jessie chuckled. "I got a feeling you and him are going to have a wonderful life together."

"Sure enough. And a long one too," I said with my chest puffed out.

Jessie stared at her feet for a few seconds. When she looked back at me, there was tears in her eyes. "Maggie, look at my hands." She held her palms up to my face.

"What's wrong with your hands?"

"Washing dishes in that hot water with that harsh soap done dried them up like prunes." She paused and grabbed my hand. "Yours look just as bad as mine. If our hands look this bad now, there ain't no telling what they'll look like in a few years."

I laughed. "Jessie, your hands and the rest of your body don't look that bad. Mine don't neither. It wouldn't hurt for you to put on a few pounds, but you still got a better-looking body than a lot of women I know. What's your point?"

"Women like us get old before our time. My mama been looking like a hag since she was in her thirties and she just turned fifty. My sisters already starting to decay and they still in their twenties—and they ain't got no husbands in sight. Me and you was lucky enough to latch onto men that cared enough to marry us. But we still can't let ourselves go to pot before our time. If our husbands dump us, it wouldn't be easy to find another one if we don't look good. Orville is real particular. He wants me to be the perfect wife. He done told me a dozen times how many other women he could have married. If me and you take care of ourselves and be good wives, I don't think we'll ever have to worry about losing our men to other women."

I was glad Jessie couldn't read minds. As much as she liked to spread gossip, she was the last person I wanted to know the truth about me and Hubert. Losing him to another *woman* was the last thing I had to worry about. He went out at least once or twice a week to spend time with his boyfriend. I looked her straight in the eyes and said with all the confidence I could conjure up, "My husband would never leave me for another woman."

Chapter 5

After I left Jessie's house a few minutes after six, I went straight home. I was supposed to give Ma Wiggins a call to confirm a few church events I had promised to help her with. She was so long-winded; I knew she'd keep me on the phone for at least a hour. I decided not to place a call to her until after I started cooking the collard greens and fried chicken Hubert had told me he wanted for supper.

While I was washing the greens, I looked at my hands and recalled what Jessie had said about them. I didn't think they looked dried out at all.

On the off chance that me and Hubert didn't stay married, I would never get involved with another man no how. But if we didn't make it, I wondered what my life would be like if I ended up alone. Would I change my mind about men and sex? After I learned more about life, and had more time to think about getting into a fake marriage at such a young age, would I want to stay married to a man like Hubert?

And then I scolded myself out loud, "Maggie, stop being foolish. As long as you and Hubert stick to the plan, there ain't no reason in the world the marriage won't last. So there ain't no chance you'll end up alone." I chuckled and pushed them thoughts to the back of my mind and finished washing my greens.

I couldn't stop thinking about the conversation I'd had with

Jessie earlier, though. It was still on my mind when Hubert got home from work a few minutes after six p.m. After he told me what a busy day he'd had, I followed him to the bedroom, where he sat down on the bed and took off his shoes. I plopped down next to him.

"How was your day, Maggie?"

"I wish it had been better."

Hubert pressed his lips together and gave me a curious look. "Oh? Did something happen at the restaurant? I hope you didn't break a bunch of plates or nothing because we sure can't afford to replace them."

"No, nothing like that. Like every day, I just didn't have much to do when I got home. Look, we been married for over a month. I get bored just sitting around the house after I come home from work waiting for you to get here," I whined.

He hunched his shoulders and gave me a dry look as he unbuttoned his shirt. "You ain't got to sit around waiting for me to come home. Get a hobby."

"Like what?"

"You like to read magazines. Do more of that."

"Come on now. I done read every new magazine I could get my hands on this month. I even rearranged everything in the closets and kitchen cabinets today, just to have something to do."

Hubert rolled his eyes, took off his shirt, and folded it real neat and set it on the nightstand. "Well, you ought to start sewing and crocheting more. That way you can make most of your clothes, like my mama been doing for years."

"I got enough clothes."

"There is a heap of things you could do to occupy yourself with. Go visit somebody, take long walks."

"You ain't helping much," I complained.

Mumbling under his breath, Hubert got up and shuffled over to the closet and got one of the plaid shirts he wore around the house. He put it on and sat back on the bed and started buttoning it, shaking his head as he gazed at me. "Maggie, you have to decide what you want to do. I can't do your thinking for you. If you bored, you have to be the one to fix that." I could tell from his sharp tone that he was getting exasperated, but I didn't care. He was the only one who could help me make my life more enjoyable.

"A baby is the only thing I can think of that would keep me content when you ain't home. I'm so ready to become a mother I don't know what to do."

Hubert suddenly perked up. "I been ready to be a daddy since the day we got married. I was just waiting on you. You said you wanted to get used to the idea of being married first. And I was trying to give you more time to get used to the idea of letting another man pester you. I'm glad you brought this up, though. I was on the verge of doing it myself."

"I'm glad we think alike on that subject. Okay, today is Wednesday. Let's put our plan in motion this weekend. We could get started Friday night after we leave your daddy's Bible study. You still want to start searching for a man in Toxey?"

"I don't care where we start, so long as it ain't in Lexington." Hubert gave me a thoughtful look before he continued. "Uh, maybe we should try Mobile first. We'd probably have better luck there, or some other big town that ain't too far. My Ford already got a lot of miles on it."

"Well, that's because you have to drive so far to be with your boyfriend," I reminded him with a smirk. When I was getting the laundry ready to wash, I'd found four love letters in one of his shirt pockets. Each one was from a *different* man. I didn't care one way or the other. The only thing I did care about was Hubert being happy with me.

"What else can I do? I can't lay up with nobody too close to home."

"Then why are you complaining about all the miles on your car?"

"I ain't complaining, Maggie. I just thought I'd mention it."

"Okay, let's move on. We said we'd try a bar in Toxey first, so let's stick to that."

"All right. That's a good enough choice to begin with, I guess. Toxey got some right handsome men. The last time I was over there, I seen two or three walking down the street that favor me quite a bit."

"That's good to know. Let's just hope that men like them hang out at that bar, and that they take a shine to me."

Chapter 6

I WAS A PROUD CHRISTIAN, BUT IT WASN'T EASY FOR ME TO FOLLOW all the rules. One I didn't like was all the time me and Hubert had to spend in church. I didn't know until after we got married that his mama and daddy had a Bible study session every Friday and that we was expected to attend. "Do we really have to go to Bible study again tonight? We just went last week and the week before. I'm anxious to get to that saloon so we can move forward with our 'manhunt,'" I whined to Hubert on Friday night right after we'd finished eating supper.

"I don't want to go to no Bible study no more than you do. But we can't change our regular routine. If we do, some busybody will get nosy. Before we know it, folks will be thinking that we up to no good."

"Well, us hanging out in bars to find a man to get me pregnant is about as 'up to no good' as you can get," I pointed out. We laughed as we rushed out the door and headed to my in-laws' house.

Several other church members usually joined us, but tonight it was just me and Hubert, his mama and daddy, and his uncle Roscoe. I felt comfortable around them, because they didn't bring up my daddy's drinking or my mama's past as often as some of the other folks we knew.

Me and Hubert sat in rickety wooden chairs in the nicely furnished living room, which was congested with all kinds of odds and ends. There was hymnbooks stacked knee-high in a corner on the floor, extra chairs, a Victrola wind up phonograph, and even a naked dressmaker's mannequin propped up in a corner. Every window in the house was covered with flowered curtains, which my mother-in-law had made herself.

Ma Wiggins and Uncle Roscoe sat next to each other on a loud green couch that had seen better days. Pa Wiggins stood in the middle of the floor with his Bible in one hand and a big white handkerchief in the other. Before he got loose, he waddled his three-hundred-pound body over to the couch and flopped down with a groan. He was already sweating, so before he spoke, he mopped his high cheekbones with the handkerchief and let out a mighty snort.

"Maggie, I know regular Bible studying is all new to you, but you'll get used to it eventually. Keeping your connection to the Lord intact will help you and Hubert keep your marriage intact. According to interpretation of the Word, we living in the last days. So Satan is working overtime. As young newlyweds with no real worldly experience, y'all will face all kinds of temptations," Pa Wiggins warned with his inky black eyes narrowed.

"Sure enough, Maggie," my mother-in-law agreed. "Especially with all the debauchery you grew up around," she added. Her heart-shaped reddish brown face was so scrunched up, it looked like she was in pain. "By the way, how is Jasper and Jeannette doing these days?" She and Uncle Roscoe was both almost as hefty as Pa Wiggins, so the couch was pretty crowded.

I was used to folks asking me that question, so it didn't faze me. But Hubert shifted in his seat and moaned under his breath. I gently tapped his foot with mine and he gave me a sheepish look. It amazed me how much he looked like his parents and uncle. They was good-looking people. If me and Hubert wasn't so squeamish, and made a baby ourselves, it would be real cute.

I cleared my throat and smiled. "My mama and daddy are doing about the same."

"No, they doing a little bit better," Hubert chimed in. "Jasper done cut back on his drinking and Jeannette is going out of her way to stay in faith."

"Is that a fact?" Pa Wiggins said with a surprised expression on his face. "Well, we'd better pray for them tonight too. It's so easy for worldly folks like them to backslide."

"Amen to that. I'm pleased to be here tonight, but can we cut out all the jibber-jabber and get this lesson going? I got a lot to do, so I hope y'all don't mind if we make this a real short meeting," Uncle Roscoe said in his husky voice. He was a year older than Pa Wiggins, and they looked so much alike, they could have passed for twins.

"I don't want to stay too long neither. I don't feel too good," Hubert piped in. "I think I should go home and get in bed before I start feeling worse."

"Hubert, I declare, I'm sorry to hear that," Uncle Roscoe said with a frown. "I was hoping you'd come join me at the mortuary later tonight and help dress them two bodies I need to prepare for funerals next week. I'd just need your help for a hour or two so I can get up out of there in a timely manner. I'm going to visit my lady friend tonight, and she don't like it when I show up real late."

"Tomorrow would be so much better. I'd like to get Hubert home so I can take care of him before he gets any sicker," I blurted out.

"Um, yeah. Tomorrow morning would be better, Uncle Roscoe," Hubert agreed, looking at me from the corner of his eye.

"All right," Uncle Roscoe said. "Be there by ten a.m."

"Humph. Boy, if you feeling that bad, why didn't you keep your tail at home?" Ma Wiggins said in a gruff tone.

"That's what I told him. He didn't want to disappoint y'all," I explained. "The next time he feels sick, we'll stay home."

Before anybody could say another word, my father-in-law cracked open his Bible and started reading, using the same loud tone he used every Sunday when he preached his sermons.

A hour after we'd gone over a few passages so many times I

had memorized each word, we ended the session with a five-minute prayer. After that, me and Hubert couldn't get out the door and into the car fast enough.

I had a black sweater on over a long-sleeved green dress with black dots, buttoned all the way up to my neck. I thought it was pretty tame. But the way my mother-in-law kept glancing at it with a deadpan expression on her face, I had a feeling she didn't think so. If we hadn't had to come to the Bible study tonight, I would have wore one of the tight dresses I'd bought today.

It was pretty dreary outside, and a little chilly. So I was glad I had the sweater.

"It looks like a storm is coming," I said in a shaky tone as Hubert cranked up the motor. It made such a racket, we had to talk loud to hear one another. "Maybe we should wait and go out another night when it don't look so gloomy. Driving in nasty weather ain't no picnic."

"Uh-uh. We said we'd start tonight. If we start coming up with excuses now, that'll set the tone for more. And it'll take even longer for us to get our plan off the ground. If you don't really want to go through with this, you need to say so now and I'll turn this car around right now. Because if you ain't sure—"

"I'm sure. Let's get going. Just be careful driving down all these narrow roads."

About fifteen minutes into the forty-five-minute drive, a great big clumsy deer jumped out of the bushes and stopped in the middle of the road, a few feet in front of us. From the stunned look it gave us, you would have thought we was in the wrong. I was glad Hubert was able to mash on his brakes in time to keep from hitting it. Hubert was shook up pretty bad. Even after the deer left, taking his good old time, we sat in the same spot until Hubert got his bearings back. Because of the delay, the trip took a extra ten minutes. I was so glad when we finally reached our destination.

The joint in Toxey was a shabby little house with tar paper on its roof on a dark country road close to the Mississippi border. The front yard was a huge sand bed. There was a pile of logs, a couple of old car tires, and other debris on the ground by the porch steps.

"This place don't look too hospitable. Since we this close to Mississippi, why don't we keep going and find a man over there? Maybe we'll find a more presentable place than this one," I said.

"Maggie, all we need to care about is what's inside this place. If we don't find nobody suitable in Alabama, then we'll try Mississippi," Hubert replied. He sounded impatient, so I decided not to say nothing else on the subject.

We parked behind a decrepit pickup truck, with no door on the passenger side. The other few vehicles didn't look too much better. One car had cardboard covering every window except the windshield. There was no telling what kind of folks we was going to find inside. I couldn't imagine no man with any class being in a place like this one. I reminded myself that we wasn't searching for a man based on how much class he had. The only thing that mattered was his looks and how willing he was to get close to me.

"I just hope this don't take too long," I whimpered.

"Stop fretting over that, sugar. If we see any men that look like what we want, we'll strike up conversations right off so we can feel each one out."

After I took a few deep breaths, we made our way up the wobbly porch steps to the front door like it was the most natural thing in the world. When we got inside, I was so nervous, my legs was shaking. In less than a minute, a man with a floppy straw hat on his bald head handed us jars filled to the brim with homemade liquor. Then he said something to Hubert in such a low voice I couldn't hear what he said. Hubert nodded, reached in his pocket, and pulled out a bunch of coins and dropped them into the man's hand.

"My, my, my! You a good tipper, so I hope you drink a lot tonight," the man boomed with a wide grin. He danced a jig away from us.

"How much did you tip him?" I asked.

"A quarter."

I gasped. "What's wrong with you? We can't afford to be leaving no quarter tip for two glasses of home brew!" I scolded.

"Baby, this is a special occasion, so let's let our hair down. Leaving big tips for drinks ain't something we'll be doing too often, I hope."

I took a sip from my glass and got a buzz right away. "That's for sure. This stuff I'm drinking now tastes like hell and smells like kerosene. I don't think I'll be able to drink any more tonight after this." I held my breath and took another small sip.

Since we wasn't used to drinking, we was still sipping on the same ones a hour later. The few men I'd seen that looked even a little like Hubert was with other women, or not too friendly.

"The women getting the attention ain't half as good-looking as you. I can't figure out these men up in here. Maybe you should have rubbed more rouge on your cheeks," Hubert whispered.

"Maybe this ain't such a good idea after all," I whispered back.

"Yes, it is. I promise you that when we finish up this deal, you'll be glad we hung in there."

The following Friday I told Hubert's mama and daddy that he wasn't feeling good enough to attend Bible study, and probably wouldn't feel well enough for us to attend church on Sunday. The real reason we couldn't go was because Friday was Hubert's boyfriend's birthday. He wanted to celebrate it with him. They was planning to have a party Friday night and supper on Saturday at a nice restaurant. Hubert planned to sleep over both nights, so he wouldn't make it back to Lexington until Sunday afternoon. My in-laws was disappointed that they wouldn't see us for a few days and told me they'd ask God to abolish whatever was ailing Hubert before he got any sicker.

Hubert was in such a good mood when he got home Sunday evening, we went to a place in Mississippi a couple of hours later. That experience was no better than the first time we went out. We'd been present for almost two hours when a man approached me while Hubert was outside with another guest trying to help him get his car started.

"I'm James," he introduced himself. He had only a slight resemblance to Hubert, but that was enough for me.

"I'm Louise."

"You look so sweet, I'd drink your bathwater. It's a crying shame you ain't available."

I batted my eyes and giggled. "What makes you think I ain't available?"

"Girl, I ain't blind. I seen how close your old shoe been sticking to you ever since y'all walked in." He whirled around and looked at the door for a split second. "I been waiting all this time for him to give you some space. I hope he don't come back and catch me."

"You ain't got to worry about him. He's just a friend I grew up with. He takes me out because I'm between boyfriends right now."

"Oh yeah? He ain't got no woman?"

"Yes, he is a happy married man."

"Humph! He can't be too much of a 'happy married man' if he got to be going out with other women. What's wrong with his wife?"

I took my time answering because I wanted to make sure I said something that made sense. "Ain't nothing wrong with her. She had a baby last night and can barely get out of bed," I explained.

"Is that right? Then he ought to be at home with her."

"He wanted to, but his wife got sick of him hovering over her. It was making her feel worse, so she told him to go out with me. I can't drive, so I couldn't come out by myself."

"Oh. Hmmm. Well, I sure would like to get to know you. And I got a feeling every other man in here feels the same way."

"Well, you available?" I asked with a wink. I was trying to act and sound as loose as some of the fast girls who lived in the low-end neighborhood I'd grown up in. It always seemed to work for them when they was trying to hook a man.

"It all depends. Why?"

"I was just wondering." Before the conversation could continue, Hubert returned to my side. As soon as he put his arm around my shoulder, James rolled his eyes and didn't waste no time easing back into the crowd.

"I'm ready to go, Hubert."

"You sure?"

"Yeah. This ain't working out and I think I know why." I spun around and headed for the door. I waited until we got in the car before I told Hubert what I thought. "You scaring the men away." He gave me a confused look, but I didn't give him time to respond right away. "The man I was talking to when you came up thought you was my man."

"I am!"

"And that's why nobody is approaching me. You should have seen how his eyes lit up when I told him you was just my friend. But when he seen you put your arm around me, he probably thought I was lying about who you was. The next time I'm going out by myself. You can either sit in the car and wait on me or go visit your boyfriend."

Chapter 7

JESSIE SHOWED UP MONDAY MORNING AROUND EIGHT, RIGHT AFTER me and Hubert had finished eating breakfast. Most of the time when she came over this early, it was because she had some gossip that was so hot, she couldn't wait for a decent hour to come tell me. "What's the news today?" I asked as she dropped down into a chair at our kitchen table.

"I just came to see if I could borrow some Epsom salt to soak my feet," she said. "But since I'm here, I guess I should tell y'all that that bowlegged woman in the house next door to me got a mess on her hands . . ."

Sometimes Jessie would take her time getting a complete story out. I figured she enjoyed keeping her listeners in suspense.

"Hubert, you going to eat that last piece of toast?" she asked.

From the impatient look on his face, I could tell he was just as eager to hear the rest of her story as I was.

"Yeah, you can have it," he said, pushing his plate closer to her. He reared back in his chair and squinted at Jessie. "Well, now, sister-girl. What kind of mess do you think your neighbor got?"

She bit off a piece of toast and took her time chewing and swallowing it before she answered. "The word on my block is, she snuck a man into the house yesterday while her husband was at work. Before the man left, they was seen in the window hugging and kissing. Somebody told her husband. I seen him leaving the house this morning with a suitcase. My neighbor ran out the door behind him, begging him not to leave. If he don't come back, she'll have to get two jobs to make all the bills."

"Hmmm. I wonder who could have blabbed on her that quick," I said as I scratched the side of my head. "They got married a couple of weeks after me and Hubert."

"I know. Anybody that starts creeping that soon in their marriage shouldn't have got married in the first place! I don't know who told on her, but I don't feel sorry for her or any woman who is so brazen and hot-natured one man ain't enough for her." Jessie bit off another piece of her toast and gave me a pensive look. "I wouldn't even want a woman like that for a friend. My mama told me and my sisters that that kind of behavior is contagious, and we shouldn't associate with them kind of women. I ain't going to let no hussy ruin my good reputation."

"I feel the same way," I mumbled. "Um, I wish I could sit longer with you, but my mother-in-law is going to do my hair before I go to work." I glanced at the clock on the wall. "I can't be late, because she got other women coming today, so I need to start stepping now."

"I'll drop you off, sugar. I need to take the car to my mechanic and get the oil changed. His place is in the same direction," Hubert said.

Jessie stood up, still nibbling on the toast. "Good. And let Sister Wiggins know I'll be making a appointment soon so she can do something with this briar patch on my head. I'm like you, Maggie. I want to keep myself looking good for my man. I ain't going to give him no reason to want another woman." Jessie tapped Hubert's arm and laughed. Me and him laughed too.

When I got to my in-laws' house twenty minutes later, Ma Wiggins had already lined up her hairdressing tools on the kitchen counter.

"Come on in and let's get going." She set the hot comb onto one of the stove eyes, which was already burning, and wiped her hands on her apron.

I dropped down into the chair she had already placed in front of the stove.

"By the way, you and Hubert must sleep real hard," she commented.

"Huh? Why do you say that?" I crossed my legs and tried to act as nonchalant as I could.

"After supper last night, I called to check and see how Hubert was feeling. It ain't like him to be feeling poorly for so many days."

"Uh . . . we went to bed early and it's hard to hear the telephone ringing in the kitchen." The only reason we had a phone was because my in-laws had paid to have one installed. With Hubert working at the funeral home and being a pastor's son, it was important for folks who had access to a phone to be able to reach him if a emergency came up. I swallowed hard and cleared my throat. I didn't like lying face-to-face to a preacher's wife, but I didn't have no choice. Besides, being deceptive was part of my life, so I had to go with the flow.

"We figured it was either that, or y'all couldn't get to the phone for some reason. It's been a long time since y'all missed Bible study and church in the same week. So I cranked up the car and drove over there to make sure everything was all right." Ma Wiggins paused and reached over my shoulder to get the straightening comb off the stove. I held my breath as I waited for her to speak again. She dragged the straightening comb through a tuft of my hair before she continued. "Did y'all let somebody borrow the car?"

"No, ma'am."

"Then where was it at? It wasn't in the driveway. When I got back home and told Leroy, he said y'all had probably gone out. I told him that didn't make no sense because Hubert still wasn't feeling well."

"Oh yeah! We decided to take a drive."

Ma Wiggins's hand froze in the air. The straightening comb was so close to my face, I could feel the heat. With that and the heat I was generating, it was pretty hot in my space.

"Then I guess Hubert wasn't so sick after all, huh?"

"Um . . . not really. I think it was mostly in his head, because right after we ate supper, he got downright frisky and wanted to get out of the house. Hubert thought a drive and some fresh air out in the country would do him good."

"Uh-huh. Well, if he don't feel better in the next few days, I'll mix up a potion of castor oil and goat's milk for him. I'll make enough for you in case you start feeling poorly too."

"Yes, ma'am."

"We can't have y'all getting sick these days. We want a healthy grandchild." Ma Wiggins nudged my shoulder and laughed. I laughed too. "By the way, Deacon Hawthorne, a new member to our church family, will be joining us at Bible study this coming Friday evening. He ain't as tolerant as me and Leroy, so I'd appreciate it if you and Hubert was to wear your Sunday best, not them vulgar glad rags y'all wore over here the last time. I declare, that dress you had on and them tight britches Hubert wore was downright worldly for humble folks like y'all."

"Okay. I'll make sure we dress right," I mumbled, using a contrite tone so she'd know I was sorry for coming to a Bible study looking "vulgar" and "worldly." I was not looking forward to this coming Friday.

Ma Wiggins called me up Tuesday right after me and Hubert had ate supper. I held my breath, expecting her to tell me not to wear no rouge to Bible study neither.

"Maggie, I hate to disappoint you and Hubert, but we won't be having Bible study at our house on Friday."

"Oh? How come?"

"I just got a call from Deacon Hawthorne. He decided that he'd rather have us come to his house for Bible study Friday evening. His daughter and her husband showed up unexpected today from Selma. They plan on staying until Sunday evening. They got a newborn and two other kids under the age of five. The deacon and his wife don't want to bring a crowd to our tiny house on such short notice. Especially since we ain't even met them yet. But he said it's okay for us to come over there, because there's a lot more room for them kids to romp around. If you and Hubert really want to go with us, I can call him back and ask him if it's okay."

I didn't waste no time replying. "Oh no! That's all right. Y'all go on and enjoy yourselves."

I was scared something else would happen and my in-laws would have the next Bible study at their house anyway, and we wouldn't be able to get out of it without causing some tension. And we wouldn't be able to leave early like the last time. That meant it would be way too late for us to go out afterward. So, instead of waiting for the weekend to resume my "manhunt," I decided to go out again tonight—by myself. I knew that the bars didn't have as many people on a Tuesday as they did on the weekends, but all I needed was one man.

After I got off the phone, I headed to the bedroom to put on the tight red dress I'd bought last week. I wanted to get a early start so I wouldn't have to drive too fast. The place I had decided to go to was in Needham, about twenty miles away. I didn't know any folks over there, so I wasn't worried about running into nobody I knew, especially at a saloon. I was surprised to see Hubert all dressed up, standing in front of the mirror combing his hair.

"Why do you have on your blue suit?" I asked as I strolled over and stood next to him.

"I'm fixing to go out," he said, not looking at me.

"Didn't I tell you that the next time I would go out alone? I was going to one of them other places I've heard about. Daddy used to talk about one across the road from a cane field outside of Needham that he visited before he wrecked that truck he used to own. He stopped going there years ago, so I won't have to worry about running into him there. He said that every Tuesday the ladies get their first drink free. And since I don't care about alcohol no how, not having to pay for it is a good thing. You can stay home and read a magazine or the Bible. I don't plan on staying out long."

"I wasn't planning on going out with you. I figured I'd go out and have a little fun myself."

"Okay. Well, I hope you going somewhere close to Needham, since we can't both use the car if we going in different directions."

Hubert held up his hand. "I took care of that already. You can take the car. My new friend is going to pick me up in a little while in that alley behind the barbecue place down the street."

"Oh? So you got a new boyfriend?"

"Yup. He's a lot more my speed than the last two. Tonight will be our second date and he's anxious to get together again. He's driving all the way over here from Mobile just to pick me up."

"That's good. He sounds real nice."

"Oh, he is! He makes me feel so special."

"I ain't surprised. You are special, Hubert." I loved it when he was in a giddy mood, because it meant he was enjoying his other life. For some reason, I believed that if he had problems in his other relationships, it would have a bad influence on ours.

And I was glad he didn't rub nothing in my face and kept the details vague. He'd mention the town each one lived in, but he never told me their names, what they looked like, or how old they was. He always referred to each one as a "friend." I didn't ask for no more information and I never planned to. I figured that the less I knew about that part of his life, the better off I'd be. Especially after all he'd already done for me so that I'd have a good life. I was happier than I'd ever been.

"Hubert, I hope you have a good time with your friend tonight."

"I will, and I hope you do too."

Chapter 8

When I got to the place in Needham, I was disappointed. It was even shabbier than the other places we'd been to. A sway-backed mule was hitched to a tree in the front yard. A few feet away was a broken-down car propped up on cement blocks. There was a bunch of other old cars and a few trucks parked outside. And it was deep in the woods. Raccoons, possums, and other creatures was roaming all over the place. I parked, took a deep breath, and then I counted to ten before I piled out of the car.

Even though the weather was chilly, the front door was standing wide-open. I had to step over a hound dog sprawled on the floor in the doorway to get inside. A stout man in his fifties greeted me.

"Hello there, new booty," he hollered as he looked me up and down. "You look like something good to eat! I declare, Christmas is coming early this year!"

Blood rushed up to my head so fast, it made me dizzy. I didn't know what to say. While I was trying to come up with a response, another man piped in. "Jackson, get out the way and let the young lady in!" The second man had a loud husky voice. It was coming from the back of the dim room. "Don't be shy, baby. Come back here and let me fix you up with a drink."

There was such a huge crowd I had to plow my way through musty bodies of all shapes and sizes until I reached the back of the room, where there was a table covered with several jars and bottles of alcohol. "Come on now!" The man who was speaking, and motioning me to join him, was in his forties.

When I got close enough, he grabbed my hand and pulled me so close to him, his hot sour breath almost took mine away. "I'm Rufus Stone. This is my place. I know you didn't come up in here all by yourself," he boomed. He grinned and squeezed my hand so hard, it hurt.

"I'm all by myself. I couldn't find nobody to come with me." I had to talk loud so he could hear me over all the noise. There was a man banging on a piano, another one blowing a horn, and folks was laughing, drinking, and dancing up a storm in the middle of the floor.

"Well, you ain't going to be by yourself long," Rufus told me. "What's your name, girl, and what do you want to drink?"

"My name is Louise and I'll drink whatever you got. I heard that every Tuesday the first drink here for ladies is free."

"Baby, a cute little thing like you can drink as much as you want and I ain't going to charge you a plugged nickel any day of the week." Rufus winked and tickled my chin.

Once he handed me a drink, I moved a few feet from him and started looking around the room. I smiled at every man who looked in my direction, hoping that would attract attention quicker. Right off the bat, I seen three different ones who looked like potential fathers for my future child. I finished my drink as fast as I could and wasn't planning on drinking nothing else, until Rufus rushed up to me with his eyes bugged out.

"Girl, you done finished that jar of white lightning already? Humph. I love to see a woman who likes to drink as much as I do. What you want next? I got some home brew that I just made the day before yesterday. It's a heap stronger than what you just drunk."

"If you don't mind, I'd just like a glass of water for now," I said as I handed him the empty glass. The liquor had rushed up to my brain and I was feeling pretty dizzy, which was not a good thing. I needed to have a clear head tonight.

Rufus gasped and done a double take. "Water? Girl, what's

wrong with you? You come up in a saloon with all this good booze, free to you, and all you want is water?" He shook his head and laughed. "If that's all you want, you should have stayed home."

Before I could speak again, another man walked over and stood next to me. "Come on, Rufus. If the lady say she only want some water, give it to her and make sure it's in a clean glass. If you want to charge her for it, put it on my tab," he said.

"Okay, then," Rufus said, shaking his head as he headed toward a door on the other side of the room.

I smiled at the man standing next to me. He looked like a real good candidate and I gave him my full attention. He wasn't fat, old, and he didn't smell like some of the other men in the place. I told myself that having sex with him probably wouldn't be too disgusting.

"I'm Scotty. What's your name, cutie?" he asked. He put his arm around my shoulder and gave me a quick peck on my cheek. This was a good sign that he was interested in more than me having a glass of water.

"Louise," I said shyly.

"It's a pleasure to see somebody as ladylike as you. I noticed that right off." He waved his hand and scanned the room. "It's a real treat after dealing with all the ferocious she-grizzlies that usually come here. You got some real class, sugar."

"Thank you. I'm glad you believe that." I giggled and rolled my eyes. I didn't need to say nothing negative about the other women on the premises. Their rowdy behavior was saying enough. One stout woman in a wrinkled black dress had kicked off her shoes and was dancing by herself, stumbling into the wall and everybody close to her. Her long, brittle hair was pointing in so many different directions, it looked like she had antlers. I overheard a couple of the men talk about what a shame it was to see such a unruly and unkempt woman in public.

One thing I knew from some of the get-togethers my parents had hosted when I was growing up was that men, even drunk ones, only went after obnoxious women when they was the only ones available. There was only a few other women in the house, and they was almost as rowdy as the dancing woman.

"I don't see dainty-looking, well-mannered women like you in this place too often. What brought you here tonight?"

"Um, I just broke up with my husband and I wanted to start moving on with my life right away. I caught him with another woman."

"Oh, so you celebrating?"

"Something like that."

"You came to the right place."

I liked this man. But if there was a chance he had a wife that might show up, I didn't want to risk getting attacked. "You married?" I cooed.

"Almost. I'm getting married next weekend. I decided to have as much fun as possible before then, since I ain't going to cheat on my wife too much if I can help it."

"Is your fiancée here?" My heart was beating about a mile a minute. I looked around the room some more.

"Pffftt! You think I'd be trying to make time with you if my woman was here?" We laughed.

"I had to ask." I giggled again. The door was still open, and the crowd had got bigger. The same dog I had to step over to get in was still in front of the door. He was wide-awake and didn't move a inch, no matter how many folks approached.

I chatted with Scotty for a hour before he invited me to go sit in his car with him so we could have some privacy. I accepted his invitation right away. When we got there, he opened the back door of a dusty Buick and we got in. He seemed surprised that I was so willing.

"Is this all right with you, Louise? I'm out for a good time tonight and I don't see no reason to be beating around the bush."

"I'm out for a good time too, so I don't want to beat about the bush neither," I said as I scooted back and got comfortable. Scotty started kissing me right away. Before I knew it, he was all over me. He slid my dress up, snatched off my undergarments, and started making them same ugly moaning sounds Mr. Royster used to make when he was having his way with me. I squeezed my eyes shut and braced myself. With Scotty already worked up, I figured it would be enough for me to just lay there and holler every now and then. That's exactly what I did for the next ten minutes.

He kept yelling at me, "Shake it up, Louise! Don't make me do all the work!" By the time I decided to get more into it and wiggle and hump a little, it was too late. Scotty was done.

When he rolled off of me, the first thing he said was, "Goddamnit! I declare, you real young, but you old enough to know *something* about making love! I could have got more pleasure humping a tree. Get your lame ass out of my sight!"

Chapter 9

I DIDN'T LIKE THE WAY SCOTTY WAS TALKING TO ME, BUT I DIDN'T SAY nothing about it. If I had told him that he was a clumsy lover, he stank, and made fun of the teeny weeny nub between his legs, I knew that that would have made him madder. What I was already doing was enough to get me killed. I didn't need to provoke him no more. Instead, I apologized. "I'm sorry. I guess I need to practice."

"That's for damn sure! And it won't be with me! Shoot!" he barked.

I put my undergarments back on as fast as I could. He cussed under his breath and shook his head as I scrambled out of his car and skittered to mine a few feet away. I started the motor and shot off like a bat out of hell. I was so preoccupied and rattled I missed the turn to get on the highway. I got lost and roamed around for fifteen minutes before I found the road back to Lexington.

Scotty's mean words rung in my ears all the way back to my house. The house was dark, so I figured Hubert was still with his new boyfriend. One thing I was sure of was that he was having more fun on his "date" than I'd had on mine.

The first thing I did when I got in the house was take off my underpants and throw them in the trash. I didn't want nothing that would remind me of a man who had been such a disappointment. I took a hot bath and turned in for the night.

I laid in the bed, stiff as a plank again, planning my next move. I couldn't go back to the same bar. The thought of running into Scotty again turned my stomach even more than having him on top of me. Now I was more anxious than ever to get this baby-making episode over with. So the best thing I could do was get with the next man as soon as possible.

When Hubert came home about a hour later, I played possum when he got in the bed. "Maggie, you sleep?" He shook my shoulder. "Maggie, wake up. I want to hear how it went tonight."

I still didn't say nothing. He finally left me alone and got in the bed. Within minutes he was snoring like a bull.

I only slept for about three hours. When I woke up at the crack of dawn, Hubert was sitting at the foot of the bed on my side. "Morning, Maggie. I tried to wake you up when I got home last night."

"Um . . . I got carried away and drunk more than I should have. I went into a deep sleep as soon as I got in the bed," I explained.

Hubert gave me a hot look and told me in a stern tone, "Now, you see here, Maggie. If you going to be having more than one drink when you go to them places, you don't need to be driving. You could have caused a wreck and hurt somebody, including yourself. Not to mention the law coming down on you for drunk driving. Lordy, Lordy, Lordy! We'd never be able to live down a scandal like that."

I sat up and looked at him with my mouth hanging open. "What do you want me to do? You want to drive me to them places and wait for me in the car like I suggested?"

"No, I don't want to do that. I ain't about to be sitting around twiddling my thumbs for no telling how long. What I could do is drop you off and pick you up later."

I shook my head. "I don't think that would work. If I go off with somebody, and they don't want to bring me back to the bar, how will you know where to pick me up from?"

Hubert crossed his legs and gave me a pensive look. "You got a point. Well, we can go back to me going out with you."

"No way. Being by myself is the only way this is going to work. Last night I wasn't in that place no time before I made a connection."

"How did it go?" he asked. I was taking so long to answer, he cocked his head to the side and raised his eyebrows. "Well, did you have any luck?"

I gave him a weary look. "It could have been better. He seemed so nice at first, and he looked the part." Just thinking about my episode with Scotty made my stomach churn, so I had to pause and blow out some air. "I didn't make him feel too good and he made sure I knew that."

"Good God! Did he get rough with you?"

"No. But if I hadn't took off when I did, he probably would have." I sighed. "I won't be going back to the place where I met that jackass, and I hope he don't show up at none of the other places I'm going to go to."

"I wouldn't worry about running into him someplace else. If you do, get the hell away from him as soon as you can." Hubert patted my leg and smiled. "Oh, well. We'll move on. There is a place on the outskirts of Mobile that Uncle Roscoe used to go to. He said he stopped going there because it was always too crowded. The men outnumbered the women five to one, so he had a hard time getting a woman to pay much attention to him."

"Maybe I should go there next, huh?"

"If I was you, I would. A girl with your looks would be able to pick and choose in a place like that."

I gave Hubert a confused look. "If you knew about this place all along, how come you just now telling me?"

Hubert rolled his eyes and shot me a hot look. "I mentioned Mobile from the start. You was the one that picked out that place you went to last night."

"Yeah. Now you say this next place got way more men than women?"

"Uh-huh. Five to one. That's what Uncle Roscoe claims. You could probably snag two or three in the same night."

"Good gracious, Hubert!" Just the thought of being around

that many men in the same place made me shiver. I suddenly felt like a lamb being led to slaughter. In a way I was. But so was the man we was planning to use for our own selfish purpose. I felt better when I reminded myself that at the end of the day, everybody involved would get what they wanted. "I don't care if they got a hundred men in that place, I don't think I could stand to be with more than one in the same night."

"I can understand that. The point I'm trying to make is that you'll have more men to pick *that one* from. Get it?"

I rolled my eyes and gave Hubert a impatient look. "I get it. But there is something else I been thinking about. When I do get pregnant, it would be nice to know who the daddy is. If I lay up with a bunch of men around the same time, I'd never know for sure. The other thing is, fooling around with a bunch of different men, I could catch the drip."

Hubert looked confused. "Is that like the clap?"

"That is the clap. From things I done heard my mama talking to her friends about, there is other nasty diseases a person can catch by fooling around with too many different folks."

Hubert shook his head. "This thing is already falling apart. If you was to catch a disease and have to go to the colored clinic to get treated, it wouldn't take no time for that news to get out. Lord knows what folks would think, especially my mama and daddy. Maybe it's time for us to start looking for a couple to have a baby for us."

"Let me go out a few more times before we try that."

Friday night, while Hubert was visiting the family of a man who had passed two days earlier to help arrange his funeral, I decided to go to the place in Mobile his uncle had told him about that had so many men.

This time I didn't wear the red dress I'd wore to that other place. I wore a white low-cut blouse and a black skirt that showed even more of my curvy shape. It was March now, so it was warm enough I didn't need to wear no jacket or even a sweater. I brushed on more rouge than usual, two coats of nut-brown face powder, and maroon-colored lipstick. I wore my hair in a French twist because I thought it made me look more attractive.

Uncle Roscoe hadn't lied. The Mobile saloon had so many men, it made me dizzy. But most of them wasn't even worth looking at. Ten minutes after I'd sashayed through the front door, five different ones approached me. Two was old enough to be my granddaddy, one weighed close to four hundred pounds, and the other two was butt ugly. When a decent-looking young man started giving me the eye, I had some hope. The only problem was, he had come with a woman. When the next possible prospect approached me, it was to ask me where the toilet was. I left right after that.

As I was driving back down the road to go home, I came across another bar less than a mile away. I parked and went in. This place was crowded too. In less than ten minutes, I had my pick of four different men who had started giving me the eye as soon as they spotted me. By now, I was so desperate I was willing to try all four in the same night, even if it meant I'd catch a disease. So long as I got a baby in the process, I didn't care. If I did catch something, I'd get treated at a clinic in another town.

It was only a few minutes past nine p.m., so I had enough time for all four men if I could get up my nerve. Before I could decide which one to disappear with first into a side room, where I'd seen a few other couples go, a fifth man approached me.

"You been pretty busy. This is the first chance I finally got to come check you out tonight," he said. "I'm Randolph."

"I'm Louise." I gave him the biggest smile I could.

I was surprised his eyes was on my face, not my bosom like with the other men who had approached me. "You must not live around here. I ain't never seen you before."

"Um . . . I live on the other side of town with my mama and my stepdaddy. My husband recently broke up with me and I needed a place to live, so I moved back in with them. The only thing is, they are real religious. They don't tolerate me bringing men to their house this soon after I broke up with my husband."

"You ain't got no job?"

Randolph's question caught me completely off guard. I silently prayed he wasn't one of them fancy men looking for a woman to put a few dollars in his pocket. Like the pimps I heard about that lived in the big cities. "Huh? Why?"

He hunched his shoulders. "Well, if you got a job, you ought to be able to have a place of your own, right?"

"Oh, I take whatever work I can get. I'll be cleaning houses until it's time to pick cotton again. I don't make enough to pay rent by myself, though. What about you?"

"I been working as one of the night watchmen at the lumber factory for ten years now. I'm a good mechanic, so I make extra money on the side working on cars. I got a pretty decent house and I'm in good health, so I can't complain about nothing. Except being lonely . . ."

"Yeah. I'm lonely too." This was going pretty good so far. A big fish had just bit my hook. All I had to do was reel him in.

"Louise, would you like to go somewhere quiet so we can talk? I really like you and I'd like to get to know you better."

"Where do you want to go?" I was hoping he wouldn't want to go lay up in his car or stretch out on the ground like I'd heard some folks did. I had already shamed myself enough by having sex with Scotty on the backseat of his car. But the back room in this joint was so busy, as soon as one couple came out, another two people rushed in. It could take hours before we could go in there. And I didn't want to be driving them spooky roads home too late by myself.

"I live about half a mile from here. My truck is right outside, but we can walk if you want to."

"I have a car. I'll follow you."

"Good. And let me tell you right off, I live by myself, so you ain't got to worry about nobody interrupting us."

"You mean like a wife or a girlfriend?"

"My wife took off last month. She's in Nashville with the man she left me for," he said in a sad tone. "I don't miss her, but I miss my kids."

"Oh? How many kids do you have?"

"With my wife, I got three boys and two girls. With the woman I was with before her, I got two more little girls. God willing, I'd like to have a few more children someday."

I had to force myself not to look too eager. But it was hard. Here was a man interested in me, who not only resembled Hubert, but who had already fathered *seven* babies! And it seemed they was all close in age, so that was proof that his baby-making batter was potent. On top of all that in his favor, being at the same job for such a long time, he sounded pretty stable and upstanding. I didn't think I'd have to worry about him getting crazy and doing something violent after I got to his house. I was young and hadn't had much education, but I wasn't stupid. I knew that everything he had told me so far could have been a pack of lies, but I didn't care. All I could focus on was getting pregnant, and I didn't want to pass up any good possibilities.

"Um . . . yeah. I can go to your house, Randolph."

Chapter 10

THE MORE I TALKED TO RANDOLPH WEBB, THE MORE I LIKED HIM. Just from his gentle demeanor and some of the things he said, he seemed like a nice man. I was glad to hear he didn't drink much and didn't go to saloons too often.

He lived in a white house with a flower bed in the front yard and a rocking chair on the wraparound porch. His living-room furniture was old and shabby, but everything was clean and well organized. There was a big box overflowing with toys on the floor and a Bible on his coffee table. Randolph seen me looking at the toy box.

"I like to have things for my children to play with when they come to visit," he said proudly.

"I'm sure they love coming over here," I commented.

"They do, but their mamas don't let them come often enough." He suddenly looked sad. He blinked and tapped the Bible and then he started smiling. "This little Good Book here gets me through a lot of rough times."

"It's got me through some rough times too."

"I make up for not being able to see my kids as often as I want to by spending time with other folks' kids. I teach Sunday school and I organize programs for kids in my neighborhood that don't have nobody giving them the attention they need."

This man was sounding better and better. I couldn't understand why his ex-wife would let him get away. However, I was only hearing his side of the story. Nobody knew better than me that all kinds of things went on behind closed doors. For all I knew, he could have been a good daddy, but a bad husband. That didn't matter to me. I was already comfortable enough to know that I wanted to get closer to him.

Randolph offered me a drink and laughed when all I wanted was water. "Louise, you seem so straitlaced, I'm surprised a girl like you would be in a bar in the first place. I'm even more surprised that you would wear such a low-cut blouse."

"I didn't have nothing else clean to wear," I defended. "Besides, my husband got so mad when we broke up, he cut up most of my clothes." Telling fibs had become second nature to me. There was times when I almost believed my own lies.

"Damn! How did you get mixed up with a jackass like that?"

I dropped my head and let out a long, weary sigh. "He treated me good at first. Then he got nutty. And, like I already told you, I came out tonight because I was lonely. I didn't care where I went, but the only other choice I had was some other joint." We laughed.

"It's a good thing for me tonight that you was lonely, and in the same place I was in." He winked. I winked back.

There was pictures on the wall facing his couch of all his children, but none of the mothers. We flopped down on his lumpy purple couch and he started kissing up and down my neck, right off the bat.

"Listen, I don't know about you, but I'm in the Church. I try not to stray too far from the Word. But . . . I'm only a man."

"I'm in the Church too. The thing is, even Christians can't live by the Word all the time."

"I'm glad to hear you feel that way." We didn't stay on the couch long. Without even asking me, Randolph lifted me up, cradled me in his arms, and hauled off and kissed me. Before I realized what was happening, he carried me out of the room. When we got to his bedroom, he set me down on a small bed with two flat pillows and a plaid quilt. I could tell he was excited. So was I. But for a different reason. I was so eager to get this hanky-panky over with, I got out of my clothes faster than he got out of his.

As pleasant and good-looking as Randolph was, I still didn't like having sex with him. I was pleased that he was gentle and that he had a nice body. His lips was soft and juicy, and the alcohol on his breath wasn't too strong. But I was glad that the session didn't involve too much kissing. That made it easier for me to do more than just lay there like a log and holler like I had done with Scotty.

I wrapped my arms and legs around Randolph and made all the moves I thought he'd like. I must have been a good enough actress because after we finished, he couldn't stop talking about how good I'd made him feel. And he didn't waste no time getting back on top of me—two more times!

"I hope I can see you again soon," he panted when I got out of bed and started putting my clothes back on. He was on his side gawking at me with a dreamy-eyed look on his face. "Maybe we could even go to a nice restaurant or something the next time. I get paid on Friday."

"That would be nice," I said. I was glad he liked me enough to want to be with me again. But I was worried about him getting too attached to me so soon. I'd heard stories about men that went crazy when a woman tried to break off a relationship with them. I was so glad I hadn't told him my real name, or where I lived. "But I don't want to move too fast."

"Move too fast? Girl, we got in the bed within hours after we met. If that ain't moving fast, what is?" He laughed.

"Yeah, we did move fast. But I don't want you to think I'm the kind of woman who jumps into bed with a man at the drop of a hat. You are the first man I've been with since me and my husband broke up."

"I didn't think you was no floozy. But I'm glad to hear that you ain't already got a slew of other men. I'd like to see you again real soon. Friday and Saturday days is the only ones I have off."

"We can get together during the day, if you don't mind."

"I thought you had a job."

"Huh? Oh! I do. But it's only part-time. I have a lot of free time during the day."

"All right. The rest of this week and Sunday, I'll be home all day, each day, until I leave for work in the p.m. I spend Friday and Saturday with my mama and daddy, and my kids when I can get them. That's when we all go to a fishing creek. Sometimes my granddaddy goes with us. If you ever want to join us, you and my mama can keep one another company. She don't like to fish much. But she likes to come and sit on the bank crocheting and going through one of them Sears, Roebuck and Company catalogs women like so much." His stressing that he was a family man made me feel even more comfortable being alone with him. "You can drop by any one of them days if you want to."

"I'll keep all of that in mind, Randolph. Now, I'd better get going."

Randolph reached up and grabbed my arm. "Can you stay just a little longer? I enjoy talking to you."

"Well, not too long. I don't like driving by myself at night."

"You welcome to stay until morning if you want to."

"No, I can't do that." I sat back down, and we chatted for another ten minutes. And then I stood up again. "I really need to go now."

Randolph put on his clothes and walked me to my car. Before I could get in, he pulled me into his arms and kissed me. "I can't wait to get together again, Louise."

"Yeah. Me too," I blurted out. "Bye!" I jumped into the car before he could say another word.

The drive home was so pleasant, I actually hummed one of my favorite spirituals most of the way. When I walked into the house, Hubert was sitting at the kitchen table with a cup and the coffeepot in front of him. He looked at the clock on the wall and then at me. "It's two a.m. I didn't think you'd be out this late," he said, gazing at me from the corner of his eye. "You must have met somebody good."

I dropped down in the chair facing him. "I did. And he was as nice as he could be. What was even better was that he looked more like you than any other man I ever seen." I kicked off my shoes and set my purse on the table.

"Oh? What's his name?"

I widened my eyes. "Why do you need to know his name? I ain't never asked you the names of your boyfriends."

Hubert hunched his shoulders. "I'm just curious. And let's keep things straight. Whoever this man you was with tonight wasn't your 'boyfriend.'"

I blew out a loud breath and rolled my eyes. "His name is Randolph Webb. Happy?"

"You going to see him again?" Hubert took a sip from his coffee cup.

"Yup."

"Hmmm. Then you must have had a really good time. I'm glad to know that. I don't want this to be too hard on you. This Randolph joker might work out just the way we want."

"Don't forget that what I'm doing is just a job to me. My payment will be a baby, I hope." I exhaled. "He was a real lonely man. After . . . we, uh . . . got in the bed and went at it a few times, he wanted me to stay a little longer just so we could talk some more."

Hubert looked surprised, which didn't make no sense. Everything was on the table, so there was nothing to be surprised about. "Oh? What did y'all talk about? I hope you didn't blab enough information so he can track you down."

"Pfffft. Is that why you looking so worried? You don't never have to fear me telling no man too much about myself. Randolph was in a bad way and needed to express hisself to somebody. See, his wife recently left him. He wanted to talk to keep his mind off how painful the breakup was. Most of the talk was about his children. He looked to be in his early thirties, but he already got seven. That was one of the first things I heard from him. He bragged about how proud he is and how he plans to have more children someday. I don't have to tell you how that got my attention. With Randolph having that many kids so close together, at least I know he ain't one of them men that can't make no babies at all. Or is real slow about getting the job done."

"Hmmm. He sounds right fruitful, all right. Let's just hope you are too . . ."

"Hubert, give me a break. Don't be bringing up stuff like that this soon in our plan. It makes me nervous and that could affect my body in ways that could slow down me getting pregnant."

"Well, it's something we need to think about. I know several women in Daddy's congregation that can't have no kids."

"I'm healthy and young, so that shouldn't be no problem. Let's try to stay positive. Things are looking up. Randolph would make a perfect daddy for us. He's everything we want, and then some. Plus, he's a hardworking man with the same Christian values we got. He don't like to go out a lot, and only drinks every now and then. He was only out last night because he was lonely. It's a good thing he ain't no hard-drinking bum with bad blood and other afflictions to pass on to his kids. From what he told me, all of his children are flawless.

"He still wants to see me again and is itching to introduce me to the kids and the rest of his family. Even if it'll be a while before I let him meet my folks."

"He wants to latch onto you like that, after just one night? This Randolph sure sounds desperate."

"Maybe he is. But I doubt if he's half as desperate as you and me."

"Yeah, but what else can we do? We want a baby more than anything. If I could get pregnant, I'd be out there myself every night looking for somebody to knock me up."

"Hubert, I know you would. But . . . well, it's harder than I thought it would be. Sex is such a odd activity. I wonder what was going through God's mind for Him to come up with something so messy and ridiculous looking?" I was glad Hubert laughed when I did. "Anyway, if things don't work out with Randolph, we'll start looking for a couple to have our baby. Hear?"

"I hear you. I don't want you to keep doing something that disgusts you so much."

"Thank you. I'm glad you see things my way." I wobbled up out of my chair, got myself a cup so I could finish what was left of the coffee, and Hubert went to bed.

I didn't want to take a bath and wash away something inside that might ruin my chance of getting pregnant. But I didn't like knowing that I still had Randolph's sweat all over the outside of my body. I went in the bathroom, soaked a bath rag in warm water, and used it to scrub myself here and there. After I splashed some of my two favorite smell-goods on my neck, wrists, and crotch, I got in the bed and started replaying a few of my thoughts.

I was serious about not going after another man if Randolph didn't come through. And it wasn't just because I thought sex was so disgusting. The truth of the matter was, during the last round of sex with Randolph tonight, I had *almost* enjoyed it. That scared the daylights out of me.

Chapter 11

THE FOLLOWING WEEK, I VISITED RANDOLPH EVERY DAY BEFORE I went to my dishwashing job. If Ma Wiggins hadn't paid me a surprise visit Friday morning, I would have visited him for a little while on that day too, hoping I'd catch him before he went fishing with his family.

Even though I was having sex, I was still very happy with my life. I was convinced that things was going to get even better.

There was a few folks who still didn't have much to do with me. But when they heard how happy I was making Hubert, some of the ones who had never spoke to me before was suddenly interested in being my friend. That pleased my mama. Every time I went to visit her and Daddy, or when they came to our house, she greeted me with a hug and a new report about something good somebody had said about me.

When I went to visit them Saturday morning, Mama got downright giddy as soon as I walked through the door. She took the unlit cigarette out of her mouth and dropped it into a empty lard can on the living-room coffee table. Then she steered me toward the kitchen, where she plopped down into a chair in front of the stove. I took a seat at the table.

"Baby, I'm glad you came before I got busy ironing that bushel basket of clothes Mrs. Lockwood just dropped off a little while ago." Mama sniffed and looked me over from head to toe.

Despite her past and the hard life she was living now, she was still a good-looking woman. I was glad I had inherited her delicate features, thick hair, and well-proportioned body.

"I hope you can stay long enough to help me get my ironing done. I still got a few items to finish for Mrs. Kesler that she brought over yesterday. I declare, white women are so lazy, they can't even do their own washing and ironing. I bet they wouldn't last a month without us."

"Be glad that's the case. If they could fend for themselves, do you know how many of us would be out of work?"

We laughed.

"You know I'll help you do your ironing, Mama. It's good practice for me. A lady I did some ironing for one time told me that I need to put better creases in the pant legs if I want her to call me again when her regular girl can't come."

"All you need to do to get them creases sharp is to sprinkle more starch. Don't worry. Now sit down and have some coffee. Your ears must be ringing because me and your daddy was just talking about you."

"Something good, I hope," I said, snickering.

"Pfffft!" She waved her hand and gave me a stern look. "You know us better than that. Everything we say about you is good," she insisted. "Anyway, that light-skinned girl who works at the meat market asked about you the other day. She said she's been hearing so many nice things about you helping out at the church and all. And she said she might ask you to join her quilt-making group to replace one of her friends that moved away."

"I'm glad to hear that, Mama. Mavis Brewster was one of the main ones that gave me such a hard time in school," I said. "I never thought she'd want to be friends with me."

Daddy was slumped in a chair at the kitchen table across from me with a quart-size jar of moonshine in front of him. Gray bristles covered his puffy cheeks and chin. Permanent dark shadows surrounded his bloodshot eyes. It had been so long since I'd seen him clean and sober, sometimes I couldn't tell when he was drunk and when he wasn't.

"Look-a-here, gal. I advise you to worry about Hubert, not

quilt-making with a setting hen like that Mavis. As long as you got him, you don't need no friends," he slurred. A mighty hiccup followed his comments. And then he added, "I'd hate for you to do something to make Hubert mad."

"There ain't nothing wrong with me having more friends," I insisted. "And what makes you think I'd do something to make Hubert mad? We ain't even been married long enough for that to happen," I snapped. "You just need to hush up!" I didn't like to sass my daddy, but I'd been doing it most of my life and he was always too drunk to realize it.

"You keep leaving your husband by hisself and you'll find out," he said with a smirk.

"What do you mean?"

"We came over to your house two evenings last week and he was there by hisself," Daddy replied as he took a long pull from his jar.

"So?"

"He told us you was 'out,' but he didn't know where," Mama added, giving me a suspicious look.

"Oh. Well, some evenings I get bored sitting around the house looking at Hubert and listening to the gramophone. So I go out from time to time by myself. He goes out by hisself sometimes too."

Daddy sat up straighter in his chair and cleared his throat. He suddenly didn't look or sound so drunk anymore. "Hubert is a man. It's natural for us to be footloose. A woman is supposed to be more sedate, like we raised you to be. I don't let your mama roam around like a gypsy by herself."

"Daddy, what makes you think I'm roaming around?"

"Girl, you old enough to know how folks in this town like to run their mouths. I been living a upright life for years and been a faithful wife, but I know from the looks I get in public that they still like to talk bad about me," Mama said with her voice cracking. "One of your neighbors told us they seen you get in the car a mess of times in the last couple of weeks and go off by yourself, all dressed up like you was going to a honky-tonk."

"And you was gone for hours. That's a mighty odd way for a newlywed woman to behave," Daddy threw in.

"What is it y'all trying to say?"

"We ain't 'trying' to say nothing—we saying it! If you want your marriage to work, you need to stay on the straight and narrow," Mama said with a heavy sigh. "If you up to no good with another man already, you need to straighten out and behave lickety-split. Me and your daddy would hate to have our only child lose her husband because she doing something she ought not to be doing. If that was to happen, I guarantee you'll never latch onto another decent man in this town."

"Y'all need to stop worrying about me and Hubert. I love my husband. I would never even look at another man. Y'all should know better. He is the only man I ever been involved with since we was kids, so why would I suddenly get interested in somebody else? The next time one of my neighbors, or any other busybody, mentions what I'm doing, tell them I said to mind their own business," I snapped. "I'll go out as often and stay out as late as I want to, so long as Hubert don't have a problem with it."

"All right, then, Miss Smart-aleck. If you that determined, you better enjoy the freedom you got left. Once them babies start coming, you ain't going to have time to be so footloose and fancy-free." Mama chuckled.

"You're right," I agreed, but only because I didn't want to continue discussing this subject.

Two hours after I left my parents' house, I headed to Randolph's place. He must have seen me coming because he came out on his front porch before I even parked. Within seconds after I turned off the motor, he rushed up to the car and snatched open the door.

"Hi," I said shyly. "I was at loose ends, so I decided to come see you again. I took a chance, because I thought you might be fishing or doing something with your family."

"I did that yesterday. I decided to spend today just relaxing and thinking about you."

"That's nice," I muttered. His comment made me blush.

"I just made a batch of tea cakes. I know you don't like to drink, but if you want something strong, I can run to the market and get some cider," he said as he wrapped his arm around my shoulder.

"Um . . . I hope you ain't got company," I said, looking toward his front door.

"Even if I did, it wouldn't make no difference. Shoot. I'd much rather see my woman." His last sentence made my chest tighten. What he said next did the same thing. "Give me some sugar, sugar!"

I tried to give him a quick peck on his cheek, but he wasn't going for that. Before I knew it, his lips was all over mine and he was grinding against me like a dog in heat.

When we got in the house, he steered me to the couch. "Now, you sit down and make yourself at home. You want some tea cakes now, or do you want to wait until I can go get that cider?"

"You don't need to go get nothing for me. Just the tea cakes and a glass of water would be fine." I sat down and took off the sweater I had on and put it on the couch arm. "I think it's going to rain, so I can't stay long."

Randolph plopped down next to me. "Baby, I know your folks is strict and all, but you are a grown woman now. It's time for you to show them that."

"I already do. I do everything I want to do."

"Everything except have your man come see you at home."

"I will let you do that as soon as enough time has passed since I moved back home. A few weeks or months maybe. By then, my folks will be ready to let me bring other men to their house. See, they was real crazy about my ex, so they need to get used to the idea of me and him not being together no more."

"Okay. In the meantime, how come I can't pick you up at your house and bring you over here? I ain't got to come in, but I'd at least like to see where you live at. If something was to happen to you while you with me, I'd like to know how to reach your folks. Besides that, I don't like for you to do all the driving. And you can at least stay all night on weekends."

Randolph caressed the side of my face. I dropped my head

and heaved out a sigh. "Um . . . I promise that in the next few weeks, I'll let you know where I live at, and I'll stay all night with you sometime on weekends."

"Why you got to wait until then? You know me well enough by now to know that I'm a stand-up man. Don't you want to spend more time with me?"

"I do. And I will. Honest to God." I planned to pray the minute I got home that I'd get pregnant before "the next few weeks" rolled around.

Chapter 12

The only reason I didn't visit Randolph again on Monday was because my period came on. As usual, I was bleeding like a stuck pig. I didn't like to go around too many folks during this time of the month because I felt self-conscious. And, since sex was the only thing I needed from Randolph, it wouldn't have made no sense for me to visit him when I couldn't do nothing. The last two times I went to his house, he'd told me that he didn't expect sex every time I came. That was the kind of man he was. But since I was on a mission, I didn't have time to dillydally. So, when he didn't make a move on me, I made a move on him.

I was glad my period had come, because I didn't want to wonder if the fool I'd been with before Randolph was my baby's daddy. So long as I was messing around with Randolph, I didn't plan on being with any other men. I felt better just knowing that if I got pregnant now, I'd know who the father was.

When my period ended, I paid Randolph a visit every weekday for the next two weeks for a couple of hours before I went to work. The first night I'd gone home with him, and almost enjoyed the sex, must have been a fluke. Because I hadn't enjoyed it since. As unpleasant as it was by now, I still enjoyed his company. He even took me to a couple of restaurants for lunch, and for a walk in the little park near his house.

We ran into some of Randolph's friends one day when we was having lunch at a cafeteria. I got nervous when he introduced me as his girlfriend and even said I was the "best thing that ever happened" to him. One of the friends told me I couldn't have picked a better man. I was beginning to feel bad about using this nice man. He was also getting kind of forward about us taking our relationship to the next level.

"If you still having such a hard time at home trying to please your folks, why don't you move in with me?" he asked on my last visit.

My jaw dropped. "Move in with you?" I gasped. "I can't do that." We had just finished having sex and was cuddling in bed.

"Then how long do you want me to be some backstreet joker you keep hid from everybody? And how long do I have to make my friends and kinfolks wait before I let them meet you?"

I rose up and looked him in his eyes. "There is something I didn't want to mention, but I guess I ain't got no choice now."

Randolph's face suddenly looked like it belonged on a puppy dog. "Please don't tell me you done decided to go back to your husband. The thing is, I'm in love with you, Louise."

I shook my head. "No, I'm never going back to him. Since my marriage didn't work out, I don't want to get too serious again until I feel like I'm ready—no matter how long it takes. Every time I do something in a rush, I end up regretting it."

"Well, you going to have to make up your mind soon. I ain't going to wait forever. I can take only so much. I done told my whole family about you. But since they ain't never met you, they beginning to think I'm making things up. Or that I'm messing around with a woman I'm ashamed of. Do you want to be somebody's child the rest of your life, or somebody's woman?"

"Randolph, I do want to be your woman. Please, just give me a little more time."

"Okay, but it ain't going to be long before I bring this up again."

The pressure he was putting on me was making me more anxious than ever. When my period didn't come in April, when it was supposed to, I got excited. When I got out of the bed the next morning, I was so nauseous, I made it to the toilet just in time to throw up. Hubert was right behind me.

"I told you not to eat all them pig ears last night," he scolded.

I stood up and sniffed. "I don't think the pig ears is making me sick," I said in a raspy tone as I wiped my lips with the back of my hand. "I think I might be coming down with a cold or something."

"Well, let me fix you some tea and then I'll rub you down with liniment before I go to work. That should take care of whatever is ailing you."

When my period still hadn't come a week later, me and Hubert got very excited. Unfortunately, it showed up the very next day. But it was not a ordinary period. Every month I had mild cramps on the first day and a heavy blood flow. This time I didn't have no cramps, the blood flow was real light, and my stomach felt like somebody was in it dancing a jig. Just as I was about to bite into a stick of the bacon Hubert had cooked for breakfast, I felt bitter fluid rising in my throat. I made it to the bathroom just in time again.

Hubert was right behind me. "Baby, you all right?" he asked.

"I ain't never puked when I got my monthly," I said in a hoarse tone. We went back to the kitchen and finished breakfast. Before Hubert left to go to work, I had to run to the bathroom again. This time I got another surprise. My monthly had mysteriously stopped. "Something is really wrong," I mumbled, shuffling back into the kitchen. "Lord, I hope I ain't caught one of them nasty sex diseases." I didn't want to get my hopes up too high and think that I was pregnant. Even if I thought I was, I didn't want to get excited until a doctor confirmed it.

"You want me to drive you to the clinic? If there is something going on, we need to know what it is right away so they can take care of it." There was a worried look on Hubert's face. "They always crowded, so we might have to wait a spell before somebody can see you." Like a lot of hospitals in the South, the one in Lexington and the towns nearby didn't treat colored folks. The colored clinics only had a few doctors and nurses, and they took pretty good care of us, though. But the staff was so overworked, I only went there when I had to.

"No, I don't want you to be late for work. I'll call the restaurant and let them know I won't be coming in today. I can take the streetcar to the clinic this morning."

I called the clinic, but the person I spoke to said they couldn't see me today. If I wanted to see one of the doctors, I had to make a appointment. There was nothing available for four days, and if I didn't come then, I'd have to wait another week. I made the appointment.

After Hubert left for work, I puked some more. I felt pretty bad the rest of the day, so I spent most of my time laying down. By the time he got home, I was feeling much better.

"You think I could be pregnant?" I asked.

"Well, there is a chance, praise the Lord. But let's not jump the gun. Do you feel well enough to go out tonight?"

"Go out where?"

"To visit that Randolph."

I gave Hubert a thoughtful look and then I shook my head. "I'd hate to get sick at his place. Maybe that ain't such a good idea anyhow. He's such a nice man. I really hate that I'm going to have to leave him high and dry when the time comes."

"If he is half as good-natured as you say he is, he won't have no trouble finding another woman, right?"

"Right," I agreed.

"Then don't waste no pity on him."

When I went to the clinic, I was jubilant when the doctor told me what I'd been dying to hear: *I was pregnant!*

I got on the streetcar and went straight to the turpentine mill to give Hubert the good news. But he had just left. It was only two p.m. and he didn't get off until five. My first thought was that he'd gone to be with one of his boyfriends. Then I recalled that he had told me last night that Uncle Roscoe had two bodies at the funeral home. Uncle Roscoe's health had been rapidly failing in the last few months, so he needed all the help he could get nowadays. A grave digger named Jerome West and a aspiring undertaker named Tyrone McElroy worked for him. They helped spruce up the bodies for funerals and burials, but

Uncle Roscoe still depended on Hubert to take care of several other details.

Hubert got his mama to do the women's makeup and dress their hair. His daddy helped the families arrange the kind of service they believed the departed would have picked out for him- or herself. It was important for Hubert to stay involved because he'd be taking over the business someday. As much as I dreaded being near that small dark dreary building across the street from the colored cemetery, I got on another streetcar and went over there anyway.

Uncle Roscoe met me at the front door, which opened into the room where they laid the bodies out for viewing before the funerals. "Hello, Maggie. It's good to see you. What brings you this way today? I know how squeamish being over here makes you." He wore what looked like a black rubber apron with a bib, and a pair of black rubber gloves.

"I need to see Hubert lickety-split. Tell him to get out here now. I got something real important to tell him," I blurted out as I looked around the spooky room. There was a thin, dark-skinned man I didn't know laying in a white coffin dressed in a white suit, a black hat, and white gloves. I could only stand to look at him for a few seconds. "Hubert is here, ain't he?"

"I sent him to Mobile to get some more embalming fluid. I got another body on the way. One of Sister Blaine's daughters died giving birth last night. Thank God the baby made it."

"Oh. Well, I'm sorry to hear about Sister Blaine's daughter. I'll drop by when I can to offer my condolences. Anyway, let Hubert know I came by."

"You want me to have him call you when he gets back?"

"No, that's all right."

"Well, tell me what you need to tell him, and I'll give him the message."

I smiled and shook my head. "Thank you. But this is something I have to tell him myself."

A hour after I got home and stretched out on the couch, Hubert came rushing into the living room with a wild-eyed look on his face. "Maggie! Maggie, what's going on? Uncle Roscoe told me you got something to tell me."

I sat up. "Why don't you have a seat?" I patted the spot next to me, but he just stood in front of me with his eyes bugged out and his mouth hanging open.

"This got anything to do with your visit to the clinic?" he asked.

I nodded. "Congratulations, *Daddy.*"

I didn't have to tell Hubert to sit down again. He stumbled and collapsed down onto the couch in tears. For the next ten minutes, we hugged and cried nonstop.

The same month I found out I was pregnant, President Woodrow Wilson declared war on Germany. Several other foreign countries were already involved in the conflict that had started three years ago. I didn't give it much thought until May. That was when we read in the newspaper that the president had signed a new law that would require all men between the ages of twenty-one and thirty-one to register for military service, starting in June. The newspaper also said that there would be more registrations later to include men in different age brackets. Hubert had recently turned twenty-one, so he had to sign up. Orville was twenty-three, but when he told the draft people about his bad heart and they checked his medical records, him and Jessie didn't have to worry about him having to serve. Me and Hubert prayed day and night that he wouldn't get drafted. We prayed just as often that we'd have a healthy baby.

Chapter 13

1918

I WONDERED WHAT RANDOLPH THOUGHT WHEN I NEVER RETURNED to his house. I felt bad about disappearing from his life without giving him an explanation—which would have been a lie, no matter what it was. The more I thought about how I'd abruptly dropped him, I felt so guilty I was tempted to pay him a quick visit. By this time I had a couple of real good lies ready. I would have told him that I was fixing to move to another state, or that me and my husband was going to get back together. After thinking it through a little more, I decided not to go to his house. For one thing, I didn't want to see his face. It was easier just to end the relationship the way I did. But I thought about him every day the whole time I was pregnant.

I didn't gain much weight and I wasn't sick much after the first month. I worked up until December. And that was only because my in-laws and Hubert made such a fuss about me staying off my feet more. "We went to too much trouble to get this baby. I ain't going to let you do nothing risky enough to cause a miscarriage. If you do, we'd have to start over from scratch," Hubert told me as he waved his finger in my face.

I looked at him like he was crazy. "Start from scratch, my ass. If something happens and I lose this baby, we'll either find somebody to have one for us, or we'll get one of them orphans from the asylum after all," I said sternly. And I meant every word. There was no way I was going to find another stranger to get involved with again. I had been lucky to find one as pleasant as Randolph.

The closer I got to my due date, the more I thought about Randolph. One night I dreamed about him. When I recalled some of the nice things he'd said to me, I really felt bad. I even thought about putting on a disguise and driving past his house for one more glimpse of it and hope to see him sitting on his porch. I didn't think about that for long, though. I knew it was better to forget I ever met him. I thought that would be easy, but it wasn't. The moment I laid eyes on my son, Claude, for the first time in January, two days after my eighteenth birthday, I was ecstatic. He looked like the infant version of Randolph. With such clear evidence staring me in the face, I knew it would be hard to put Randolph completely out of my mind.

My life was complete now and I was going to enjoy it even more. Me and Hubert was so happy, but Hubert's mama and daddy was even happier. My mother-in-law insisted on staying with us the first week, even though Jessie, Mama, and several ladies from church and the neighborhood came to the house every day to see if I needed help with anything.

The first few weeks was so hectic, I could barely catch my breath. I took a leave from work and didn't know when I'd be ready to go back. With all the company we had coming and going, me and Hubert didn't have the privacy we enjoyed so much before I had Claude. Not even at night. When my in-laws didn't insist on making a pallet on the living-room floor and spending the night, Jessie or my mama did. I couldn't wait for all the excitement to die down so I could get used to being a mama, and not have a bunch of other people telling me what I needed to do, and what I didn't need to do.

When a day went by that somebody didn't show up, I was relieved. My relief never lasted long. As soon as I got comfortable, sure enough, somebody would come over before they went to work or after they got off work. Some days they dropped in when they was on their lunch break. Since my mother-in-law did her hairdressing in her kitchen, one day she brought her tools to our house and had her clients meet her there.

The one time I didn't open the door when she knocked yesterday, she sat on our front porch for three hours waiting for me. And all during that time, I had to hide out in the bedroom and keep the doors closed so she couldn't hear Claude crying. After she left, I thought it was safe to go back to the living room. Twenty minutes later, she was back. I had unlocked the front door and cracked it open to let in some fresh air so I couldn't hide from her this time, and I didn't really want to. I felt bad about doing it the other time. I decided to let her fuss over my son as much as she wanted.

My in-laws showed up again this morning at seven. The front door was unlocked, so they came in without knocking and went straight to the kitchen, where I'd put Claude's bassinet. Me and Hubert was still eating breakfast. I had just finished feeding Claude and now he was in his crib passing gas and cooing like a dove.

Ma Wiggins picked Claude up and flopped down in a seat at the table. My father-in-law hovered over her shoulder, grinning like a fool.

"Claude looks exactly the way Hubert did when he was a baby," Ma Wiggins insisted. "Look at them sparkling eyes, that thick curly hair, and that high forehead." She hugged Claude so tight, he squirmed and thrashed around like somebody having a fit.

"This boy is the spitting image of his daddy!" Pa Wiggins hollered. His comment sent a sharp pain through my chest. "Coochee coochee coo." He tickled Claude's chin and then he pulled him out of Ma Wiggins's arms and started hugging him real tight too. Not only did Claude squirm and thrash around some more, he screamed like a banshee.

"Y'all going to spoil the child," Hubert warned.

"What do you expect? We couldn't wait for Hubert to get married and give us a grandchild. If you don't want us to spoil this one too much, I advise y'all to get busy and make another as soon as possible!" My father-in-law laughed.

"I agree," my mother-in-law said, smoothing down the sides of Claude's hair.

My mama and daddy was happy to have a grandchild too, but they didn't come around as often as my in-laws. Daddy was usually too sick from drinking too much, and Mama was too busy working and taking care of him. He had got so bad, she had to get neighbors or somebody else who didn't work to watch him when she had to work outside of the house. That was one of the main reasons she had started taking in more laundry and ironing that she could do at home.

"I hope Jasper and Jeannette spend a lot of time with Claude while he still real young," Ma Wiggins said in a dry tone.

"They will when they can. Mama told me she was going to try and find a house closer to ours to move to so she could come over more often," I replied.

I left Claude with my mother-in-law when I needed to go shopping or when I needed some time to myself. As much as Mama wanted to spend time with him, I was reluctant to leave Claude at her house and I had a good reason. The last time I had, Daddy almost dropped him on his head.

"I don't want to hurt my folks' feelings by not letting them watch Claude too often. But I can't risk him getting hurt over there," I told Hubert. I didn't tell him about Daddy almost dropping Claude. I knew he would have never allowed me to leave him alone with them again, period.

"Your mama would make sure he'd be safe," Hubert said. "We want to keep everybody happy, so what you need to do is take him over there more often. But only when you will be there the whole time."

I didn't have to worry about Claude's safety with my parents for long. When he was eight months old in September, Daddy got sick one Saturday afternoon and couldn't keep no food down for the next two days. He swore he would never drink again. But it was too late. A day later, he had a seizure and died on the way to the clinic.

We found out later that the alcohol had done so much damage to his liver, his doctor wondered why he hadn't died years ago. Or how come he hadn't caught that deadly virus that the newspaper said was going around killing folks all over the world, especially ones in bad health like he was. Before I could get used to having only one parent, Mama caught that virus. She died two months after Daddy. Ten days later, Uncle Roscoe had a massive heart attack and died.

Hubert was now the owner and director of the Wiggins funeral home, but he wanted to keep working part-time at the turpentine mill. He was such a good worker that his boss had put him in charge of supervising the colored workers, which meant a bigger salary. With him bringing in more money, I could take my time going back to work. And I wasn't going back to the restaurant. I planned on doing more housekeeping and laundry because the hours was more flexible, and I could even do ironing at home. That way I could spend more time with my baby.

Uncle Roscoe, bless his sweet generous soul, had left his house to Hubert too. It was all paid for, so having to pay rent was one bill we wouldn't have to worry about no more.

We already knew most of the neighbors in our new neighborhood. They was all hardworking Christians like us. The only problem with our new location was a crabby old man directly across the street from us named Mason Burris. He was so mean, people crossed the street when they seen him sitting on his front porch in his rocking chair, looking like he was mad enough to cuss out the world. He threatened people and spit chewing tobacco on them if they got close enough. His wife was one of the sweetest ladies I knew. She did washing and ironing in her home for a couple of wealthy white families. She was afraid to leave her husband in the house by hisself because he kept his shotgun nearby and wasn't afraid to use it.

The first week we lived in our new residence, Mr. Burris shot out the window in the house next door to his. He didn't like how loud his neighbors was playing their music. Me and Hubert decided we'd avoid having contact with him as much as we could. I didn't spend too much time fretting over Mr. Burris. I had way more important things on my plate.

Losing so many loved ones in such a short period of time had depressed me for quite a spell. I was so sad the next few weeks that when Claude started walking and talking as well as a child twice his age right after he turned a year old, I didn't enjoy them milestones as much as I thought I would.

I had too much to be thankful for, so I eventually bounced back. Before I knew it, I was even happier than before.

Chapter 14

1920

EVEN THOUGH I WAS SURROUNDED WITH LOVED ONES, I STILL missed my parents. As much as it had bothered me to see Daddy falling-down drunk and Mama so tired from working long hours, I would have gave anything in the world to have them back. I regretted not telling them more often how much I loved them.

I'd lost two friends and three neighbors this year too. They'd caught the same virus that had killed Mama. The epidemic got so bad, undertakers was collecting two and three bodies a week. On top of trying to stay healthy, me and Hubert went to more funerals in a month than we used to go to in a year. This tragedy made me appreciate life and the loved ones I had left even more. I took life one day at a time and didn't take nothing for granted.

Now that Claude was the only blood relative I had left, I was going to cater to him more than ever before. Even though he was walking as good as me and Hubert, his feet almost never touched the ground. I kept him in my arms as much as I could. I couldn't stand in the kitchen and cook, or even walk around the house, without holding him on my hip.

When I left the house, even if Hubert was at home, I took Claude with me. I enjoyed all the attention he got from the people I ran into, and he did too. He was such a happy and friendly baby, even people I didn't know couldn't stop themselves from coming up and tickling his chin. I heard "coochee coochee coo" so often, I started hearing it in my sleep.

"Maggie, you need to lighten up on that boy. If you don't stop being so clingy, you might damage his disposition and he'll be as spoiled as a month-old tomato," Hubert warned. Claude was two years old now and more lovable and handsome than ever.

"Aw, hush up! How can I not cling to such a perfect, wonderful, sweet baby boy? This is the only child I'm ever going to have, and if I want to spoil him, I will. And you can't talk! Every time I turn around, you picking him up and bouncing him on your knee." I laughed, but I gave Hubert a hot look too. We was sitting on the couch. Claude was snoozing in his bedroom.

"Yeah, but I don't overdo it. The way you treating him could give the boy some unnatural ideas."

"Your mama and daddy spoiled you! You turned out all right."

"My daddy didn't dote on me too much. But my mama acted almost as giddy as you. I think . . ." Hubert stopped and looked away. "She braided my hair and spoke baby talk to me until I was eight. Them kind of things can confuse a young child and even turn them . . . funny."

"I don't believe that! I'm sure Ma Wiggins ain't the only woman in Lexington that paid so much attention to her baby. Other than that man they ran out of town years ago, we don't know any other 'funny' men, or women, in Lexington."

Hubert blinked and gave me a dry look. "That don't mean there ain't none here. Shoot. Nobody knows about me. For all we know, there could be a dozen more men in Lexington just as funny as I am."

"You could be right. But I still think a child should be showed a lot of love. If he or she turns out funny, it was meant to be."

"Listen to me, Maggie. There ain't nothing wrong with you, or me, showing Claude a lot of love, so long as we don't overdo it. But we don't need to pamper him to death. I do believe that if my mama hadn't done that to me, maybe I wouldn't be what I am today."

What Hubert just said was so disturbing, I could barely catch my breath. "You think your mama spoiling you is the reason you like men now?" I wheezed.

"I don't know for sure if that's what caused it, but it's a damn good guess. You ain't got no idea how disgusted I was with myself when I realized I was . . . unnatural. There was times I couldn't sleep. When I felt real bad, I even thought about . . . doing away with myself."

I reached over and rubbed his back. "Hubert, I'm sorry you been tortured for so long. But I don't think your mama is the reason you turned out the way you did."

"Regardless, I don't want to take a chance on you spoiling Claude to the point of turning him into a sissy. If he ends up like me, I don't know what I'll do."

"You worry too much. Go make yourself some tea and read the Bible. I'm going to pay Jessie a visit. She ain't been feeling so good lately. Claude should stay sleep until I get back, but look in on him every few minutes or so."

Jessie had found out a month ago that she was finally pregnant. I was so happy for her, but at the same time I was sad. Her baby would know who his birth daddy was, mine never would.

Jessie had a normal pregnancy, but she gave birth two weeks early at home to her son, Earl. She was by herself when her water broke at half past noon that day. She didn't have no telephone, so she'd stumbled to the house next door and had her neighbor send her teenage son to the honky-tonk where her footloose husband usually hung out. Nobody had seen Orville.

The same neighbor sent her son to get a midwife who lived two streets over. That was usually what colored women in one-horse towns like ours did instead of going to the clinic. The midwives only charged a dollar for their services, a dollar and a half if it was twins. If the parents didn't have enough money, they gave the midwife a home-cooked meal or something from their garden. It cost three dollars to give birth at the clinic, which was a lot of money for folks scrambling to get by from day to day.

The only bad thing about giving birth at home was that if

something went wrong, the midwives wasn't much help, and the mama and child usually ended up at the clinic anyway. I hadn't wanted to take no chances and end up having problems that could cause my baby to be born afflicted or dead. That was the main reason I'd given birth to Claude at the clinic.

Orville didn't show up until everything was over, eight hours later. I was standing next to the midwife when he shuffled into the bedroom, with a scowl on his dark, mulish face.

"Damn! What's with all this caterwauling? Can't I come home to some peace and quiet?" Orville griped as his wife laid on the bed moaning and groaning.

"You got a baby boy," I told him with my jaw twitching.

"Oh yeah? Humph! It sure took Jessie long enough to do something right. But that ain't no reason for her to be making such a racket! Shoot. Women have babies every day." He snorted and looked from Jessie to the midwife. "Miss Mona Lisa, you do whatever you need to do to get her up on her feet so she can fix me something to eat before I go to bed. I ain't ate nothing since noon."

"I made gumbo yesterday and there's plenty left. I'll go home in a few minutes and get you a bowl," I told Orville.

"Good! The way Jessie is wallowing in the bed, I got a feeling she ain't going to be cooking nothing no time soon. You need to bring me enough of that gumbo so I'll have some for tomorrow. And when you get back, wet a rag and help sop up the mess Jessie done made in this bed."

"Have some respect and compassion, fool! Jessie's still in a lot of pain!" the midwife blasted. Miss Mona Lisa was a middle-aged, sharp-featured woman who didn't take mess off nobody. Not even muscle-bound, strapping brutes like Orville. People was still talking about the time she sliced a man twice her size across his face at a party one night because he'd slapped her for spilling a drink on his new shoes.

"I d-didn't mean n-no harm, Miss Mona Lisa," Orville stammered. "You know I'm just playing."

"Come meet your son," Miss Mona Lisa said gently. She smiled and lifted the blanket off the baby's face.

Orville leaned over, glanced at his son, and grunted. "Humph. I declare, he sure is a puny little rascal. He looks like a naked squirrel."

I couldn't let that comment go without putting in my two cents. "He look just like you," I said with a smirk.

Orville glared at me like he wanted to bite my head off. "Maggie, don't you never stay home?"

"I should be asking you the same question. The neighbors sent for me when they couldn't find you!" I snapped.

"Well, I'm home now, so you can drag your uppity tail back to your own house." Orville paused and squinted at the midwife. "That go for you too, doctor woman."

"I ain't going nowhere until you give me the money y'all owe for my services," she shot back.

"I ain't got no money. I lost my latest job last week, and don't know when I'll be getting another one," Orville whined.

"I got it," I said as I pulled a dollar bill out of my brassiere. I had started doing washing and ironing jobs at home a few times a week, so I had extra spending money. Miss Mona Lisa snatched the dollar out of my hand and stuffed it down in her brassiere. Then I turned to Orville. "You can pay me back whenever you work again."

Most of the married men I knew was upstanding and easy to get along with. That was why I didn't let a jackass like Orville get under my skin. Besides that, he had a real bad heart. If he got too upset, he became so weak he had to go to bed and stay there for days at a time. I didn't want to upset him, because I was scared he would have a heart attack. He'd had one last year, and the year before. When he had to stay in bed, Jessie had to pay somebody to watch him, which meant she had to work more hours at the restaurant and take extra jobs if she could find any. If Orville had to stay in bed for a while during a time when I was not working, I looked after him for free.

"You still want some gumbo, Orville?"

"Yeah. And I hope I don't have to wait too long to get it. I'm hungry." When he stopped griping, he pursed and poked his bottom lip out so far, it looked like a beak.

Unfortunately, Jessie's son had some serious complications from the beginning. Earl had stopped breathing for a few minutes right after his birth, and he had to be fed goat's milk because he couldn't keep none of Jessie's down. He'd been born with skin a walnut shade of brown. A few days later, he was a shade lighter. But by the end of the first week, he was almost as yellow as a lemon. I spent as much time as I could at Jessie's house. She had returned to work and was still paying most of the bills, so I minded Earl for free when I didn't have to work. No matter how much I helped her out, Orville was usually rude to me. This Saturday evening was no different.

"Good gracious. Every time I look around there is puke all over the place. I didn't sign up for no sickly baby," Orville complained, stumbling into the house with a fishing pole in one hand and a bucket of catfish in the other. "Especially one that keep changing colors like a chameleon!" He laughed.

Me and Jessie occupied her living-room couch. She was breast-feeding Earl, who was a month old now. Claude was with my in-laws. I greeted Orville in the most cheerful voice I could manage, but he ignored me and kept on ranting.

"Earl is doing a lot better than he was a couple of weeks ago, praise the Lord," Jessie said in a voice that sounded so weak and tired, I was surprised she was able to speak at all. Then her voice suddenly got loud and angry. "You couldn't wait to have a son, Orville. Now you got one, so be thankful."

"I am glad I got a boy and you better take good care of him. If you don't, I'll have to take him to the clinic to get doctored on. And I might have to take you there for the same reason," Orville warned, wagging his finger in Jessie's face. He laughed, but I had a feeling he was serious.

Chapter 15

1923

THE OLDER CLAUDE GOT, THE MORE I CLUNG TO HIM. THE TIMES when Hubert stayed out all night with one of his friends, I let Claude sleep in the bed with me. I let him have his way most of the time, but when he misbehaved, I gave him a whupping—but never one as harsh as some of the ones I got growing up. I didn't use switches or belts; I used the palm of my hand and baby-tapped his bottom.

"Mama, stop that. You tickling me," he said, laughing, after I chastised him this morning. We had just celebrated his fifth birthday a week ago. "Shoot! All I done was chase Sister Goode's old cat that keeps trampling on your flower bed."

"And you called Sister Goode a witch," I accused.

"But ain't that what she is?" he protested. "She is the only old lady I know with warts on her face and a black cat. And she gives kids mean looks. Just like the witches in that book of fairy tales you gave me for my birthday."

"I don't care how many warts Sister Goode got, or how many mean looks she gives kids. You do not disrespect grown folks. Would you rather wait for your daddy to come home and get a real whupping from him?"

"No, ma'am," Claude mumbled, his voice trembling. "I'll go next door and tell Sister Goode I'm sorry." Not only did he apologize to our neighbor, he ran errands for her for a whole week, and refused to accept the pennies she offered.

It was important to me to raise my child right, because I wanted to be proud of him. Especially after all I'd been through to get him. Every time I went out in public with Claude, folks complimented me on my skills as a mother; he was so polite and behaved well. As much as I wanted to brag about him, I didn't. Especially when I was with Jessie. She hadn't been as lucky as I was.

Jessie's son, Earl, didn't walk until he was two years old and didn't talk until he was three. And he didn't talk that often. Some days he would sit on her couch and stare at the wall for hours at a time, and never say a word. Claude tried to bring him out of his shell by attempting to include him in activities with him and some of the other kids, but it did no good. Orville was so disappointed, he had very little to do with the son he'd wanted for so many years.

When Earl went a whole week without talking, Jessie finally took him to the clinic. That's when she found out he was mentally retarded. I'd gone to the clinic with her. When we got back to her house, she put Earl in his room, and me and her sat down on her living-room couch.

"Orville is going to have a fit when I tell him about Earl," she said with her voice trembling.

"Don't worry about that. He's always going to find something to gripe about," I said as I rubbed her shoulder. "But I hope he don't blame you for Earl's condition."

That was exactly what Orville did. He shuffled in a few minutes later from the sugarcane field where he was working. Jessie didn't give him time to say or do nothing before she blurted out what the doctor had told her. I had never seen a man's face droop and nostrils flare as fast as his did.

"Woman, if you hadn't been gobbling up so much pork when you was pregnant, that boy would be just as normal as I am!" he blasted. His eyes was darting from Jessie to me and back. The way he was glaring at me, you would have thought I'd had something to do with his son's condition too.

"How do you know it was my fault? You got a slow-witted cousin in Birmingham," Jessie shot back.

"Leave my family out of this mess. My cousin got kicked in the head by a mule when he was little and that's what caused his problem!" he yelled, shaking his fist. "Besides, my other son—" Orville stopped and covered his mouth with his hand.

Jessie grunted and froze up so stiff, I was surprised she was still able to move her lips. "So it's true what I been hearing about you and that Simmons woman," she said in a voice that sounded like it was coming from beyond the grave. "You low-down, whorish dog."

Busybodies was always telling Jessie that Orville was fooling around with other women. It was easy to believe he already had a child with another woman. And, knowing him, he probably had more than one.

"Aw, hush up! That's your fault too! If you was doing your job right, I wouldn't have to get no poontang on the side. Shoot. You probably fooling around yourself, so don't you start on me, woman," he growled. "I'll put something on you a doctor can't take off."

"You'd hit me right in front of company?" Jessie said, nodding in my direction.

"'Company'? *Maggie?* Shoot! Maggie ain't nobody," Orville snarled. He was looking at me with so much contempt, I figured he wouldn't hesitate to put something on me a doctor couldn't take off too. "Jessie Lou, you know I been having chest pains off and on all week," he whimpered as he rubbed his chest. "You push me too far, you'll be sorry."

Not only was I scared, I was embarrassed after his "poontang" comment. "Um . . . I'd better get back home so I can make that gumbo I promised Hubert we'd have for supper this evening," I said as I stood up.

"Can you come back later?" Jessie asked with a pleading look in her eyes.

"I think so, but only after me and Hubert and Claude eat." I cleared my throat and looked at Orville. He was standing in the middle of the floor with his hands on his hips. "And as long as it's all right with you, Orville."

The mean look was no longer on his face. He was actually smiling now. "I don't mind so long as you bring me a bowl of your world-beating gumbo. I ain't had a decent meal this month. Uh . . . Maggie, don't pay me no mind when I go off. You know my bark is way worse than my bite."

I gave Orville a dismissive wave. "Pffftt! I never pay much attention to you when you act up."

We laughed.

"Good. I hope you never do. In the meantime, I'm going to go lay down for a spell. I loaded so much sugarcane today, my bosom feels like I swallowed a sword. Wake me up as soon as you get back over here with that gumbo."

I left right away. I didn't want to return, but I was going to, for Jessie's sake. Because if a good meal would help calm Orville down, I was all for it.

Jessie was sitting on her living-room couch rocking Earl when I let myself back in. I had brought a huge bowl of gumbo so there would be enough for Orville, Earl, and Jessie to have more than one helping. "Is Orville still laying down?" I asked, glancing toward the hallway that led to their bedroom.

"Yeah, and I hope he stay in that bed for a while. I ain't in the mood to deal with him right now," she told me as she raked her fingers through Earl's hair.

I set the bowl on the coffee table. Then I plopped down next to Jessie and gently massaged her shoulder. Earl was already asleep, but she was still rocking him. "He's a sweet little boy, Jessie. And keep in mind that every child is a gift from God."

"I know, Maggie. One good thing about Earl being slow is, I won't never have to worry about him growing up and leaving me. He won't never get married or even have a girlfriend, but so long as he's happy, I'm happy." She paused and gave me a pensive look. "Claude ain't even started school yet and these little girls around here love him to death. I pity you when he reaches his teenage years. Before you know it, he'll get married and some other woman will take your place."

Jessie's prediction sent shivers up my spine, but I managed to stay composed. "Ha! I ain't about to let that happen! So long as I continue to treat my baby as good as I been doing since the day he was born, he won't be able to function without me when he gets grown. With or without a wife, *I* will *always* be the most important female in my baby boy's life."

PART TWO

1936–1939

Chapter 16

1936

NOT LONG AFTER GETTING HIS HIGH-SCHOOL DIPLOMA, CLAUDE landed a job at the local sawmill. He helped with the sorting, cutting, and processing of raw logs into timber products. He didn't make much money at first, but me and Hubert gave him a few dollars when he needed it, which was usually to do something special for one of his girlfriends. He was so popular, he never stayed with the same girl more than a few weeks. So I wasn't worried about him getting serious anytime soon. I dreaded the day he would decide to get married. Until then, I was going to let him enjoy his young years. But I planned to keep a hawk's eye on him to make sure he didn't do nothing stupid.

The house we lived in now was about a mile from the one we'd lived in when we got married. I liked it more because the rooms was bigger and there was more closet space for Claude to store all the nice clothes and other things we bought him. The other thing I liked about our house was that it was closer to the funeral home so Hubert could walk to work when he felt like it. And the bus stop was within walking distance. Buses ran every day except Sunday, but service was very limited where colored folks lived.

So many jobs had disappeared because of the slump the economy was in. But there was still a lot of work on the farms when the crops was in season, though. And the white folks that still had money always needed housekeepers, mammies, maintenance men, cooks, and drivers. Most of them jobs didn't pay as much as they used to. With so many banks and other businesses gone, the best jobs that was left went to white folks. With Hubert still working at the turpentine mill, running the funeral home, and me working when somebody hired me, we was doing all right.

We liked to do as much as we could for folks that needed a little help, like some of our neighbors, the church, and Claude. I'd just been laid off a week ago from a farm where I'd helped spread horse manure to fertilize the crops. I'd been going on interviews, but nothing had panned out yet. Before I had time to get too discouraged, things started looking up a few weeks after Claude's high-school graduation.

I happened to be standing in my mother-in-law's kitchen one Monday afternoon the second week in July. I had been raving about the ribs she had served at our family Fourth of July celebration last week.

"Maggie, I can cook some ribs, but can't nobody make as mean a pot of gumbo as you do."

"Thank you, Ma Wiggins. I learned everything I know about cooking from my mama," I said, beaming brighter than the naked lightbulb hanging from her kitchen ceiling.

"I wish Jeannette had lived long enough for me to get to know her better," she said with a heavy sigh.

"I wish she had too." The last thing I wanted to discuss was my mama. As much as I missed her and Daddy, I didn't like to dwell on the past. Especially in front of my mother-in-law's company. A woman named Maxine King, our church secretary, had just flopped her three-hundred-pound self into the metal chair my mother-in-law used when she did somebody's hair. Ma Wiggins had just started to heat up the straightening comb on the stove so she could press Sister King's long gray mane. The smell of hair grease and smoke was so strong, I couldn't even smell the turnip greens and pig feet cooking on the same stove.

Sister King had severe arthritis in her left knee. To ease the pain, she had to elevate her leg when she sat down. I was squatting down, helping her prop her leg up on the footstool Ma Wiggins kept in the broom closet.

"Maggie, how old are you now?" Sister King asked.

Her question caught me completely off guard. This woman had known me all my life and knew that her youngest son and I was the same age. I gave her a puzzled look for a few seconds until I remembered she had started having problems with her memory. I stood up. "I'm thirty-six, ma'am."

"Then you got quite a few good years left to work. Clarice tells me you between jobs again."

"I am. The man I was working for lost his farm to the bank last week."

Sister King turned around to face my mother-in-law.

"What's wrong now?" Ma Wiggins asked. "Is the comb too hot?"

"No, it ain't. Can you get me a pencil and a piece of paper?"

Ma Wiggins left the room and came back with a nub of a pencil and a piece of paper and handed them to Sister King. She didn't say nothing while she was writing. With a crooked smile, she handed the paper to me.

"You call this lady. She's real sweet and a Christian to the bone. Her name is Mrs. Dowler. This her phone number and address. I did her laundry for twenty years. But because of my bad knee, I recently had to quit."

I gazed at the piece of paper for a few moments.

"Girl, don't stand there like a stump. If you want a job, you best call up this lady posthaste before somebody else gets to her first. Everybody I know would love to work for Mrs. Dowler. She is itching to replace me. She called me up last night and begged me to come back and stay on until she got another girl. When I told her I couldn't, she cried."

I looked at the paper again. "Okay. I'll give her a call the minute I get back home."

My mother-in-law nudged my arm with her elbow. "Shake a leg, girl. Go in yonder to the living room and use the phone on the end table. You need to call up this lady right now," she insisted.

I skittered into the living room and dialed Mrs. Dowler's number. She picked up on the first ring. "Blood of Jesus" was how she greeted me in a tone too stern for a lady who was supposed to be "a Christian to the bone."

"Hello, can I speak to Mrs. Dowler, please?"

"This is she."

"I'm calling about the laundry job. My name is Maggie Wiggins."

"I see." She sucked on her teeth for a few seconds. "May I ask how you heard about the job?" She didn't sound like no lady itching to hire somebody.

"Mrs. Maxine King just told me—"

Mrs. Dowler cut me off and the tone of her voice was so warm and pleasant now, it sounded like I was talking to a different lady. "Holy moly! Maxine gave you my number? Bless her! Can you be here in an hour?" She was talking so fast, her words nearly ran together like one long sentence.

"Well, I guess I could. I did laundry for a few other ladies and I can bring their names and phone numbers in case you want to call them up and check—"

Mrs. Dowler cut me off again—so abruptly, my lips froze. "Pshaw! I don't have time for that. I need somebody to get over here lickety-split. If Maxine referred you, that's all I need to know. Can you get here in an hour or not?"

"Yes, ma'am. I believe I can," I mumbled. "Mrs. King gave me your address."

I left right after I hung up the telephone. I didn't even bother to go home and change clothes. I went straight to the bus stop and hopped on the bus that would carry me to Mrs. Dowler's part of town.

Chapter 17

THE ECONOMY WAS STILL PRETTY BAD IN 1936, AND PRESIDENT Roosevelt had started calling it the Great Depression. But some white folks seemed to be doing all right. Mrs. Dowler was one of them lucky folks. She lived in a big white house with the neatest lawn I ever seen. There was a great big weeping willow tree in her front yard and a shiny black Ford in the driveway. I'd worked for several well-to-do ladies over the years. But nary one lived on as grand a scale as Mrs. Dowler. Most of the houses in her neighborhood was two stories high, a few was three. You could tell where the people who had lost their money used to live. Them houses had signs on the front lawn with the name of the bank that had took them over.

Just as I was about to knock on the back door, it swung open. A elderly white lady stood in the doorway with a blank expression on her face. She had on a blue bibbed apron that had so much starch in it, it probably could have stood up by itself. I didn't know if she was a maid or what. And with times being so hard, a lot of white women who had been living like queens was doing domestic work now. After gawking at me for several moments and not saying nothing, she finally said, "Yes."

"Hello, ma'am. Good afternoon. Um . . . I got a appointment to see Mrs. Dowler. I'm here about the laundry job."

"I'm Mrs. Fern Dowler. You must be Maggie Wiggins." The face powder Mrs. Dowler had smeared on her face from her forehead to the top of her neck, two or three layers deep, didn't hide none of the lines on her face. And her skin was so stiff, it looked like it had as much starch in it as her apron.

"Uh-huh. You told me to come see you right now."

There was a tight smile on her face now. "Are you always this punctual?"

"Yes, ma'am."

"Good! I do not tolerate tardiness," she gushed. "Come on in, honey child."

Mrs. Dowler waved me in and led me to the biggest living room I had ever been in. She motioned for me to sit down on a dark blue settee, facing the long white couch she plopped down on. There was great big lamps on each end table and on another table sitting in front of a side window. Next to that window was a large bookcase with all five shelves filled to the gills with books. I had expected to see a woman in her fifties or sixties. Mrs. Dowler was in her eighties, but was as spry and healthy-looking as a woman half her age. Her fluffy white hair reminded me of cotton. Even with the wrinkles, I could see that she was still a good-looking woman. She had wide brown eyes and rosy cheeks, and a nice firm-looking body for a woman her age.

"I'll need you to be available all day, every Monday and Tuesday. Some Mondays I'll have great big loads for you to wash, other Mondays I may have only a few pieces. On Tuesdays I'd liked some of my things starched and ironed, especially my hankies, bloomers, and most of my Sunday-go-to-meeting frocks." She was speaking in such a loud tone of voice now, I wondered if she was hard of hearing, or thought I was. "You think you can handle that?"

"Yes, ma'am," I replied. "I've done that for several other ladies, and they was real pleased with my work. I can give you their telephone numbers if you want to give them a call."

"Gnat butter!" Mrs. Dowler screwed up her face and threw her hands up in the air. "References don't mean anything to me. I've had workers with great references who did lousy work. And it took me only a few days to realize I'd made a mistake. But if

Maxine King sent you, you're worth a shot. If you don't suit me the first few days, I'll send you on your way. Is that fair enough?"

"It is. Um . . . I'm a pretty good cook too. Everybody tells me that I make a mean pot of gumbo." I wasn't the best cook in the mix, but when it came to making gumbo, I didn't have no competition. Neighbors beat a path to my house when they heard I was cooking gumbo.

"I don't need you to cook. I'm a whiz in the kitchen and I like to do most of my own cooking. But since I have such a busy life, I have a girl come in three days a week to throw a few things together. You'll probably never meet her, or the man who takes care of my yard and keeps my car clean and running smoothly. Now, next." She lifted her hand and wagged a finger in my direction. "I may ask you to tend to my garden yonder in the backyard. I've always had problems with pests. Are you scared of weevils and lizards?"

"No, ma'am. I used to catch them to play with when I was a little girl."

Mrs. Dowler looked at me like I'd just took off all my clothes. "Eeyow! I hope that doesn't mean you'll have a problem helping me get rid of those little devils. They've been stuck in my craw since I was a little girl. I will ask you to sprinkle arsenic in my garden on an as-needed basis."

"Yes, ma'am."

"By the way, I do my own driving. I never liked having a chauffeur hauling me from here to there so I got rid of him right after my husband passed. I feel as free as a bird when I'm behind the wheel! I like to take frequent jaunts to clear my head and get some fresh air. I do my own shopping. I have a lot of friends and a very active social life, so I may leave you on your own for hours on end some days. But washing and ironing are two things I can't tolerate." Mrs. Dowler lowered her voice and leaned forward. "It's because my mama made me do so much of it when she took to her bed after her stroke. I was the oldest girl in the family, so naturally I got stuck with chores Mama could no longer do. We had several servants, but nary one could do the washing and ironing well enough to please my mama." Mrs. Dowler leaned back in her seat and blinked. And then she asked a few questions about my family and mundane things about my background. "Maggie, I can tell that you are a very intelligent and charming gal. Just from what you've told me, I can also tell that you and I will get along just fine." I had barely been able to get a few sentences into the conversation. But I'd told Mrs. Dowler all I wanted her to know for now.

We spent the next two hours sitting in her living room. My butt got numb from sitting in the same spot so long, but I didn't want to offend her so I didn't say nothing. I just kept smiling and listening. She jibber-jabbered about world affairs, relatives she couldn't stand, and the price of everything from meat to rouge. When she finally took me to the kitchen, I was so relieved I could have hugged her.

Standing in a corner in the back of the room was a large wringer washing machine. On a big round table next to a huge refrigerator was a box of detergent, and a bushel basket filled to the brim with dirty laundry. Before I could do anything, Mrs. Dowler started telling me about an upcoming tea party she was going to attend. She went on for ten minutes. "Now, let's stop lollygagging so you can get to work. You'll find the washboard and bar soap in the pantry by the side of the stove. That's what you'll use to wash certain items, like my hankies and bloomers. Any questions?"

"Um, what about my pay?"

"What about it?"

"You didn't tell me how much I'd be making."

"Oh yeah. Well, when I get people I like, I go out of my way to keep them happy, so they won't want to take off and leave me in a lurch. Whatever you made on your last job, I'll pay you double. I'll get some paper so I can put it in writing."

"My goodness! Thank you, ma'am!" Double pay! I liked this lady already.

"The only reasonable thing to do with money is to spend it while you can. My daddy was very rich. Would you like to know how much money he left behind when he died?"

"Yes, ma'am. If you don't mind telling me."

"All of it. The point I'm trying to make is, I can't take any money with me when I pass on. And, at my age, I have everything I need and then some. I'd rather see my money do some good. I own several properties in Lexington. The rent I collect goes straight to charity, one hundred percent."

"That's very nice of you, Mrs. Dowler."

"Well, let's move on." She folded her arms and nodded at the basket on the table with the clothes waiting to be washed. "I want you to get this first load started. Then join me in the living room so we can chitchat a little more."

"You want me to start working right now?"

Mrs. Dowler gasped. "Of course, I do. Why else do you think I was so eager to get you over here today? Nothing has been washed or ironed since Maxine had to abruptly quit, so you got your work cut out for you."

"Oh, that's all right. I don't mind working hard," I chirped.

"Now, you use all the elbow grease necessary to get everything showroom clean. Is that clear?"

"That's real clear, ma'am."

Mrs. Dowler loved to talk so much, after I finished washing and hanging everything on the clothesline in her backyard, we spent another hour in her living room. She repeated some of the same stories two or three times, but that didn't bother me.

We sipped tea, munched on tea cakes, I nodded when necessary, and howled with laughter each time she said something funny (even if it wasn't funny). I wanted to make a good enough impression because this job sounded like one I could really sink my teeth into. Some of her stories was funny, some was sad. But each one was interesting just the same. Her favorite subject was her large extended family. She was the only one still in Alabama. But her three daughters and four sons and their children and grandchildren lived in Atlanta, where her family was from.

Her only remaining sibling was her baby brother, Oswald. He lived in San Francisco, California, with a wife Mrs. Dowler described as a "shrew" and a "trollop." I was too embarrassed to admit that I didn't know what them words meant. I had learned a heap of words that white folks used by reading magazines and listening to the radio on a regular basis. But she'd just used two that I had never heard before. I made a mental note to buy a dictionary the next time I went shopping.

One thing I knew how to do good was make people feel good about themselves. The best way was to bombard them with compliments. When Mrs. Dowler told me she was eighty-seven, I gasped and said, "My goodness! You look ten years younger."

Mrs. Dowler looked horrified. "What woman wants to look seventy-seven?" she hollered.

My heart started beating so hard, I was surprised I didn't keel over. "I . . . I . . . I didn't mean no harm, ma'am—"

She cut me off with a loud laugh. "Honey, don't be so sensitive. I know you meant well."

"It's just that you do look younger than you really are. Nobody would ever know your real age if you didn't admit it," I whimpered. "When I spoke to you on the phone, I thought you was in your fifties or sixties . . ." Lies had got me so far, I planned to tell them as often as I had to.

Them comments made her blush and giggle. "That's better," she said, giggling some more. I was glad she had a sense of humor on top of all her other good qualities.

When I told her how beautiful her house was, and that she had the style and grace of a film star, she got as giddy as a teenager. She served me more tea cakes and insisted on pouring me a glass of her most expensive red wine. I didn't have the nerve to tell her that I hadn't had more than two or three drinks in the last five years, and that had only been because I'd been at a wedding.

When Mrs. Dowler took a break to go use the bathroom, I trotted across the room to the bookcase and got the dictionary, which was the only book on the shelves bigger than the Bible next to it. I flipped the pages as fast as I could to find "shrew" and "trollop." They meant exactly what I thought. When she came back and repeated the story about her baby brother's wife to me again, I enjoyed it more, because this time I knew what she meant.

"By the way, from now on, I want you to use the front door, coming and going."

"Ma'am?" I had never entered a white person's house or business through the front entrance. It could have got me arrested. "Y-you mean that, Mrs. Dowler?"

"Of course, I do! If anybody questions you about it, you tell me, and I'll straighten them out right away. My house, my rules. Period."

"Thank you, ma'am." My head couldn't swell up no bigger and I couldn't puff out my chest no farther. Mrs. Dowler whirled around and strutted out of the kitchen. I looked around the room and smiled. I had a feeling I was really going to like this job more than all the others put together.

Chapter 18

With all of the many blessings I already had, I thought my life was as good as it was ever going to be. I was wrong. Mrs. Dowler changed me in ways I never could have imagined. By the end of the third week, it felt like I had been reborn. Me and her had already become the best of friends.

Mrs. Dowler reminded me of President Roosevelt's wife, Eleanor. She had graduated from a fancy college, traveled all over the place, wanted colored folks to be treated better, and socialized with people in high places. I started doing things I seen Mrs. Dowler do on a regular basis. I spent more time reading books, listening to Mrs. Roosevelt's programs on the radio—which was a welcome change after listening to nothing but gospel music for most of my life. I was learning new words and ways to be more ladylike.

I started doing things I'd never done until I met Mrs. Dowler. I kept my fingernails trimmed and buffed, stuck my little finger out when I drunk from a cup, and I smiled so much now that by the time I went to bed, my cheeks would be aching. I was learning stuff faster from Mrs. Dowler than I'd learned in school. I had a whole new outlook on life and that made me feel better about myself and enjoy life even more. With my family and my new job, it felt like I'd already died and gone to heaven.

Mrs. Dowler had introduced me to some of her friends, who also treated me like I was as good as they was. But there was a fly in the ointment and it was a big one. She had warned me that many people in her family was racist and would torment colored people for little or no reason in the blink of a eye. I hadn't had no problems with the few I'd met, so I knocked on wood every day.

I didn't know how rich Mrs. Dowler was, but she was good about sharing her wealth. On top of paying me more in two days than I'd made in a whole week at some of my other jobs, she gave me a cash bonus when I did something that really impressed her. Like the first time I gave her a foot massage. From that day on, every time I clipped her toenails and gave her a foot massage, she gave me a huge bonus. She was generous to a lot of other folks too. I couldn't count all the times I seen her write out checks to various charities, white and colored.

One afternoon while we was sipping tea, I casually mentioned that my church was raising funds to buy new pews. When I got ready to go home, she walked me to the door, gave me a hug, and handed me a check for the whole amount to pay for the pews! When I took the check to my father-in-law, his eyes got so big, I thought they was going to pop out.

"I heard that the Dowler woman was a generous soul. I had no idea she was this generous," he hollered. "Let me get on this phone right now so I can call her up and thank her."

White folks wouldn't be found dead in a colored church, but Mrs. Dowler showed up at ours just before the morning service the very next Sunday, dressed to kill. She had on a black wide-brimmed hat with a red feather on the side, a flowing white dress with puffy sleeves, and enough makeup and jewelry for three women. The way the congregation was gawking at her, you would have thought she was a carnival sideshow freak. Some folks had looks on their faces like that deer Hubert had almost hit on our way to that first honky-tonk. But being gazed at didn't bother Mrs. Dowler one bit. She was as gracious and friendly as she could be.

When Pa Wiggins called her up to the pulpit so he could praise her, she skittered up there like a frisky squirrel. Then she spent the next forty-five minutes telling some of the same stories

I'd heard half-a-dozen times. Mrs. Dowler never attended our church again, but she continued to dole out donations to us, left and right. It was a mystery to me how she could be the way she was, when so many other white folks was doing all they could to make life miserable for colored folks.

1939

As close as me and Mrs. Dowler had become since I started working for her three years ago, Jessie was still my best friend. I was glad she had a job she loved now too. She had been hired to join the night shift crew at a nursing home last month. She did everything from mopping floors to answering phones at the front desk when the receptionist wasn't available. I drove her to work some nights at eleven o'clock, Monday through Friday, and she took the bus back home each morning. She usually left Earl with her mama or one of her other relatives. When they couldn't watch him, I did. I never asked her to give me money for gas or pay me for minding him. Each time she offered to pay me for either one, I refused. I was glad I was able to help her out any way I could. Orville still only worked here and there, now and then. He didn't help Jessie much with their bills or anything else, so I was glad to help her out for free.

Jessie was still the biggest gossip I knew. I enjoyed our conversations as much as I always did. She'd recently moved a block away from us. Since we lived closer now, we started spending even more time together.

Our routine had been the same for years. We'd sit and chat for hours at a time, several times each week. This particular Friday afternoon in May, we occupied her front porch steps. We had just finished shelling the peas she was going to cook for supper. Orville was nowhere in sight and Hubert was visiting his mama and daddy. Earl was in his room playing with the same toys he'd been playing with since he was a little boy. Claude had gone to visit a new "friend" he'd told me about a hour ago. Just hearing him refer to one of his girlfriends that way made my chest tighten because that was what Hubert still called his boyfriends.

Jessie had already updated me on all the latest gossip. I had no telling what she'd share with me next. Her next question caught me off guard.

"Maggie, don't you get sick of Claude running around with so many different girls?"

I rolled my eyes and waved my hand. "Pffftt! He is just doing what every other young man his age around here is doing," I said, chuckling.

"Not my boy," she said in a low tone.

"I'm sorry. You know I would never say nothing about Earl that would hurt you."

"I know what you meant."

"But Claude is having fun, and as long as he ain't hurting nobody, I ain't going to say nothing about all the running around he's been doing lately." I snickered. "I'd be more concerned if he didn't have no girls chasing after him."

"Oh. I'm glad to hear that what he's up to these days ain't bothering you . . ."

I didn't like the mysterious look on Jessie's face. It was the look that always meant she had something juicier to add to a story.

"What do you mean by that?" I asked, gazing at her from the corner of my eye.

She cleared her throat and gave me a pitiful look. "I guess you ain't heard what Daisy is going around town saying—"

"Daisy who?" I scratched my head. "Hmmm. The only Daisy I can think of is Daisy Wallace, the only female bootlegger in town. She was in a bad car wreck five years ago and I thought she was dead."

"That woman ain't dead, but she been in a coma since the wreck. She ain't the Daisy I'm talking about, though. Keep thinking."

I spent a few more seconds tuning up my brain so I could

think faster. "Oh yeah. That young couple at the end of the block had a baby girl last year and named her Daisy."

"Think some more."

I didn't know why Jessie had such a deadpan expression on her face now.

"You got me. The only other Daisy I know is that wild man-eating Compton woman. She's thirty-two and that's way too old for Claude."

Jessie gasped. "Then you ain't kidding me by playing dumb? You really didn't know?"

"Jessie, I don't have time to be playing games or acting dumb. You either pee or get off the commode. It ain't like you to beat around the bush."

"Maggie Wiggins, if your boy got any crazier about Daisy Compton, y'all would have to sign him into the nuthouse."

My jaw dropped and my ears started ringing. "Do you mean to tell me that *that* juke joint jezebel is messing with *my* baby boy? I been hearing wild stories about her for years. Folks say she is the most ill-tempered woman in town. No way! I don't believe it! Whoever told you that got it wrong. Maybe they made a mistake and is talking about another Claude."

"Maggie, they talking about *your* Claude." Jessie gave me another pitiful look. "Sugar, it pains me to tell you this, but I seen them together myself last night at that rib joint on Patterson Street. He was kissing up and down her neck."

I gasped so hard; my tongue felt like it was about to slide down my throat. "But why would he do that? Just last week he went to a fish fry with that cute Richardson girl. And last night some other young girl called the house for him. What would a woman Daisy's age—with *four* kids—want with a young boy like Claude?"

"The 'young boy' is twenty-one years old, Maggie."

I was in such a state of shock, I didn't know what to say or think. I sat as stiff as a board with thoughts buzzing around in my head like bees. Each thought felt like a sting. Daisy was the type of woman that mothers warned their sons about. Now that

I had so much prestige and good standing in the community, I wasn't about to let my son get caught up with somebody that folks made fun of almost as much as they had done me in the past.

Daisy's daddy had run off years ago. Four of her six brothers was sharecroppers and they spent most of the money they made on gambling, women, and alcohol. The other two was in prison. Nary one had even attended school for more than a year or two, so they couldn't even read or write. Daisy had dropped out in the third grade and could barely read and write herself. Her two sisters was just as shady as she was when it came to using men. They were in their late twenties and still living home, and mooching off their mama.

The only saving grace in the Compton family was Daisy's mama. Sister Compton was practically a saint. She went to church every Sunday, didn't smoke, cuss, or drink. She was so dedicated to taking care of her family, she took jobs you couldn't even get a chain gang to do. Right now, she was lucky enough to be working as a cook in the kitchen at the colored clinic. Every weekend and most evenings, she kept Daisy's kids. The oldest one was just twelve. I heard she'd been trying to get Daisy to give her custody of them for years, because she neglected them, beat them way more than they deserved, and flat out chose her men over her kids. But all of Sister Compton's good qualities still didn't make no difference to me.

"I can't believe my child is involved with that family! W-why ain't you told me this before now?"

"As close as you and Claude is, I thought you knew. You told me yourself that he don't keep nothing from you. I was waiting for you to tell me about it."

"I didn't know nothing about him and that woman! Well, I'm going to put a stop to it—"

Jessie held up her hand and cut me off. "Maggie, for your own sake, stay out of your son's business. If he is anything like the rest of these young men around here, he'll use Daisy as long as she'll let him. And believe you me, then he'll move on." She stood up and stretched. "You better pray he don't get her in the family way. Because if he do, she and the child will be in his life, and yours and Hubert's, from now on." Jessie started walking toward the door. "By the way, I got a ride to work tonight so you don't have to take me. And Earl is spending the night with Mama. Now you sit tight. I'm going to get us some more cider."

Chapter 19

I DIDN'T WAIT FOR JESSIE TO COME BACK OUTSIDE. AFTER WHAT SHE had told me about my son and Daisy, I couldn't sit still. I stumbled off the porch and trotted all the way back to my house.

A hour later, Hubert came home from the funeral home. He had been there preparing thirty-year-old Jimmy Jackson for his service. He'd fell in a lake and drowned two days ago. On the days that Hubert had a body, he didn't go to work at the turpentine mill. His supervisor never had a problem with him taking off whenever he needed to. I immediately went out on the porch.

"Hurry up and get in the house! We need to talk!" I yelled as he piled out of the car.

He started walking fast toward me with a frightened look on his face. "What's wrong?"

"We got a problem! A serious problem."

"Oh, shit! W-what is it?" His voice was trembling and blood was rushing from his face.

I knew what he was thinking, so I squashed that thought right away. He thought somebody had found out he was funny. "Don't worry. It ain't what you think. Nobody knows the truth about you."

He looked relieved as he rushed into the house behind me. We stopped in the middle of the living-room floor. "Then, is somebody sick or did somebody else die?"

I shook my head. "Do you know who our son is fooling around with?" I didn't give him time to answer. "Daisy Compton."

Hubert rolled his eyes, waved his hand, and let out a mighty sigh. "Is that all? You made my blood pressure shoot up to the roof over something like that?" He shuffled over to the couch, plopped down, and crossed his legs. You would have thought it was just another leisurely day to him.

I stomped like a bull up to him and stood there with my arms folded across my chest. "Is that all you got to say? Hubert, that woman is a low-down, low-life hussy eleven years older than him!"

He uncrossed his legs and held up both hands. "What do you want me to say, Maggie? The boy's been courting for years."

"He ain't never messed around with a woman like Daisy. I know you done heard all the gossip about her. She's still involved with her kids' daddy, and she roams all over town with other men. On top of that, people say she's got a mean streak a mile wide. Did you know that she bounced a brick off one of her men friend's head? His mind ain't been right since."

I was glad to see that Hubert looked more serious now. "Say what? I declare, I didn't know that."

"Well, you know it now."

Hubert sighed. "Well, like I said, the boy is grown. We ain't never interfered in his personal life with women, so it's too late for us to be doing that now. Do you think he would listen to us?"

"He ain't got no choice!" I hollered, wagging my finger in his face.

"Maggie, let this go. Claude needs to find out about real life firsthand so he can learn from his mistakes."

"Oh, you can sit here and say that. It's easy for you not to be concerned because he ain't your son!" The second them words left my mouth, I wished I could take them back. The hurt look on Hubert's face made my heart skip a few beats. "I'm sorry," I said, flopping down next to him. I attempted to hold his hand, but he pulled it away.

You would think by now that I would know not to get too handsy with him when we was alone. But sometimes I couldn't help myself. The closest we ever got when we was alone was still in the bed, each one facing the opposite direction. And, like from day one, it was only to keep each other's back warm.

"You know I didn't mean that."

"You ain't got to be sorry. What you just said is true, at least nature-wise. But that boy is as much mine as he is yours, and I love him as much as you do. The last thing we want to do is make him so upset he'll turn on us."

"Why would he turn on us when we are just trying to keep him from getting hurt?"

"If he got feelings for Daisy, we can't change that. Now, I suggest you calm down. When he get home from work, we'll feel him out and go from there. I'm sure it ain't nothing too serious."

Claude got home two hours later, about a hour later than usual. He was whistling when he walked through the front door and strolled into the living room.

"Hey, y'all," he greeted. Me and Hubert was still sitting on the couch. He looked as chipper as ever, but my face was as tight as a drum.

"Son, we need to talk to you," I blurted out.

Claude chuckled. "It'll have to wait, because I'm fixing to go back out. I just came home to wash up and change clothes." He stopped walking and stood in front of us with a smile that reached from one side of his face to the other. "I got a big date tonight." He winked. I cringed.

"With who?" Hubert asked.

"Oh, she is a real special lady," Claude answered. He was beaming like a lightning bug.

"I hope it's the Richardson girl. She's so sweet," I commented.

"Hazel Lou? Pffftt!" Claude waved his hand and let out a long, loud laugh. "She done outlived her usefulness. I got bigger and better fish to fry."

I held my breath for a few seconds, and when I let it out, I asked real quick, "Is it true you been fooling around with Daisy Compton?"

"Yup," Claude admitted with a smirk. "I wouldn't call it 'fooling around,' though. I'm serious about her, and she's serious about me." He glanced at his feet and started shifting his weight from one foot to the other. There was so much sawdust on his shoes, I couldn't tell what color they was. Any other day I'd have him take off his shoes and I would get a warm wet rag and wipe them clean. Today I wanted to wipe that annoying look off his face.

I leaped up off the couch and grabbed him by his shoulders. "Son, have you lost your mind? That woman ain't no good!" I screamed.

Before Claude said anything else, he gave me a disgusted look, removed my hands off his shoulders, and moved a few steps away from me. "Mama, you ain't got no right to be saying nothing like that." Then he turned to Hubert, who was looking so hopeless now. "Daddy, what you got to say about Daisy?"

"She is kind of long in the tooth," Hubert replied.

"I don't care how old she is. All them young girls I been seeing is so silly and stupid. I need a woman who already knows the ropes. I'm in love with Daisy. A older woman like her can teach me a lot," Claude insisted, moving away from me even more.

I couldn't tell who gasped the hardest, me or Hubert. Now that he'd heard that Claude was "in love," he was taking this thing serious. "Why *this* older woman, son?" he asked with his voice sounding so raspy and weak, I was surprised he was able to keep talking. "She got four kids, and folks say she can get right ornery to her men if they make her mad."

"Well, I love kids and I hope to have a bunch myself someday. I already care about Daisy's just as much as I do her. And if she did chastise some of her men friends, all I can say is that they shouldn't have made her mad."

My legs felt as wobbly as jelly and my head was throbbing like mad. "Let's go eat supper. We can discuss this some more then," I said gently.

"Didn't I just say I had a date? Let me stop running my mouth. I need to get changed so I can get back to Daisy by the time I told her I would. If y'all don't want *me* to get mad, I advise y'all to stay out of my business!" He sprinted out of the living room and headed toward the hallway.

Me and Hubert was so stunned, we couldn't even speak.

Claude had never been this disrespectful before, so I knew we had a major mess on our hands. Because of Daisy Compton—a woman I wouldn't let date my dog—he was acting like a fool. Forty-five minutes later, he strutted out of his room wearing the Sunday-go-to-meeting suit I'd bought him for his twenty-first birthday. We felt helpless as he rushed out the door without saying another word.

"Well!" Hubert said. "I guess this is worse than I thought, huh?"

"I guess it is," I muttered.

When Claude came home Saturday evening, he marched into the kitchen while me and Hubert was eating supper. Without giving us a warning, he dropped a bombshell I never seen coming.

"I'm glad I got here before y'all went to bed. Uh . . . I'm fixing to move in with Daisy today."

I decided not to open my mouth. I knew that the wrong words would shoot out like bullets, and a situation that was already out of control would go through the roof. And, if Claude provoked me, I would probably break a switch off our pecan tree and give him a whupping! I hadn't had to do that since he was a little boy. It was the last thing I wanted to do now. Instead, I stayed as cool as a cucumber. But inside I was blazing like a blowtorch.

With a puppy-dog look on his face, Claude said, "Y'all please don't be looking so downhearted. I don't want to make this no harder than it already is. But . . . um . . . I just came to get some of my work clothes and a few other things. I'll get the rest later. I probably won't be coming to church tomorrow, so don't look for me. I want y'all to know right now that it was Daisy's idea for me to move in with her. I went along with it because she threatened to break up with me if I didn't. I don't want to lose her just when we was really beginning to enjoy each other's company. And I agreed to move in with her because I didn't want to make her mad." Claude paused and gave us a sorry look. "She's used to getting her way."

I gasped so hard, I choked on some air. I couldn't get a single word out. Hubert's mouth dropped open, but he didn't say nothing neither. It was hard to believe, not to mention disturbing, that a boy who had always been so levelheaded would agree to do something as serious, and out of the blue, as moving in with a woman he barely knew.

Claude coughed to clear his throat before he continued. "Daisy's brother is outside with his truck waiting to help me haul my stuff. I'll come get the rest of it once I get settled. So this won't be so painful if y'all just sit there and don't try to interfere." He didn't wait around to hear what we had to say. I didn't know what was running through Hubert's mind, but I was speechless. Claude shuffled on to his room.

"We . . . we done lost our baby, Hubert," I said with a sob stuck in my throat.

"It don't matter who he is with. He is still our boy," he declared.

We didn't move from the kitchen table when Claude rushed out the door carrying a armload of clothes and a shopping bag bulging with other items. That was the last thing I remembered before I hit the floor.

When I opened my eyes, I was laying in my bed. Hubert and my in-laws was standing over me. From the grim expressions on their faces, you would have thought they was looking at me in my coffin.

"What happened?" I wheezed, looking from one face to the other.

"You fainted. As soon as Hubert called us, we headed over here as fast as we could," Pa Wiggins replied.

I must have hit the floor pretty hard; I was aching all over. But none of my body parts was in as much pain as my heart.

"Where is Claude?" I whimpered.

"At Daisy's house, I guess," Hubert said with his voice cracking.

"How did y'all let something this unspeakable happen?" Ma Wiggins asked. Her eyes had narrowed and her hands was on her hips.

"What was we supposed to do, Mama?" Hubert asked. He was wringing his hands so fast and hard, I could hear his knuckles cracking.

Ma Wiggins gave Hubert a disgusted look. She looked even more disgusted when she turned to face me. "I can't believe y'all couldn't talk no sense into that boy!" she shrieked with her lips quivering.

"We just found out about Daisy yesterday. We did try to talk to him, but it didn't do no good," I said, sitting up. I was surprised to see that Hubert had dressed me in my nightgown.

"I ain't going to sit back and watch him ruin his life with that . . . that strumpet!" Pa Wiggins blasted. In all the years I'd known him and listened to his fiery sermons, I had never seen him sound so riled up. The only women he'd ever mean-mouthed in my presence was the juke joint jezebels and the ones in the Bible who had misbehaved.

"I got a good mind to go over there with a switch and make that boy get his tail back in this house," Ma Wiggins hollered as she stomped her foot.

"Mama, please don't do that. It would only make matters worse. I think the best thing we can do now is wait for this mess to run its course," Hubert said.

He didn't look too hopeful about what he'd just said. And I didn't feel hopeful at all.

Chapter 20

Me and Hubert didn't go to church on Sunday. We had stopped going regularly about five years ago, so my in-laws was used to us not being there every week. My father-in-law had recently stopped having Bible study every Friday. My mother-in-law had got sick of them and put her foot down and told him enough was enough. I was surprised to find out that she'd hated them sessions almost as much as me and Hubert. Pa Wiggins was still preaching his foot-stomping sermons at church, though. He was still working for our late mayor's brother because they paid him good money and treated him like family.

I didn't miss going to church so much or attending Bible study. But me and Hubert still prayed on a regular basis. We got on our knees several times Sunday night and asked God for guidance.

I didn't sleep a wink when we went to bed. And I cried off and on for hours. But I got up at daybreak Monday morning, like I always did, so I could get ready and go catch the bus to Mrs. Dowler's house. I never drove our car to work for several reasons. One was because I didn't want none of her neighbors to think I was being uppity by rolling up in a car nicer than some of theirs. A lot of colored housekeepers rode to work on the same bus with me so I had made a few new friends, and I got to see people I didn't see that often otherwise. We exchanged everything from gossip to recipes. I even took the bus when I was going to visit folks or when I had to go downtown. Even though the rides was never that long, I had enough time to read a few pages in a magazine or rear back, close my eyes, and just enjoy the ride. Another reason I relied on buses was because Hubert usually drove our car to his job at the turpentine mill, especially on the days he wanted to go straight from work to visit his boyfriend. Even when he left the car at home, I only drove when somebody needed a ride or if I didn't feel like walking somewhere and the buses had stopped running for the day. Whenever Hubert had to leave the car with his mechanic for a few days to have some work done, he rode to the turpentine mill with one of his coworkers. When he couldn't catch a ride with somebody, he drove the big black hearse that had belonged to Uncle Roscoe. I was glad that when he didn't have to use it, he parked it at the funeral parlor.

Other than spending time with my family and Jessie, working for Mrs. Dowler was the highlight of my week. Because of her age, I knew that the job was only going to last so long, and I wanted to enjoy it for as long as I could. I looked forward to each Monday, especially today.

"Why don't you give Mrs. Dowler a call and tell her you need to take the day off," Hubert suggested when he came out of the bathroom already dressed.

"I'd rather go to work. It'll keep my mind off Claude," I muttered.

"All right, then. But please try not to fret too much. I talked to Daddy this morning. He's going to call up some of the most devout warriors in his congregation and get a prayer chain started."

"Thanks, sugar. We need all the help we can get."

As soon as I walked into Mrs. Dowler's living room, she wobbled up off the couch. "Don't move!" she ordered, holding up her hand. And then she turned around real slow to show off a new outfit, a crisp white floor-length cotton dress with gold ruffles at the end of the sleeves. "How do I look?" she asked.

"Like a film star, like always," I told her. I stood there while she turned around some more. Mrs. Dowler liked to spend money. Two weeks ago, when she'd bought a new washing machine, she'd also bought a new stove and refrigerator. She spent a ton of money on clothes too. Some was downright outlandish, like the outfit she had on now. Like a lot of folks, colored and white, rich and poor, she liked to walk around barefoot. Her long narrow feet, which she had me massage and slather with calamine lotion at least once a week, looked like raw chicken feet. When she stopped turning around, she cocked her head to the side and gave me a puzzled look.

"Maggie, you look terrible! What's the matter?"

"It's a family matter, ma'am. I don't want to burden you with it," I told her in a weak tone.

She followed me into the kitchen, where she had placed two baskets of dirty laundry on the floor next to the brand-new washing machine.

"Listen here now." She shook her finger in my face. "I'm your friend. Don't worry about burdening me. That's what friends are for. Tell me what the problem is, and if nothing else, I can say something that'll make you feel better."

"Don't you want me to do the washing first?"

"You can do that later," she insisted. She folded her arms and narrowed her eyes. "Now spit it out."

"All right, then."

She ushered me back to the living room. When we got there, we dropped down onto the couch. Mrs. Dowler didn't say another word until I finished telling her everything that was going on with Claude.

"Well, I declare. You and your husband have sure got a mess on your hands. I hope your boy sees that woman for what she really is before she causes him too much trauma."

"I hope he does too. Claude is our whole world. I'm worried that when he sees she ain't the woman for him, it'll be too late, and he'll be wallowing in misery."

"There is not much you can do at this point. I advise you not to spend too much time fretting over it, because then you'll be the one wallowing. Keep yourself busy. That'll help. But if the boy truly loves this woman, I advise you not to interfere."

"I can't just let my only child ruin his life and not try to stop him!" I hollered.

"Sugar, by meddling, you'll only be pushing him toward that woman even more. Just let nature run its course."

"Is that what you'd do if you was in my shoes?"

"Honey child, I've worn your shoes before. My middle boy, Buford, took up with a gal that was a tawdry piece of work. Maizie Hancock was her name. She was as cute as a button on the outside, but bad to the bone inside. She lied like a rug, cussed like a convict, and spent my poor child's money like it grew on trees. Her daddy and all of her brothers were moonshiners and the biggest hell-raisers I'd ever known. Her mama had run off with a foreigner when Maizie was still a teenager. When she came back home, she was pregnant with that man's child. Her husband shot her dead right in front of Maizie, and she never got over that. She went loony and stayed that way for years. By the time she was eighteen, which was when she got her hooks in my son, she had been married twice and already had two children. They ended up with her mama's folks in West Virginia."

"Is your son still with Maizie?"

"A year after they got married, when she was twenty, she took off with a suspicious-looking man from New York. Or was it Connecticut? Hmmm. Anyway, she was in some Northern state with a different man, a gambler. And she'd had two more kids."

"I bet you was happy she was out of your son's life."

"Bah! The whole time she was in the wind, Buford wrote letters to her and begged her to reconcile with him. I don't know what all he said to woo her back, but she agreed to it. Only if he'd come pick her up, though. The same day Buford was supposed to drive to whatever state Maizie was in, that gambler choked her to death. My son was devastated and hasn't been the same vibrant and well-rounded man he used to be since that fiasco. He lives with my daughter in Atlanta now, because he's too weak and vulnerable to live on his own. All because of that woman."

"My Lord," I gasped. "I think that's a shame."

"I don't think so! Maizie getting herself killed, I mean. If I'd been able to get my hands on her before that gambler, I would have choked her to death myself! My whole family was glad she was out of our lives for good. And the best part of it was that Buford hadn't had any children with that floozy. Lord knows, it would have pained me tremendously to have reminders of her in my life." Mrs. Dowler sighed and touched my arm. "Now, Maggie, I hope that what I just told you doesn't make you feel different about me. You know I'm a Christian woman, but I am not perfect."

"I don't feel no different about you. I would probably feel the same way if something happened to Daisy that would get her out of our lives for good . . ."

Chapter 21

CLAUDE HAD BEEN GONE TWO WEEKS. AS DEPRESSED AS I WAS, I never let it interfere with my job. Mrs. Dowler was a good distraction. There was no telling what I would have done without her.

It seemed like the older Mrs. Dowler got, the friskier she got. She was so busy, I got tired just watching her go about her business. One day she changed all the curtains in the windows in every room. The day after that, she scrubbed down the walls in her living room and didn't even sweat. I wondered what her cleaning woman did if Mrs. Dowler was doing so much around the house. I didn't want to ask because it was none of my business. And one thing I was happy to say about myself was "My mama didn't raise no fool." There was no way I was going to speak out of turn to a woman who was so good to me.

On almost every Monday afternoon, ladies from Mrs. Dowler's garden club and members of her church dropped in to have lunch and tea. She did so much shopping, one of her walk-in closets had dozens of outfits with the price tags still attached. Even when she wasn't expecting company, she liked to dress up. Some days she'd change clothes two or three times before I left. Every now and then, a guest stayed overnight, or a relative came to visit for a few days. She would put fresh linen on every bed in all five of her bedrooms whether they'd been slept in or not. There was some Mondays when half of the laundry I did was linens and underwear.

Mrs. Dowler also had me pull weeds and chop grass from between the rows of beans, tomatoes, and cabbage in her backyard garden. The weevils and other pests was so bad, I sprinkled arsenic whether she told me to or not. That was one of the first things I planned to do today. Before I could get started, Mrs. Dowler came in the kitchen, where I was, and started telling me more stories, mostly the same ones with a few slightly different details.

This time we occupied her kitchen table. I knew that if I didn't stop her, she'd talk for hours and then I'd have to rush around like a headless chicken so I could get all my chores done so I wouldn't miss the last bus.

"Well, I guess I should get up and get to work," I said, already easing up off my chair. "You expecting any company today?"

"No, sugar. But I will be having kin here later in the month."

"Oh? One of your kids?" I'd only met one of her daughters and a few of her grandchildren.

"Remember I told you I had a brother in California?"

"Yes, ma'am. Oswell, right?" I sat back down.

"Oswald. He's the youngest of the boys. As a matter of fact, he's the youngest one in the family. I was in my twenties and a wife and mother myself when Mama had him, so he's more like a son to me." Mrs. Dowler rolled her eyes up in her head and snickered. "He behaves like one too."

"How long is he going to stay with you?"

"Well, I have a feeling it'll be longer than I want. His wife is divorcing him and he's so overwrought about it, he had to quit his job. Can you believe that? He had only one year to go before he could retire!"

"He must really be upset."

A glazed look was on Mrs. Dowler's face now. She got up to get a glass of water. This usually meant she was about to go off on another tangent that would drag on for several more minutes, so I shifted in my seat and got more comfortable.

"He's floundering in a cesspool of discontent. When we talked on the phone last night, ten minutes into the conversation he went to pieces. I declare, he cried so much, he started babbling gibberish and I couldn't understand a word he was saying. For a minute I thought he'd lost his mind. But he's very fond of the drink, so it was probably the alcohol."

"That's a shame," I remarked.

"Part of his problem is, he's very sensitive and doesn't have much ambition. So I don't expect him to get back up on his feet anytime soon," Mrs. Dowler said.

This brother was sounding more and more like trouble brewing for me. But I pushed that thought to the back of my mind. I had such a good thing going with Mrs. Dowler, he'd have to be meaner than a rattlesnake to me before I'd consider complaining to her, or quitting. "I can't wait to meet him." Telling such a flat-out lie made my lips quiver.

"I wanted you to know about him up front before he gets here." Mrs. Dowler let out a long, loud sigh and gave me a woeful look. "I know you've met my daughter and her grandchildren, and they were nice to you. I've mentioned it to you before, but it behooves me to remind you that most of my family has never been too kind to colored folks. I was fourteen when Lincoln freed the slaves. I enjoyed playing with the slave children, and I loved the woman who was my mammy as much as I loved my own mother. My mammy's name was Annie Pearl and she gave birth to sixteen children. My daddy was the father of her first four. So I had two brown-skinned half brothers and two brown-skinned half sisters to play with too." Mrs. Dowler stopped talking and wiped a tear from her eye.

Despite how she kept me from getting my work done in a timely manner and talked my ear off, I didn't mind listening to her stories. Even the ones that was painful to listen to.

"Uh, I can see that this subject is hard for you to talk about. You don't have to tell me nothing else about it," I said gently.

Mrs. Dowler shook her head. "Uh-huh. I want to get it all out." She sniffed and started talking again. This time there was so much emotion in her tone I wanted to hug her. "Setting the slaves free caused such a uproar. I remember how mad it made my daddy, and almost every other white person I knew. Oswald used to listen to all the stories his granddaddy and other relatives regaled him with about how it was the slaves' fault for the war and for some white folks losing everything. Therefore, he may give you a fairly hard time, but"—Mrs. Dowler paused and raised her hand and held it in midair—"only until he gets to know you. Once he sees what a nice woman you are, I'm sure he'll come around."

I smiled. "Don't worry about me getting along with your brother. I've dealt with racist folks before. Things will be fine."

"I sure hope so. With your boy acting like a fool, you've got enough to fret about these days. Oswald is spoiled and always wants things his way. One of the things he's particular about is his booze. He will only drink whiskey. And only Glenfiddich, which he thinks is the best. He won't touch wine or beer with a stick, no matter how bad he wants to indulge. Other than the red French wine I've been so fond of all my life, whiskey is the only other spirit I still keep in the house nowadays. It was also all my husband would drink before his health declined. When friends and family who wanted something different came to visit us, they had to bring their own bottle. That's still true today." Mrs. Dowler shook her head and chuckled. "So I'll have to always remember to keep the special-brand whiskey in stock for Oswald. But I do have to warn you, when he's drinking, he might be a little more fractious than usual."

"Fractious" was another word I had to look up. From the way she said it, I had a pretty good idea what it meant. "You mean 'grouchy'?"

"Precisely. When that comes up, and if it's for something that makes you uncomfortable, let him know. And you can tell him that that's what I advised you to do. If he don't like it, he can lump it!"

"Yes, ma'am." I didn't care what Mrs. Dowler said, but a little voice in my head was telling me that I was fixing to have another mess on my hands.

Chapter 22

By the time June rolled around, I was a emotional wreck. I couldn't tell if I was coming or going. I didn't want to be around too many people because each day it got a little harder for me to hide my pain. Hubert, Jessie, and Mrs. Dowler was the only people I felt comfortable around.

One of my neighbors invited me and Hubert to have supper with them three weeks after Claude had moved out. We went, but it was so hard for me to put on a happy face. When we got home, I told Hubert I wouldn't accept no more invitations until we got things sorted out with Claude.

We hadn't seen or spoke to Claude since he moved out. I was half out of my mind with worry and angrier than I'd ever been in my life. Hubert tried to act strong and positive, but several nights when he thought I was sleeping, I heard him praying out loud, begging God to bring our son back to his senses.

I called Daisy's house every evening and each time she told me Claude was not at home, or that he couldn't come to the phone. When Hubert called, she told him the same thing. She had even trained her children to repeat the same information. I called this morning and told her point-blank that I just wanted to let my son know we was thinking about him and that we missed him.

"I'll let him know," she said in a smirking tone. Before I could say another word, she hung up.

A few more days went by and we still hadn't heard from Claude or been able to reach him. He hadn't even communicated with his grandparents and they was as upset as I was. Each time Claude's name came up in Ma Wiggins's presence, she cried up a storm.

"This done gone on long enough," I told Hubert. "We need to go to Daisy's house. It might not do no good, but if we don't go, we'll never know."

"Baby, I agree with you all the way."

I was glad Hubert felt the same way. If he hadn't, I would have gone over there by myself anyway.

When we pulled up in front of Daisy's little brown house that Saturday afternoon, I seen her peeping from the front window. But when we knocked, she ignored us. We stood in front of her door for ten minutes before she finally opened it and came out on the porch.

"What's wrong with you people? Y'all can't be showing up over here without calling."

Daisy had on a bathrobe and fuzzy slippers, and here it was the middle of the day. I could see traces of face cream on the sides of her face and the top of her neck. The tone of her voice was so cold, you would have thought we was bill collectors. She was a petite dark-skinned woman with a beautiful heart-shaped face and thick black hair halfway down her back. It was easy to understand how she had caught Claude's eye. She had wrapped her bangs around a brown paper bag curler. Bobby pins held the rest of her hair in place.

"How would y'all like unexpected company showing up at your house?" she asked with her big brown eyes narrowed.

"Unexpected company shows up at our house all the time and it don't bother us one bit," Hubert said through clenched teeth.

"Daisy, we been calling and calling for weeks and it ain't done no good," I reminded. "All we want to do is talk to our son."

"Why? So y'all can talk bad about me to him some more? Ain't y'all done enough of that?"

"Look, lady. Put yourself in our shoes. You got children. How would you like it if somebody kept you from seeing them?" Hubert said.

The way Daisy leaned her head back and parted her lips, I thought she was going to laugh. It was a good thing she didn't, because I wouldn't have been responsible for my actions. I was teetering so close to the deep end; it wouldn't take much to make me go off it. She sniffed. And then with a smug look on her face, she said in the same cold tone, "I ain't stopping y'all from talking to Claude. That's on him. He don't want to talk to y'all."

"All right. Just let him know we came by. And you let him know that we'll be paying him a visit at his job." I was the one sounding smug now and I could tell that it bothered her; her demeanor changed right away.

"Y'all going to pester him at the sawmill?" she whimpered. She covered her heart with her hand. I wondered if hers was beating as hard as mine was.

"And we'll do that as many times as we have to, until we can talk to him," Hubert added.

What we'd just said ruffled Daisy's feathers. There was a worried look on her face now. "Don't do that!" She blinked and started shaking her head so hard, the paper curler came undone and fell to the ground. "Claude's already having enough problems at work. I don't want him to lose his job. He wouldn't be able to help me get out of debt like he promised."

Me and Hubert looked at each other, then back at Daisy. "What kind of problems is he having at work?" I asked. I was just as concerned about him "having enough problems at work," but I'd deal with that issue later.

"Ask him," Daisy said with a sneer.

Before anybody could speak again, a dusty black truck stopped in front of the house and Claude piled out. It was the same truck he'd left our house in when he moved out. When he seen us, his face lit up. He trotted up the walkway, grinning from ear to ear. He stopped in front of us and started shifting his weight from one foot to the other. I wanted to hug him and slap him at the same time, but I couldn't bring myself to do neither one. I was disappointed that he didn't make no attempt to show me and Hubert no affection, other than that grin on his face.

"Mama, Daddy! I thought y'all was still mad at me! Y'all ain't called the house or nothing."

"We been calling and calling. You never called us back, so we figured you wasn't getting the messages," Hubert said.

Claude scratched his head and gave us a puzzled look. "I guess the kids forget to tell me."

I was tempted to let him know that almost every time we'd called, Daisy had answered the phone. But I decided to try and keep things on a low level for the time being. If we made her too mad, I was sure she'd take it out on Claude after we left.

"I guess they did," I mumbled. "Um, me and Hubert would love to have you and Daisy come have supper with us. The kids can come too," I said, forcing myself to smile at Daisy.

"We going to be busy for the next few days," she claimed. The smug look was back on her face.

"Okay." I looked her straight in the eyes. For her peepers to be so big, I had a feeling there was nothing behind them but a dark mass. Which was probably the same thing in her chest where her heart was supposed to be. "Well, when y'all get some time, please let us know. We'll be going now."

"Y'all don't want to come in the house?" Claude asked, nodding toward the front door, which Daisy had closed when she came out. "Daisy got the place fixed up so nice. I just bought a new couch."

Daisy threw up her hand and shook her head. "Not today. The house is a mess. Them kids got toys and whatnot scattered all over the place. Some other time would be much better." She pressed her lips together so tight, it looked like she had glued them shut.

I guess this was her way of letting us know she was done talking. I was stunned when she opened the door and ushered Claude into the house and skittered in behind him. I gasped when I heard the lock click. Me and Hubert stood there for a few moments with our mouths hanging open.

We shuffled back to our car in silence. Before we drove off, I seen Daisy peeping out her front window again.

"Well!" Hubert boomed as he started the motor. "What did you make of that? If I wasn't a gentleman, I would have snatched that hussy bald!"

I didn't even look at Hubert when I spoke. "I wanted to do a lot more than that. Get me out of here before I lose my religion."

Four more days went by before Claude called. "Mama, I'm sorry things ain't going too good with you and Daddy and Daisy. It might take Daddy a while to come around, but you being a woman, I know you understand these things better. Can you do me a favor and try to get to know Daisy? I sure would appreciate that."

"Son, I'd like that myself. And so would your daddy. She's the one that's so busy she don't have time for us."

"Well, she got a notion in her head that y'all don't like her and don't want her to be happy."

It made my blood boil to hear that Daisy was making me and Hubert out to be the bad guys. "I'm sure that if she gave us the chance to get to know her, she'd change her mind about that. We want her to be as happy as we want you to be."

"Why don't you take her to lunch or something? She likes to eat at that fish place around the corner from her house."

As much as I hated to, I went for his suggestion. "I'll do that. Would you like to come too?"

"No, not yet. I think you and her need to get better acquainted first. Mama, I hope you can find it in your heart to accept the woman I love. She ain't going nowhere and I ain't neither. If you accept her, you'll have to include the kids too. I know you always wanted a big family, and since I'm your only child, having some ready-made grandchildren will have to do until I become a daddy."

"You're right, son. I'm sure everything is going to work out just fine, if we all work at it."

I had planned to call up Daisy in the next day or so and invite her to lunch whenever she was available. But first, I called up Ma Wiggins and Jessie to get their feedback. They encouraged me to go through with it. Hubert did too. Just as I was about to pick up the phone to call her Wednesday morning, a few minutes after ten, it rang. I was shocked when I heard Daisy's voice.

"Hello, Maggie. Claude told me you wanted to treat me to lunch." Now she sounded so sweet, it was hard to believe she was the same mean-spirited woman I'd seen a few days ago.

"I do. He told me you like that fish place on Liberty Street. We could go there, or some other place real nice. You choose."

"Eating out these days is expensive," she pointed out.

"I know. That's why me and Hubert don't eat out that often. A good lunch could cost a pretty penny."

"Uh . . . instead of you spending a pretty penny, why don't you just give it to me? We sure could use it."

My ears felt like they was going to explode. I had never heard of such a odd and selfish request. "Y'all need money?"

"All the time. The light bill is past due, and Claude won't get paid until next Friday. The lady I been cleaning for is on vacation for the next two weeks. When I don't work, I don't get paid."

"I see. I can do that if it's what you really want. I'd hate for y'all to get your lights cut off, with all them kids in the house."

"Good. When can you give me the money?"

"You can come get it right now if you have the time. That way I can fix lunch and we can eat here." I didn't know how I sounded to her, but to myself it sounded like I was groveling. And I was. I was willing to do whatever it took to stay on good terms with my son. Even if it meant it would cost me every dime I had.

Chapter 23

As "BUSY" AS DAISY CLAIMED TO BE, SHE WAS AT MY DOOR TEN minutes after our phone conversation. She almost stepped on my foot as she stumbled through the front door. I couldn't believe the first words out of her mouth.

"I'm glad to see that your house looks better inside than it do outside."

"Well, it's a very old place. And Uncle Roscoe really let it go."

"He sure did."

"It don't matter none to me and Hubert. We had a few things done when we first moved in. But since we plan on staying here for life, we got plenty of time to get it fixed up more."

"That's good to know. I'd hate for me and Claude to get stuck with a expensive chore like that when y'all pass on."

This heifer had no shame. She'd only been with my son for a few weeks and she was already plotting to move into our house when we died!

"We'll eat in the kitchen." Keeping a fake smile on my face wasn't easy, but I was determined not to let her get to me today.

"Thanks, Maggie. I can't stay too long, so can we move right along?" The way she casually plopped down at the kitchen table and crossed her legs made it look like she wasn't in no hurry.

"Yeah," I mumbled.

I reached in my brassiere and fished out the five-dollar bill I had set aside. Her eyes lit up like lightbulbs when I handed it to her.

"Good gracious! It wouldn't cost no more than two or three dollars for us to eat at the most expensive colored restaurant in town, and that would include drinks, extra side orders, and dessert."

"I always leave a good tip when I eat out," I explained. I wouldn't miss the five dollars. Mrs. Dowler had gave me another bonus last week for helping her find a brooch she had misplaced. "And I wanted you to have enough left over after you pay your light bill so you can get the kids some candy or playpretties. I got cider, or would you rather drink something else? Like buttermilk or tea?"

"You ain't got no beer?"

"We don't keep alcohol in this house," I said firmly.

"Well, Claude drinks like a fish when he's with me. That's one of the reasons we was short of money this month."

"My son drinks? I ain't never seen him drink nothing stronger than buttermilk." It was bad enough Claude had stopped teaching Sunday school since he met Daisy. If she had him drinking now, there was no telling what else she'd drag him into if I didn't stop her.

"Look, Maggie, I don't know what your son got you thinking, but believe me, he ain't the Goody Two-shoes you think he is. I didn't come after him, he came after me. I told him he was too young and that I needed a man who was willing to help me out with my finances."

I glared at Daisy when she reached for one of the ham sandwiches I had already set on the table. "He promised me that he'd do everything I asked him to if I gave him a chance. So far, he been true to his word."

"Men his age make a lot of snap decisions. They can change their minds at the drop of a hat."

"I ain't going to worry about Claude doing nothing like that." She bit off a plug of her sandwich and chewed like a cow, never taking her eyes off my face.

Somehow I managed to smile. I sat down across from her, but I ignored the sandwiches.

"Ain't you going to eat, Maggie?"

"I guess I ain't as hungry as I thought."

"Okay. Then if you don't mind, wrap them sandwiches up and I'll take them with me. And how about a glass of that cider you mentioned?"

In less than fifteen minutes, Daisy had gobbled up three of the six sandwiches and sucked up half of the pitcher of cider. "I guess I should be getting back home now. Thanks for such a nice lunch." She let out a mighty belch and rushed out the door so fast, you would have thought the house was caving in.

I didn't tell Hubert I'd gave Daisy money when he got home from work. But I did tell him that I'd fixed lunch for her. That pleased him.

"That's a start. If Claude is so crazy about her this soon, there must be something good about her."

"Folks say she's real good to her mama," I said.

"Hmmm. Well, anybody that's good to their mama can't be all bad."

"I agree with that. But that don't mean she can be a good thing for our son."

"Well, for now, we'll just have to bite the bullet and go with the flow. So long as we keep things in perspective, I'm sure we'll get through this mess without losing our minds. Let's try and give her the benefit of the doubt."

I was going to bend over backward to tolerate Daisy. But Saturday night when Jessie started laying out more bad news, I didn't think I could do much bending after all.

We was sitting across from one another at her kitchen table, sharing a fresh pot of coffee.

"Maggie, that woman was at that bootlegger's house on the corner of Lomax Street last night. She was doing a brag about how she got Claude and you in the palm of her hand. That's what Orville told me first thing this morning. He was there and heard it with his own ears."

"What? Maybe that's where she got Claude, but she's wrong if she think I'm fool enough to let somebody like *her* hoodwink me. I don't know why Daisy would say something like that."

Jessie gave me a sideways glance. "Maybe it's because you paid her off when she came to your house to have lunch with you . . ."

"'Paid her off'? That heifer! If you talking about me giving her the money I was going to use to spend on her lunch at a restaurant, I wasn't trying to pay her off. She claimed they needed the money to keep their lights on."

"Daisy also bragged about what a good meal ticket Claude was. She's already in charge of all the finances. When he got paid the last time, she took what she wanted and gave him the change."

I had always loved listening to Jessie's gossip. Because my son was the main subject this time, it was painful. But I knew that if I stayed on top of everything unpleasant going on in my Claude's life, it would be easier to figure out how to get things under control and keep them there. That was the only reason I didn't change the subject or leave then.

"I don't understand why she's running her mouth so much. She should know that eventually somebody is going to tell me or Hubert, and we'll get mad."

"I think that's what she really wants. She done also told a few folks she can't stand you and Hubert, and that she is going to make you and him real sorry for the misery y'all done caused her."

I narrowed my eyes and stared at Jessie. "What misery? We been trying to be friends with her from day one. She is the one causing all the misery. I wonder how long it's going to take for Claude to see what a low-down, conniving heifer she really is!"

"You better hope it's soon. Like so many colored folks around here, she's been talking about packing up and moving North so she don't have to keep living under these segregation laws."

I breathed a sigh of relief. "Her leaving town would be a blessing. I hope she decides to do that. Good riddance! I'd even help her pack her bags."

Jessie let out a loud sigh and gave me a pitiful look. "That'll make things harder on you and Hubert."

"Harder how?"

"She done already said she is taking Claude with her. She said that a smart, ambitious colored man like him could go real far up North."

When I heard that, I almost jumped out of my skin. "To hell with that notion! Daisy Compton, or no other woman, ain't taking my baby nowhere!" I stood up and started pacing back and forth.

"You can't stop her, Maggie."

"When is this move supposed to take place?"

"Well, I heard she said she didn't want to do it before her wedding . . ."

Now on top of being mad, I was confused. "'Her wedding'? Who is she going to marry? This story is getting crazier and crazier."

Jessie took a long pull from her coffee cup before she replied. "Maggie, use your head. Ain't you been listening to everything I said in the last few minutes? Who do you think she's plotting to marry?"

I was about to take a sip, but I set my coffee cup back down so hard, coffee splashed out onto the table. "I know it ain't Claude," I said in a low, raspy tone. "Is it?" I dropped back into my seat.

"Yup." Jessie nodded and grabbed a dishrag and wiped up the coffee I'd spilled.

My jaw dropped so fast, every muscle in my neck and jaw immediately started throbbing. "I know the boy is love-struck, but I don't think he'd go that far! I don't believe it! I won't believe it until I hear it from him!"

Jessie's news flashes was making me sick. I was starting to get mad at her for delivering such unspeakable information.

"Um . . . I was hoping I wouldn't have to bring this next thing up. But you are my best friend and I think you need to know." Jessie cleared her throat and continued. "Anyway, Daisy is still in love with her kids' daddy. He done already gone North and she wants to join him."

"Then why don't she take her cheesy black ass up North to be with him?"

"I can't answer that, but I suspect she thinks that if she can get up there, her ex will eventually come around. I'm telling you, she ain't about to turn Claude loose until she gets all the help she can from him. One of the reasons she ain't headed North already is because she ain't got the money to do it with. But . . . well, Claude is the golden-egg-laying goose she needs."

I raised my hand and stood up again. "Jessie, I done heard enough."

"You don't want to hear the rest of what folks is talking about?"

"You done told me all the worst stuff and I feel bad enough already."

"I hope you and Hubert can turn Claude around before Daisy do something real drastic to keep him under her thumb."

I waved my arms and shook my head. "Like what?"

"Well, me and you both know how some folks around here use hoodoo to get what they want. When I was younger and didn't know no better, I had considered using it myself to get pregnant, remember?"

I gasped. "You talking about *witchcraft*! Oh, Lord. Don't tell me that woman fools around with something that dangerous! I don't know if any of these hoodoos in Lexington is really all they cracked up to be, but I don't want to have to find out. You telling me that Daisy is using hoodoo on my child?"

"I don't know if she is or not. But it wouldn't surprise me if she did. I heard that some of her relatives dabble in it, so it wouldn't be no stretch for her."

Before either one of us could speak again, Orville walked through the front door. He glared at me and shook his head. I had spoke to him so many times and been ignored, now I only said something to him when I felt like it. I didn't feel like doing that today.

"Hi, pig face," he growled, glaring at Jessie.

She gave him the evil eye, but she didn't say nothing. I sure would have. Especially when the only pig in the room was him. I had never heard any other man low-rate his wife or girlfriend in such a mean way. Orville laughed and kept walking.

"He's lucky I'm way too holy now to pay a hoodoo to straighten him out," Jessie said in a low voice. "I don't know how much longer I can put up with his mess."

"I seen him walking down the street the other day with that boy he had with his girlfriend," I mumbled.

"Which one?"

"He got more than one?" I felt bad for Jessie, but I was glad to be discussing her problems now instead of mine.

"Girl, where you been? He got another son with some other woman, ten years younger than Earl. I just found out last month."

"Did you get on him about it?"

Jessie nodded. "He didn't deny it. When I threatened to leave his ass, he slapped my face so hard, I seen stars. Then he cussed a blue streak and said if I ever left him, he'd kill my mama. And then he'd track me down and kill me."

"Lord have mercy. Well, I better get on home. If I hear any more bad news, I'm going to have a fit."

More bad news was waiting for me when I got home. Hubert was standing in front of the living-room window with a distressed look on his face. Claude was sitting on the couch with one of the biggest smiles I'd ever seen on him.

Before I could say anything, or give him a hug, he told me, "Mama, Daddy, me and Daisy is fixing to get married. I came over here as fast as I could because I didn't want y'all to hear it from one of them gossips."

Chapter 24

I'd had some bad dreams in my life, and I hoped that I was having one now. But I wasn't. Claude's announcement slammed into my head like a brick.

The house was so quiet now, it was scary. Hubert's jaws was twitching, and his eyebrows was scrunched up. I was glad I wasn't near a mirror because I didn't want to know how bad I looked. After a few more moments, Hubert stumbled across the floor and stopped in front of Claude, with his arms folded across his chest.

"Boy, did I just hear you say you going to marry that Daisy woman?"

"That's what you heard, Daddy," Claude whimpered, scooting back farther on the couch.

I just stood there as stiff as a statue, praying in my head that I'd be able to speak again before I collapsed. Hubert shook his head and slapped the side of his ear, like he couldn't believe what he was hearing. I was too overwhelmed to react as fast as he had.

"Y-you asked her to m-marry you?" he stammered.

Claude stood up and said in a tone so casual, you would have thought he was asking what I was cooking for dinner. "No, sir. I didn't ask Daisy to marry me. She asked me. I told her I wasn't sure I was ready for marriage yet and that upset her. She said I'd led her on, and that she ain't never let no man dupe her and get away with it. I felt bad when she busted out crying. So I apologized and told her I'd marry her. She stopped crying right away."

I was glad I was finally able to speak again. And I came out swinging. My voice was so loud and hot, the insides of my mouth felt like they was on fire. "You going to go through with it? Even after admitting you didn't know if you was ready for marriage? Boy, you must be too weak!"

"I ain't weak, Mama—"

"Then you must be crazy! That's the only way this nonsense is making any sense! We didn't raise you to let no woman take over your life the way Daisy is doing!"

"Y'all raised me right, and I plan to raise my kids the same way. But y'all also raised me to be my own man and make my own decisions. Well, the thing is, I love Daisy and I don't want to lose her. If I don't marry her, she might run off with somebody else. She told me she'd been thinking about that anyway."

"Claude, don't you know that everybody in town knows that woman got a few loose screws? Why would you want to burden yourself with somebody like that?" I asked.

Claude inhaled with his mouth opened so wide, it looked like a dipper. "'Burden'? Daisy *ain't no* burden. Besides, like I said, I love her."

"You ain't even old enough to know what real love is," I insisted. I didn't want to move closer to him and have him move even farther away. That would have made me feel even worse.

"Don't be telling me nothing about me being too young! You and Daddy was both younger than me when y'all got married!" Claude reminded. He waved his hand in the air and then he wagged his finger in my face. "I knew I shouldn't have come over here. I'm going to go back home."

"Home? You already at home!" I boomed. I rushed up to him and grabbed his arm. "This done gone on long enough. You get your behind in your room and read the Bible! You stay there until we—"

I didn't even get to finish my sentence. Claude spun around and took off running toward the door.

After he dashed out the house, me and Hubert skittered to

the door. By the time we got outside, Claude was crossing the street at the corner.

"Claude, baby, please come back!" I hollered.

As soon as I got the last word out, lights started coming on in the houses closest to us and people started peeping out their windows.

"Hubert, we done run him off," I said, sniffling. "We got to go get him."

"Maggie, we can't do that. We'd only make things worse." Hubert's voice was so feeble now, I was amazed that he was still able to speak. "Let's go back in the house. We done already gave the neighbors enough to start gossiping." He wrapped his arm around my shoulder and guided me back inside. "Let's just wait and see what happens next."

We decided not to tell Hubert's mama and daddy yet about this tragic turn of events. We didn't want Pa Wiggins to know that the prayer chain he had organized wasn't working.

I cried off and on for the next two days. When I crawled out of bed Monday morning, my eyes was so red and puffy, it looked like somebody had clobbered me. I hadn't slept much since Claude took off, and I knew Hubert hadn't either. He'd tossed and turned and cried almost as much as I had.

"You want me to fix you some eggs and bacon?" he asked in a raspy tone when I joined him in the kitchen at half past seven a.m.

I shook my head. "Thank you. But I ain't got no appetite."

"You look terrible, sugar pie. Why don't you stay home today?"

I glanced at the clock on the wall above the counter. "I can't. All I'd do is mope around here and cry some more. Being with Mrs. Dowler today will take my mind off this situation."

When I got to Mrs. Dowler's house at nine a.m., I was shocked when I seen the way she looked. Her eyes was almost as red and swollen as mine! As bad as I was feeling, I started feeling sorry for her right away. She was so good to me, I cared a lot about her.

"Lord have mercy, Mrs. Dowler! What's the matter?" I took her by the hand and led her to the living-room couch and we plopped down at the same time.

"It's my baby brother, Oswald. The one in California I told you about." She choked on a sob and dabbed at her eyes with a white lace handkerchief.

"Did he decide not to come stay with you?"

I was hoping that was the case. With all the stuff I had going on in my life, I was not looking forward to dealing with a bigot who would probably take over Mrs. Dowler's house and cause me some grief.

"He called me up day before yesterday and told me that he had to change his travel plans. Instead of coming later, he's coming sooner."

"How much sooner?" I asked with my heart racing.

"He'll get here in the next day or so. He got on the train yesterday morning."

"What happened to make him change his plans?"

"The man his wife dumped him for beat him up when he tried to talk her into staying with him. He was told to leave lickety-split, or face serious consequences. Like another beating, or worse. He packed all he could carry and told his wife he'd be back to get the rest of his belongings when he found somebody with a car or a truck. She wouldn't let him take his truck, even though it's in his name. When he did find a friend to bring him back and help him load up his stuff, she had packed everything he owned and set it outside on the ground. That was bad enough. But before he could collect it all and put it in his friend's vehicle, it started raining cats and dogs. All of the nice suits he owned were totally ruined. So were several family heirlooms that can't be restored."

"Oh, my God. She's meaner than I thought."

Mrs. Dowler nodded. "Oh, Maggie. You should have heard how hard he was crying on the telephone. He hasn't boo-hooed like that since he was a baby! He said he didn't know if he wanted to keep on living." Mrs. Dowler grabbed my hand and squeezed it. "My dear husband committed suicide. It almost destroyed me. I declare, I couldn't go through it again and not go crazy!"

"I don't think your brother will do nothing that desperate."

"That's debatable. I've told him numerous times that there are enough fish in the sea that he shouldn't pin all his hopes on one woman. I advised him to find someone new as soon as possible. He pooh-poohed my suggestion and continues to moon over his wife. Oswald can't stand being without a mate. He's been with his wife since they met in college. And he claims he never looked at another woman since he married her."

"I hope him and his wife can patch things up and at least stay friends. It'd be a shame for a man who's been with the same woman for so long to end up by hisself."

"We've got a lot of other kinfolks scattered here and there. But he's the only one who got up enough nerve to move to a faraway Babylon like California. I'm surprised he hasn't come to his senses and left that place before now. But his wife rules the roost and I'm sure she was calling all the shots. I'm sorry his marriage failed, but at least he'll be coming home to somebody who loves him. Thank God he's still got the bulk of his inheritance. Daddy left us all well taken care of. My brother will be able to pay his own way and not have to depend on me.

"He is no angel, though. I swear to God, that man is so persnickety and hard to get along with, Jesus would weep. But I love him to death and I'd never turn my back on him. He won't be alone as long as there is a breath in my body. He told me that he only wants to stay with me until he finds a job. I told him that at his age, that wouldn't be so easy. Can you imagine someone a year from retirement still wanting to work? I declare, this situation is driving me stone crazy!"

"Mrs. Dowler, I am so sorry for you. I'll do all I can to help you get through this."

She started crying some more. I patted her shoulder until she stopped. Then she sucked in a deep breath, rubbed the side of her head, and gave me a serious look.

"Enough about me. It's your turn."

"My turn, ma'am?"

"You can't hide anything from me. What's got you looking like a deserted puppy?" she asked, sniffling and squinting.

I updated her on Claude, and I didn't leave nothing out. When I stopped talking, she gave me a sympathetic look.

"Isn't it quite a coincidence? We both have loved ones in serious distress on account of a female."

I sighed. "That's for sure. Me and my husband tried to talk some sense into my son's hard head, but it didn't do no good."

"And it won't. At this point, I advise you and Hubert to try and repair the damage you've already done to your relationship with your son. Try to accept the woman and things might work out better than you think."

"I am trying to get to know her better and give her a chance. She told somebody she couldn't stand me and my husband, but I'm going to overlook that and try to accept her anyway. I've . . . um . . . even gave her some money."

Mrs. Dowler gasped so hard, she choked on some air. I had to slap her on her back to help her catch her breath. She looked at me with a mortified expression on her face.

"You did what? Good Lord in heaven. Why would you give money to a woman like that?"

"Because she asked for it and I thought it would help our relationship." My answer was as dumb as could be, even though it was true.

"Listen, Maggie. I'm a heap of years older than you, and there are probably things you know that I don't know. But I can tell you one thing, you can't buy love or friendship. If you start paying this woman off, she'll expect it. The more you give her, the more she'll want. I've known folks like her. They don't stop milking a cow until it's bone-dry. Before you know it, you and Hubert will be in the poorhouse and that woman still might be wreaking havoc in your son's life."

I gave Mrs. Dowler a thoughtful look. "I don't know what to do now. If they go through with the marriage and move to another state, me and Hubert won't have a chance of getting him back."

"When is this wedding supposed to take place?"

"I don't know. But the way things have been moving so far, something tells me it's going to be soon."

"Lord Almighty! In the meantime, do everything you can to

make peace. Spend time with her before the wedding if you can. Maybe you'll be able to convince her to wait a few months. That would give your boy more time to see her for what she really is. What activities does she like best?"

"I don't know her well enough to know much about that."

"Get in touch with your son and apologize for upsetting him. First chance you get, grill him on some of the things she likes. If she likes to cook, share some of your recipes with her. If she likes to keep her hair looking good, take her to your mother-in-law so she can fix her up with a real nice do. Invite her to your house for supper. It'll make her feel special and might make her behave better."

"I'll do all of that if I have to." I was sniffling. "But what if none of them things work?"

Mrs. Dowler stared at the floor for a few seconds. When she looked back up, there was a look in her pretty brown eyes that I would never forget. For a split second, I thought I was gazing into the eyes of Satan. Not only was the pupils two shades darker, they had swelled up almost the same size as a dime. Well, I was in such a state of panic myself, maybe I was just imagining that was the way they looked. Even if that was the case, I had never seen anybody's eyes look so evil. I knew that Mrs. Dowler wasn't evil. She was just as devoted to her religion as I was. But people like us could be pushed just so far.

When I rubbed her hand, she started talking again. "If the things you try on Daisy don't work, you'll have to find a way to get rid of her. If you don't, she's going to cause you even more grief. Mark my words."

Chapter 25

I SHED A FEW TEARS DURING MY BUS RIDE BACK TO MRS. DOWLER'S house Tuesday morning. I was so distracted I missed my stop. I was glad I wasn't too far away when I realized that. By running, I was still able to get to work on time.

Mrs. Dowler met me at the front door and ushered me into the kitchen. "Please keep your voice down. My brother is upstairs unpacking and getting settled into his room and I don't want to disturb him. I fixed him some grits and eggs, so he'll be down momentarily."

"I'm glad to hear he made it here," I said in a dry tone.

"I am too. But I do wish he could have worked things out with his wife so he could have remained in California." Mrs. Dowler started wringing her hands and breathing through her mouth. I had never seen her acting so jittery.

"Do you want me to go back home? That way you and him can have more time alone today."

Mrs. Dowler inhaled suddenly with her mouth hanging open. "Oh, heavens no! Don't you even think about going back home." She started to wring her hands even harder. "He's not the best company, even when he's in a good mood. Having you here today would make it much easier for me to start sorting out a routine with him."

"All right, then." I glanced around the kitchen. There was a bushel basket on the floor with the items I had washed and hung on the clothesline yesterday. "Do you want me to start the ironing now? I like to take my time with your hankies so I can get the creases nice and sharp."

I was glad she had stopped wringing her hands. "Yes. Wait a few more minutes, though. I want you to know up front that you may have to make a few small adjustments to accommodate my brother from time to time." She abruptly glanced toward the door and then back at me with mournful basset-hound eyes. "He'll be down in a few minutes. He was in a grouchy mood when I picked him up at the train station this morning. And with good reason. They held the train up in Texas for two hours, and the food they fed him wreaked havoc on his bowels. He's spent most of his time since he got here, sitting on the commode. With that and everything else that's happened to him, he'll be considerably grumpy for a while."

I wanted to wring my hands the way Mrs. Dowler had done. But I didn't want her to know how concerned I was.

"Then I'll make sure I don't do or say nothing that might upset him."

"I'm pleased to hear that. He may not be too friendly toward you at first. For my sake, please don't let his behavior bother you too much, though. I can assure you that once he gets to know you, he'll take a right smart shine to you."

The smile on Mrs. Dowler's face didn't fool me. I had a feeling she was just as concerned about how her brother was going to treat me as I was.

"Okay. I'm sure me and him will get along just fine, so don't you worry about nothing." I didn't know how convincing I sounded to her, but to myself, I didn't sound sure of nothing. Talking about this miserable brother made me feel awkward, so I decided to change the subject. "By the way, I forgot to tell you yesterday that I seen a lizard in the garden while I was hanging out the wash. He was right stout, so I know he could do a whole lot of damage."

"Is that a fact? Hmmm. You know, you've been maintaining my garden very well and I do appreciate it. You are so thorough.

I'm sure you'll take care of that stout lizard and any other creatures that might pop up." Mrs. Dowler's face bloomed as large as the sunflowers in a vase sitting on one of her living-room end tables. "I'm so pleased to have you around."

"Thank you, ma'am. I'm pleased to be here."

Mrs. Dowler raised her finger in the air. "One more thing. Before you do the ironing, I want you to get that arsenic out of the pantry and go out to the garden and sprinkle a mess of it in each row, end to end."

"That's another thing I need to let you know. There ain't but a smidgen of arsenic left. I meant to tell you before now, but with all the things I got going on at home, it slipped my mind. I'm sorry."

"You don't have to be sorry. I fully understand what you're going through, and you have my undivided sympathy. I thank you for still being mindful enough to keep tabs on our supplies. We're low on arsenic, you say? Damnation!" Mrs. Dowler cringed and screwed up her mouth and exhaled from one side. "I tell you what, take the keys to my car and go over to that hardware store on Morgan Street and get some more. Get the largest can they got. No, make that two large cans."

I held up my hand. "Mrs. Dowler, that store don't like to serve colored folks. When they do, they're real mean. The last time I went in there, the cashier shortchanged me. When I brought it to her attention, she threatened to call the police and say I was harassing her."

Mrs. Dowler leaned her head back and widened her eyes, like she was hearing news like this for the first time. "My Lord!" she wheezed. "I am so sick of these Jim Crow laws and all this race-dividing foolishness. You would think that by now the lawmakers would realize that it'd be easier for everybody if they treated colored folks like human beings. The money y'all spend is as good as the money white folks spend! Do you think I care if a colored person eats in the same restaurants I eat in, or sits next to me on the bus? I don't know how your people make it in this world without going crazy!"

"I been asking myself that for years." We both sighed. "There's a colored man on Noble Street who sells all kinds of stuff out of his backyard shed. He got white friends who do a lot of favors for him. They been picking up merchandise for him to sell, as far back as I can remember. The last time I was in his place, he had some arsenic," I said.

"Bootleggers and all kinds of other unsavory characters have taken over that whole vicinity. I wouldn't dare ask a pretty little thing like you to go over there by yourself. Not with all those husky men on the loose. You could get ravaged."

"I been going over there all my life and ain't none of them men ravaged me yet."

"Maybe not, sugar. But there is a first time for everything. I'll go to the hardware store on Morgan Street myself," Mrs. Dowler said, removing her apron. "I'd invite you to ride with me, but somebody needs to stay here for when Oswald comes down in case he needs something. I hope you don't mind."

"No, ma'am. I don't mind," I said in a shaky tone.

Less than a minute after Mrs. Dowler left the house, I heard footsteps padding down the staircase. I held my breath when a skinny white man with skin that looked as tough as shoe leather shuffled into the kitchen. He stopped in the doorway and slapped his hands onto his narrow hips. He had on a brown suit, a white shirt, and a brown plaid necktie. There was such a friendly look on his face, I couldn't imagine him rocking the boat for me after all. When he smiled, I felt even more at ease. And then his mood changed in the blink of a eye. Now he was looking so distressed, you would have thought I'd stepped on his foot.

"Who the hell are you? And how did you get in this house, gal?"

Chapter 26

I WAS SO CAUGHT OFF GUARD, MY FIRST THOUGHT WAS TO RUN OUT the back door and keep on running. But common sense told me that that would have been a big mistake. I couldn't leave Mrs. Dowler in a lurch. My lips was quivering, but I managed to smile and say in the most cheerful tone I could manage, "Good morning, Mr. Oswald. I'm Maggie Wiggins. I do the laundry for your sister, every Monday and Tuesday. She just left to go pick up something from the store."

I was so nervous I started sweating right away. I reached out my hand to shake his. The way he looked at it, you would have thought I had a wart on every finger. He grunted and dismissed me with a sharp wave.

"Uh . . . she fixed you some breakfast, but she said if you want anything else I'm to take care of it."

Mr. Oswald let out his breath and looked me up and down. His gaze stayed on my bosom way longer than it should have. I didn't know what to think when he winked at me and smiled.

"When I want something from you, I'll let you know. Now you get!"

I scurried into the pantry to get the iron and the board. I figured if I took long enough, he'd be gone by the time I got back to the kitchen. So, to kill time, I rearranged all the canned goods on the shelves, twice.

Ten minutes later, when I thought it was safe to leave the

pantry, that sucker was still in the kitchen and was just putting a bowl of grits and a cup of coffee on a tray. This time when he looked at me, he didn't look so mean.

"And another thing, don't you ever enter my room without my permission. I got valuables lying about, and I want to keep them. Do you hear me?"

"Yes, sir." I didn't even look at him as I set up the ironing board.

Mr. Oswald heaved out a loud breath and headed back toward the staircase.

I didn't want to jump the gun, but I had a feeling he had something nasty on his mind that involved me. That was usually the case when a man looked at a woman's body the way he'd looked at mine. I immediately pushed that thought to the back of my mind. I didn't think he would be brazen enough to take advantage of me in Mrs. Dowler's house. But he had already got it in his mind that I was a thief! I had never stole nothing before in my life, and I was not stupid enough to start by swiping things from white folks now.

This was going to be a long day. A little voice in my head told me that every other day was going to be just as long with Mr. Oswald living in the house.

It never took me more than a couple of hours to do all the ironing. After I had done that, I went out to the garden to sprinkle the arsenic Mrs. Dowler had returned with. She had bought two real large containers so she wouldn't have to buy any more for a while. It was a good thing she did, because now snakes had decided to invade her garden.

"You ain't got to worry about them creatures for now," I told Mrs. Dowler when I got back in the house.

She was in her living room slumped in a corner on her couch, drinking mint julep and fanning her face with one of the many hand fans she owned. "Good! I got enough to fret about."

The worried look on her face worried me.

She glanced at the doorway and said in a low tone, "Oswald said you sassed him while I was gone. Is that true?"

My mouth dropped open. My heart was beating so hard, it felt like it was trying to bust out of my chest. "Huh? I would never sass him!"

"Well, he must have misconstrued whatever it was you said. Just be careful from now on. I don't want him to get any more upset than he already is."

"Yes, ma'am." I was glad that Mrs. Dowler had not harped on what her brother had told her. But I knew there would be other times when I said something he "misconstrued." In the meantime, I planned to continue catering to Mrs. Dowler. "Do you want me to bring you some of them tea cakes you made this morning?"

"No, thank you. I'm fine for now, sugar."

"You look like you could use some pampering, ma'am. Do you want me to tend to your feet?"

Nobody loved to get a foot massage as much as Mrs. Dowler did. According to her, nobody did it as good as I did. It was a unpleasant chore. But I didn't mind doing it. Besides, it was nowhere near as unpleasant as scooping up lizards and weevils and whatnot and disposing of them.

"A foot massage would suit me just fine. Wait until I finish my mint julep, though."

"All right. While you doing that, I'll get a bucket and go back out to the garden and scoop them critters up. It don't take but a few minutes for that arsenic to work, so they should be nice and dead by now. Do you want me to dump everything in the trash can this time, or make a pile and set it on fire like you had me do the last two times?"

"I'd rather you put everything in the trash. And that's what I want you to do from now on. The last time you set a fire, the neighbors complained about the stench. But you don't have to do that right now. Before you go back outside, come sit with me for a little while." She patted the spot next to her.

I eased down and took her hand in mine. "Do you mind if I ask why you looking so sad? Is it because of what your brother said about me sassing him?"

"No, it's not. It's just . . . well, I'm a bit melancholy because today would have been my husband's ninety-first birthday. I just want some company, if you don't mind. Oswald and my husband never got along, so I can't expect any sympathy from him."

"I know you must miss your husband something terrible after being married to him for sixty-five years."

"I miss him dearly. After he passed, I had a few men friends, but I knew I'd never get married again. Nobody could take Billy Jim's place." Mrs. Dowler whipped a frilly handkerchief from inside her brassiere and dabbed at her eyes. "Um . . . when he found out he had cancer and only a few months to live, he couldn't go on. He didn't want to suffer, and he didn't want to be a burden to me. I told him we'd get a full-time nurse, but he didn't want anything to do with that. He didn't want his family and friends to know about his illness, since he never wanted pity."

Mrs. Dowler sat up straighter and cleared her throat. "When the economy started going downhill a few years ago, a lot of bankers and other businessmen preferred suicide to living like paupers, and nobody was surprised. Some folks thought that suicide was more honorable than living in poverty, especially the ones who'd been living on easy street for so many years. My folks had always had money, so we were all right. With my inheritance, and the rent I collect from the properties I own here, I'll never have to worry about money."

"If your family still had money, why did your husband kill hisself?"

"*I* had money, Billy Jim didn't. His folks had lost everything in the War Between the States. My husband was a proud man. He had a fine education and was very shrewd, so he did quite well in real estate for years. People came to him when they were in need, and that made him feel very important and honorable. He would have never accepted handouts for himself or lived off my money. Nobody in my family knows the real reason he killed himself eight years ago. To this day, everybody—including the family—think he died of a broken spirit because he'd lost his real estate business. He made me promise I would never tell anyone that he'd taken his own life because he didn't want to suffer. He was afraid they would think of him as a coward. You are the only person I've ever told this to."

"I appreciate you sharing something so serious with me. You ain't got to worry about me telling nobody," I said. "And I thought I had problems."

"But there's hope for you. If this woman who has mesmerized your son is as wretched as you say she is, maybe you'll get lucky and one of her other men friends will solve your problem."

"You mean, one might kill her?"

Mrs. Dowler laughed. "I don't think you'll get *that* lucky. I was thinking that maybe she'd get tired of your son and take off with another poor fool. Now, until *when* or *if* that happens, try to get along with her." Mrs. Dowler looked toward the doorway again and shook her head. "My poor brother. I hope he finds himself another lady friend before too long. I don't know of any other man who hates being without the love of a woman as much as Oswald."

"Oh, I'm sure he'll find somebody eventually. Didn't him and his wife have any kids?"

"Just one. A boy they named Richard. He died in the military when he was only nineteen, in the Great War. His wife had developed a medical condition so they couldn't have any more. I'm so grateful I had seven. If I lost one, I'd never get over it. But at least I'd have the others to fall back on." Mrs. Dowler gave me a pitiful look. "Do you ever wish you had more than one?"

"Every day." I got sad so quick, I had to blink hard to hold back my tears. "Having one child is a blessing and a curse. We tried and tried to have more, but nothing happened. I don't know what me and Hubert would do if we ever lost Claude." I couldn't imagine what Mrs. Dowler would say if I told her me and Hubert had never made love to each other.

Chapter 27

ONE OF THE FIRST THINGS I DID WHEN I GOT UP WEDNESDAY morning was try to reach Claude. Daisy answered the phone.

"Hello, this is Maggie," I said, speaking in the sweetest tone of voice I could manage. At the same time I had the nastiest taste in my mouth I'd ever had. I was determined to get along with this woman, no matter what I had to do.

"Maggie who?" she asked. The she giggled. "Oops! I'm sorry. I didn't recognize your voice. Claude ain't home."

"Oh, that's all right. I called to talk to you."

"*You* want to talk to *me*? What in the world about?"

"I . . . I was wondering if you'd like to go have lunch with me one day this week? I'd still like to try that fish place." I held my breath because I expected her to ask me to give her the money again instead of spending it on lunch.

"Well, I'm busy and I will be for the rest of this week. And I'm fixing to go pick blackberries in a little while before Claude and the kids get home this evening."

"Really? What a coincidence! I was thinking about doing the same thing myself today. I like to pick mine in June right after they get good and ripe. Me and Hubert don't like berries as much after they been hanging on the bushes too long because they ain't as juicy and fresh then. Which patch do you go to?"

"I been going to the one down the road from that pig farm near the highway. It's the only one close enough to walk to from here. Which one do you go to?"

"I like that one off of Sawburg Road. The berries is real plump and plentiful." I sniffed and added, "Most of the folks I know don't like to go that far."

"That patch is along the railroad tracks, so you can't get there in a car. And that's a long walk from this part of town. Especially for a woman your age . . ."

If her crack about my age was made to make me feel low, it didn't work. I looked younger than thirty-nine, but some folks thought Daisy was at least five years older than she really was! "Well, I don't mind. I need the exercise. Besides, it'd give us a chance to talk."

She took her time responding. "What do you want to talk to me about?"

"You don't have to worry. I'm done sticking my nose in my son's business. He loves you so much and I know you make him happy, that's enough for me. There's a heap of other things we can talk about."

"Hmmm. Let me finish washing my dishes and do a few chores. It's ten now. I should be done by eleven. Is that a good time for you?" she asked.

"Uh-huh."

"Good. Then be here at eleven sharp. If you going to be late, call me back and let me know. Otherwise, if you ain't here when you supposed to be, I might take a notion and go off somewhere else."

"You ain't got to worry about me being on time. I'll be there with bells on," I answered.

Daisy was taking too long to say something else and that made me nervous. It was important for me to get to know her well enough so I could figure out the best way to get her out of my son's life.

"You that anxious to go pick blackberries, or to spend some time with me again?" she inquired.

"Both. I been meaning to go pick blackberries for a few days now. And I was going to invite you to come over and eat lunch again so we could converse some more. This way I can do both."

"All right, then. By the way, I got a favor to ask you."

My stomach knotted up. I held my breath because I thought she was going to ask me for more money. And I was prepared to give it to her.

"Do you mind coming in through the back kitchen door when you get here? I don't like folks trampling on my living-room floor. It's hard enough to keep it clean with me and Claude, the kids, and my folks in and out. I ain't going to put up with nobody else tracking in sand and other debris no more."

"Is that the favor?"

"Yup. You got a problem with it?"

"No, not at all."

"Okay, then. I always leave the kitchen door unlocked, so when you get here, just walk right in. And make sure you wipe your feet first," she said.

The back door! This woman never ceased to amaze me. "All right," I muttered. It was a wonder that my seething resentment hadn't reached the boiling point. I told myself to keep my anger under control because it wasn't going to last too much longer. "I don't have no problem coming and going through back doors. I'm used to it."

And I was.

The white-owned businesses that did serve colored folks made us come in through back doors. We had to ride in the back of the bus, even if we was the only passengers on it. When we went places where you had to stand in line, we always had to get in the back and wait until every white person had done their business before we could get waited on. The last time I went to the post office, when I finally made it up to the front of the line, it was closing time. I had to go back three more times just to buy a few stamps.

I was used to all the mistreatment we had to put up with. Besides, it was the law and there was nothing we could do about the way things was. But I never expected that kind of third-class treatment from a colored person! If this was what I was going to have to put up with if my son stayed with this woman, me and

Hubert would probably have to start drinking like fish just to tolerate her.

Before I could leave the house, Daisy called me up to say she couldn't go to the blackberry patch today. According to her, "something came up" that she had to go take care of right away and she wasn't sure how long she'd be gone.

Me and Hubert sat down to eat supper a little before six-thirty p.m. Since this mess with Daisy started, he didn't go visit any of his men friends as often.

"When do you plan on making gumbo again, Maggie?" he wanted to know.

"Why? You don't like them black-eyed peas," I teased as I pointed to his almost-empty plate.

"These peas is scrumptious, like everything you cook. But I'm like everybody else—I can't get enough of your gumbo. I could eat it two or three times a week."

I felt my face get hot. I blushed when I got embarrassed or when somebody teased me.

"Well, I'll make it again in a few days, just for you."

We laughed.

Before either one of us could speak again, we heard somebody open the front door. Hubert looked at me with a puzzled expression on his face. I shrugged. I assumed it was Jessie, but it was Claude who stumbled into the kitchen. He looked like he had been mauled. His shirt had been ripped in the front. There was a knot the size of a walnut on his forehead, and blood was trickling from his lip. Me and Hubert jumped up out of our seats at the same time.

"What in the world happened to you?" I hollered.

I ran up to Claude and grabbed his arm and steered him to a chair at the table. He shuddered when I grabbed the napkin I'd been using and started wiping his face.

"Nothing serious," he panted, pushing my hand away. "Can I stay over here tonight?"

"Boy, who hit you?" Hubert yelled, with a frantic look on his face, as he hovered over Claude.

Claude was breathing hard and rubbing the knot on his forehead. It took him a few moments to respond. All the while, me and Hubert stood there with our mouths hanging open.

"I got a ride home from work with one of my coworkers. We drove past a house where a new bootlegger just started doing his business at. The next thing I knew, Daisy sashayed out, all hugged up with some joker!"

"Did you get out of that car and go get her?" I asked as I wiped blood off his lips.

"No, I didn't have a chance to. I went on home. When she got in, I asked her about the man I seen her with and she jumped on me," he whimpered. "She poked me with a fork and then she bounced a skillet off my head!"

"I can't believe my ears!" Hubert hollered.

I had never seen him in such a agitated state. His eyes was darting from side to side and he was breathing through his mouth.

"See there! We tried to tell you that woman ain't no good!" I screamed. I sounded like a crazy woman and probably looked like one too. "Thank God we got you back before she done any real harm."

Claude's eyes got big. "Oh, Mama, don't overreact. She didn't mean to hurt me!" He had the nerve to say that, with a chuckle no less.

"Boy, what's the matter with you? She came at you with a fork and a skillet. If she didn't mean to hurt you, what did she mean to do?" Hubert asked.

Claude gave us a weary look. "This ain't as bad as y'all making it out to be. If Daisy really wanted to do me some harm, she would have done it by now."

"I think a knot on your forehead and one of your best shirts ripped to pieces is doing you some harm!" I hollered.

"Aw, Mama. I know Daisy better than you do. She . . . she would never go too far. Last week she pulled out a gun and put it right up to my head. All because I told her I didn't want her to go out at night to drink without me."

"*What?*" Me and Hubert shrieked at the same time.

"Like I said"—Claude paused and looked from me to Hubert with the same weary look on his face—"if she wanted to do me some real harm, she would have done it by now."

Chapter 28

I WAS SURPRISED I DIDN'T FAINT AFTER WHAT CLAUDE JUST TOLD US.

Hubert covered his mouth with his hand and swayed from side to side. I was too stunned to move. I tried to say something, but I couldn't get the words out. My head felt like somebody was inside hitting my brain with rocks.

When Hubert was able to stand up straight, he stomped his foot and balled his fists. "That's it! This thing done got way out of control! I'm going to go over there and give that heifer a piece of my mind!"

Claude rolled his eyes and threw his hands up in the air. "Aw, come on, Daddy. Don't you dare do that. This ain't no big deal. I'm still going to marry Daisy." He was just as cool and calm as he could be.

I was finally able to talk again. "Boy, that woman pulled a gun on you! What you waiting for her to do next, put a noose around your neck and string you up from a tree?"

"Now, don't go making up stuff," Claude said with a dry look on his face. "She likes to bluff. I ain't worried about her going too far. I wish y'all would stop trying to get involved. Maybe I shouldn't have told y'all nothing until the day after the wedding."

I was horrified when he laughed. Me and Hubert was going to pieces and he was laughing!

We looked at Claude with our eyes as wide as saucers. "Why

did you come over here if you didn't want us to get involved?" I asked.

"I came over here so I could give her time to cool off," he replied.

I was glad he had stopped laughing.

"But I don't think I want to spend the night over here after all. She was crying and begging me not to leave when I ran out of the house, so I'm sure she is sorry for what she done. She claims that man I seen her with was her cousin," Claude said.

"Is she so hot she's hugging up on her cousins?" I wanted to know. "Only a fool would believe that cock-and-bull story!"

Claude gave me an exasperated look. Then he stood up and started moving toward the door. "Then I guess I'm a fool," he mumbled. "I'm sorry I came over here and riled y'all up. I won't do it no more."

When he left, me and Hubert looked at each other and shook our heads. "What do you think we should do now?" he asked.

Like this was a question I could answer? Shoot. I was just as dumbfounded as he was.

"I don't know. But I would like to know if you still think I should try to get close to Daisy?" I said with a smirk.

He took his time answering. "Believe it or not, I still do. Most young couples have their ups and downs. It ain't unusual for them to come to blows from time to time."

"Me and you been married over twenty years. We ain't never 'come to blows,'" I pointed out.

"Maggie, if Claude don't think this is such a big deal, maybe we shouldn't. Lord have mercy."

Hubert blew out a long, loud breath and rubbed the side of his neck. I had never seen him look so tired and defeated.

"This mess done just about wore me out. I'm going to go in the bedroom and listen to the radio for a while." His voice sounded so weak now, and he looked like a man who was ready to give up the fight. Maybe he was, but I wasn't.

I paced back and forth in the living room trying to decide what to do next. One thing I already knew was that I was prepared to fight this battle to the very end—even if it took my last breath away. At the end of the day, I'd rather be dead than lose my child. I knew now that saving Claude was up to me. With everything I'd heard about him and Daisy, I'd be a fool if I didn't take action. I couldn't wait to talk to Jessie about this again. I rarely took her advice, but just talking to her always made me feel better when I was downhearted.

Jessie's brother had recently started a new job at a logging company near the nursing home where she worked. It was only part-time, but he worked a night shift like she did. On the nights he had to go in, he gave her a ride to work and she didn't need to depend on me. And, when her mother decided to go to Birmingham to visit her sister last week, she took Earl with her. They would be gone for another week, so Jessie didn't need me to watch him neither.

Other than Mrs. Dowler, Jessie was the only person I really liked talking to about my problems. I decided to go to her house to see if I could spend a little time with her before she went to work. I was in such a tizzy, I had to do something that would help me calm down. I was disappointed when she didn't answer her door.

On the walk back to my house, I thought that it might be better if I went to the source of my pain: Daisy. The minute I made it back into my kitchen, I dialed her number. If nothing else, I could at least try to settle our differences by trying even harder to be nice to her. I was glad Hubert was still in the bedroom listening to the radio. I didn't want him to hear my end of the conversation in case I got ahold of her.

Just as I was about to hang up after ten rings, she answered.

"Oh, Maggie! Praise the Lord, I'm so glad you called," she greeted. She really did sound like she was glad to hear from me. "Me and Claude had a little misunderstanding and he said he was going to spend the night with y'all. Well, I guess he thought it over because he's back now and everything is all right. We done kissed and made up. He went to go get me a catfish sandwich. I want you and Hubert to know that y'all ain't got nothing to worry about. Claude had the wrong idea about something, but I cleared it up. And he apologized for making me mad. Bless his heart."

I wanted to scream my head off. If I could have jumped through the telephone, I wouldn't have been responsible for my actions. I could picture my hands around her throat. By the grace of God, I managed to sound cool and calm. "Daisy, don't worry about nothing. I'm sure you and Claude will work things out on your own."

"I'm glad you feel that way, Maggie. If I'm going to be part of your family, I want us to get along."

"I want the same thing, Daisy," I managed to say. My heart was beating so fast, I massaged my chest. That didn't slow down my heart, but I felt a little better.

"You still want to go pick blackberries? We can go tomorrow. I'd like to go to that patch you been going to."

"Yeah. I'd still like to go. I was planning on going anyway in the next day or so. Tomorrow works for me."

"We'd have to go early in the day, though. I want to surprise Claude and the kids with a blackberry pie when they get home tomorrow. So I would appreciate it if you don't let nobody know we going. Okay?"

"Okay." Just talking to the woman who was causing so much distress in my family was one of the hardest things I ever did. It was going to take a miracle for everybody involved to be happy. But at least I was trying. "I'll be at your house around ten in the morning."

"That's a good time. We'll be back home in plenty of time so I can get all my cooking and other chores done. Just remember to come through the back door, like I already told you."

"No problem." I chuckled. "And, Daisy, I do want us to be friends. Me and Hubert tried for years to have another baby, hoping it would be a girl. Things didn't work out for us, so having a daughter-in-law would be the next best thing." I was so used to lying about me and Hubert's attempts to have another child, I had almost started believing it myself.

"You think so?"

"I know so."

"I ain't got much in common with you and your church friends. And I'm going to be honest with you, I ain't going to change to please other folks this late in the game."

"Daisy, please just be yourself. I'd rather have you be honest and up front about everything. That way I will always know where we stand. Once we get more acquainted, I want you to join us for supper with Hubert's mama and daddy. But that's only if you want to. I don't want you to feel pressured about doing nothing just to please me and Hubert." Just saying them words almost made me vomit.

My ears burned, my stomach churned, and my chest tightened when I heard what she said next.

"Maggie, I'm glad you finally came to your senses. And it's a good thing you doing that *now.* If you hadn't, when Claude got back from the fish place, I was going to make him cut *all* ties with y'all."

This woman was worse than I thought! Was she so stupid she thought I'd let her cut us off from Claude completely and not do nothing about it?

"I'm glad I finally came to my senses too. The last thing I want is to lose all contact with my son permanently."

"All right, then. Let me get off this phone so I can finish rolling up my hair. I'll see you in the morning."

"Yup," I chirped. The taste in my mouth was so sour, I had to hold my breath to keep the puke from rising in my throat.

Chapter 29

I HAD HEARD MORE THAN ONE PERSON SAY, "IF YOU KICK A DOG LONG enough, that dog is going to bite you." Daisy had turned me into a dog, and she'd kicked me long enough. Well, it was time for me to bite her. I couldn't think of no other way to stop her from what she was doing to my son, but to kill her.

I never thought I'd see the day that I would be planning to kill somebody. I had never even wanted to hurt another human. Not even the mean kids who had picked on me in school. The only person I'd ever got violent with was a boy at church I'd slapped for touching my titties when I was a young girl. I'd felt bad about it later. But if I hadn't chastised him, I knew I would have felt even worse for letting another person put their vile hands on my body and take advantage of me.

But it was my son I had to defend now, and murdering Daisy was the only way I could end the nightmare she'd put my whole family in.

As much as I hated to admit it to myself, I was convinced that Claude truly did love Daisy. At the same time my instincts was telling me it wasn't healthy love. I knew that deep down he was wishing he'd never got involved with her. Being the considerate man that me and Hubert had raised him up to be, he didn't want to hurt Daisy's feelings. Another reason I believed she had him minding her like a obedient puppy was because he was afraid of her. What man wouldn't be scared of a woman who'd pulled a gun on him?

When I woke up Thursday morning, I already knew how I was going to kill her: in the blackberry patch today. Most people I knew who went there usually went late in the day or on weekends, so I wouldn't have to worry about no witnesses. The best part was, there was a abandoned well near the spot where I always picked berries. This was a area a lot of folks avoided because it was where one of the old plantations had been located during slavery days. The only thing left was the well, surrounded by grass, tall weeds, and blackberry bushes.

Most of the abandoned wells in Lexington was just big round holes in the ground now. The logs that had been stacked a few feet high to border them when they was dug had been destroyed in the War Between the States, or blown away by tornadoes. The wells that didn't have no markings, had been covered over with planks to keep folks from accidentally falling in. But when we had tornadoes, which was almost every year, the planks got blown away. So far, nobody had fell into any of the wells that I knew of.

Before me and Hubert got married, I'd read in the newspaper that the city had used sand to fill up all of the old wells where the white folks lived. They'd only filled up a couple for us and that happened ten years ago. I knew that they'd take their time taking care of them all, if they ever did.

Last June, when I visited the patch I was going to today, the planks was missing. I searched around until I found them and put them back in place. Jessie recently told me that when she'd visited the same patch two weeks ago, the planks had been blown off and scattered around again. She'd collected them and put them back in place.

Before I could leave my house, Ma Wiggins called me up. It was a few minutes past nine-thirty a.m.

"Good morning, Maggie. I was wondering if you wanted to go to the notions store with me and help pick out some fabric for that dress I promised I'd make for you?"

I gasped real loud on purpose because I wanted her to hear my distress. "Oh, I forgot about that! I woke up with the worst cramps I've had in months. I done threw up twice. I'd better stay close to the house today. I'm going to fix myself some ginger tea and go back to bed in a little while."

"That's a shame. I'm sorry to hear you ain't feeling well. Don't you worry, though. I'll come over right away. You need to stay off your feet, so I'll make you some tea and take care of fixing supper for you and Hubert. I got a couple of ladies coming to get their hair done, but I'll reschedule them."

"That's all right," I blurted out as fast as I could. "I don't want you to change your plans on my account. Uh . . . the lady who lives across the street is coming over."

"Not that Burris woman, I hope."

"No, it's a lady who just moved here from Tuscaloosa. You ain't met her yet."

"Good. I don't want you to get too close to that Burris family. With that grouchy old grandfather, it ain't a good idea. I'd have a conniption fit if that old man done something crazy to you. I've had a bad feeling about him ever since that first time he shot out the window next door to him because they was playing their music too loud. You remember that he did that?"

"I've had a bad feeling about him since the first day I met him. I'm glad he ain't never hit nobody with them shotgun blasts."

"He will, sooner or later. Just don't you and Hubert do nothing to set him off and have him start shooting at y'all." I could hear Ma Wiggins sucking on her teeth and blowing out loud breaths. "All right, I might come after your company leaves."

"That's all right. When she leaves, I'm going to go back to bed and I'm going to stay there until Hubert comes home."

"Okay, sweetie. I'll let you get your rest then."

I still hated lying, especially to people as nice and saintly as my in-laws. But since I'd been living such a huge lie all these years anyway, it didn't bother me too much no more. Now that I'd told this one, I'd have to make sure my mother-in-law didn't find out otherwise. That meant I couldn't let nobody know I even left the house today.

* * *

It was warm outside, but I tied a scarf around my head anyway. I owned a pair of sunglasses, which I hadn't wore in a while, and I put them on too. When I looked in the mirror, I was satisfied that I wouldn't be recognized by any of my neighbors when I walked down the street. If somebody did know it was me, I prayed they didn't stop me. Everybody I knew was so long-winded, I'd have a hard time making it to Daisy's house by the time she'd told me to be there, even though she didn't live but a few blocks away.

I hadn't met any of her neighbors, so I wasn't worried about running into any of them, coming or going. One good thing about where she lived was that her house was at the end of the block and there was a vacant lot facing it. Behind her house was a deserted building that used to be a restaurant.

"Daisy, I'm here!" I yelled as I entered her kitchen. I was surprised to see how clean and neat it was. She was the kind of woman I expected to be barbecuing a possum on a rack in her kitchen sink, like my mama used to do. She came stumbling in right away while I was still scanning the room. "It sure is quiet around here. On my block we got dogs barking at all hours and noisy cars and trucks cruising up and down the streets."

"I'm glad we ain't got to put up with all that. That's why I love where this house is located." Daisy had on a black skirt and a sleeveless green plaid blouse. She stopped in front of me and did a double take. And then she looked me up and down. "Don't you think it's too warm for a blouse like that?"

I had on a brown skirt and a long-sleeved white blouse. "I know. But I always wear long sleeves when I go to a blackberry patch now. I don't like my arms getting pricked by them thorns. And the sun is already so bright today, I decided to wear my shades."

Daisy narrowed her eyes and looked me up and down some more. "I better put on some sunglasses too. My eyes is real sensitive." She left and came back a few minutes later with a pair of dark glasses in her hand. "The lady I been cleaning for this month gave me these glasses. She picked them up last month when she went to Miami to celebrate her birthday. When she got back home, come to find out, her son had already bought her a pair of the same glasses, so she gave these to me."

"That's nice. Uh . . . you ready to go?"

"Yeah. I—how come you ain't got no bucket?"

"Bucket?"

"What you going to put your blackberries in?"

I had been in such a hurry to get out of the house, I had forgot all about bringing a bucket. "Shoot! I left it sitting on the kitchen table. Do you have one I can borrow?"

"Yeah. Just don't forget to bring it back." Daisy opened her broom closet and got me a bucket. "And make sure you wash it out before you do."

"I sure will," I said.

Chapter 30

All kinds of thoughts was going through my head. The inside of my mouth was so dry, my throat ached when I swallowed. My chest was tight, and my stomach was in knots. My head was throbbing on both sides, and in the front and back. I wondered if all killers went through so many changes before they committed murder.

"I'm kind of glad to be doing this. Picking blackberries can be so much fun. Besides, it'll give us a chance to have a woman-to-woman talk and have some fun at the same time. Besides, I'd rather tell you what's what to your face than over the phone," Daisy said as we started walking down the street.

"I feel the same way. I'm too old to be bickering."

"That's what I told Claude. I couldn't understand why you was making such a fuss about him being with me in the first place."

"Well, you got four kids, Daisy, and you still young enough to have even more. Claude is the only one I'll ever have," I said in a low tone. I didn't like how this conversation was going.

"I don't think it matters how many kids you or I got."

"It matters to me."

"He's your son, but he's also my man. You told him what to do when you was in control, now that's my job."

She was crazier than I thought! It took all of my strength to keep from attacking her now. One of the reasons I didn't grab her around the throat was because it would have been way too hard to drag her body to the well. We still had to walk several more minutes before we got there. And we was still too close to the road, so anybody driving or walking nearby could have been a witness.

"Claude never liked being controlled," I pointed out, speaking in the sweetest tone I could use without choking on the words. "He was a pretty good kid growing up, but I still had to whup his behind every now and then to make him mind me. I think I did a pretty good job of raising him."

"Maggie, your job is done. You need to realize that and cut Claude some slack."

I hated the self-satisfied look on her face. "What do you mean?" I asked.

"It's up to him to decide who he obeys now."

"'Obeys'? What do you mean by that?"

"Well, I done told him over and over that as long as he's my man, he's going to mind me. I ain't never let no man get the upper hand, and I ain't going to start now."

We had to stop and let a man on a mule wagon pass before we could cross the road and go into the field where the patch was located, which was only a few more yards by now.

What she had said so far had riled me up a lot. I was scared that I wouldn't be able to keep from saying something that might spook her enough to turn around and go back home. So I decided to let her do most of the talking the rest of the way. What was said next riled me up even more.

"I'm trying to get pregnant. I know that once I give Claude a child, he'll be even easier to control." She paused and gave me a wistful look. "He told me how bad you and Hubert want a grandchild."

"Yeah, and I hope he gives us a bunch. I wish I had been able to have more kids."

"Well, some of us get blessed more than others."

The smirk on her face almost made me lose my religion. If this woman didn't die today, I was afraid that I would have a fatal heart attack because of all the stress she was causing me.

"Daisy, don't get mad. But if it's all right with you, can we drop this subject? I thought we was supposed to be trying to have a better relationship. What we talking about now ain't helping none."

"Uh-uh. Let's get everything out of our systems now. Or as much of it as possible."

"I'm sorry you feel that way, but I've said all I'm going to say on this subject for the time being," I said firmly. Even with the sunglasses on, I seen red. It was a shame that I'd only be able to kill her one time.

"Well, in that case, I'll let it go for now. Ain't no sense in me going on and on, if you ain't going to say nothing else about it. At least I got a better idea where you coming from. We'll pick up where we left off some other time. How is that?"

"That's fine with me, Daisy." I smiled at her, praying it would be for the last time. I refused to think things wouldn't go as planned. If something happened and she got loose after I'd started the attack, there was no telling what would happen next. She could overpower me and I'd end up at the bottom of the well! Another scary possibility was that if she got away, she could go home and get her gun and come after me. Well, one way or the other, one of us was not going to be alive after today.

We finally reached the blackberry patch. From the looks of things, not too many folks had started picking this year's crop. Every bush I could see was loaded down with some of the plumpest, blackest berries I ever laid eyes on. Some had even fell to the ground.

"Look at all these healthy-looking bushes with them plump berries! This looks like a good spot!" Daisy squealed.

It was a good spot. The abandoned well was just a few feet in front of us. We was far enough away from the road that even if somebody drove by, they wouldn't see us.

"I wish I had brought a bigger bucket," Daisy said. She ran over to one of the biggest bushes and gazed at it like it was a pile of gold.

Daisy was so distracted, she didn't notice when I slid the planks off the well. I picked up the biggest one and walked up behind her and brought it down on the back of her head as hard as I could. She hit the ground so fast, she never knew what hit her.

Daisy didn't move or make a sound. I looked around and didn't see or hear nothing but a few squirrels ripping and running about. I was going to hit Daisy with the plank a few more times, to make sure she was dead, but then I seen a rock the size of a coconut laying on the ground a few feet away. It was harder than the plank, so I knew I'd only have to use it one time.

I picked it up and hit her on the head again. I struck her so hard, her skull cracked wide-open. I was surprised to see that she had such a big brain. It was a shame she hadn't used it to make better decisions.

I outweighed Daisy by at least twenty pounds, and I was half a head taller. It was easy to drag her body to the well and slide her in. But I was so ramped up, even if she'd been twice my size, I wouldn't have had no trouble getting the job done. I was just that mad. She hit the bottom with a loud plop. I tossed in the bucket she'd brought with her, as well as the one she had loaned me. After I put the planks back on the well, I left the patch, running. When I got back out to the road, I slowed down and started walking.

Once I got back to Daisy's house, I went in through the kitchen door again. I was in such a state of bliss, time seemed to be standing still one minute, and flying by the next. I knew it was still early in the day and it would be a while before Daisy's kids and Claude got home. But I didn't care how much time I had left to work with, I had to move fast.

I trotted into the living room. She had a lot of nice stuff: a brown-and-white plaid couch with a matching settee, brocade curtains, and a huge radio on top of a cherrywood table by the front door. These was things she couldn't have paid for by cleaning houses part-time. But I wasn't the least bit surprised that she had so many nice things. When it came to flimflamming folks, Daisy had it down pat. On top of being a shoplifter (according to a secondhand story Jessie had shared with me), she had my son and no telling how many other men giving her financial help.

Jessie had also told me that Daisy's mama and other members of her family helped her too. One thing I had to say about this wench was that she had to be able to talk a good game to have so many folks under her spell. I was surprised she bothered to work at all. As big a she-devil as she was, she had the nerve to have a great big picture of Jesus at the Last Supper on her living-room wall.

When I got to Daisy's bedroom, the one where she had flummoxed my baby boy, I went straight to the closet. It broke my heart to see some of the clothes I had bought for Claude hanging next to hers. I grabbed as many of her frocks off the racks that I could and stuffed them into a pillowcase. I was about to leave when I realized it wasn't going to be enough just to take some of her clothes. I had to really make it look like she'd run off with another man. And the best way to do that was to leave a note. I cussed at myself for not thinking about this detail before now.

I had never seen Daisy's handwriting. The next thing I had to do was find a sample. I found a bunch of letters folks had sent her, but nothing she'd wrote. I was about to give up when I noticed a Bible on her nightstand.

"Why would a devil like her need a Bible?" I asked myself out loud. Everybody I knew wrote important information in their Bibles. On one of the blank pages before Genesis, she'd jotted down her kids' birthdays, and comments about mundane situations she'd experienced. It was going to be easy to copy her handwriting. It looked like something a chicken had scratched. I couldn't find nothing to write on in the bedroom, but I found a notepad in the kitchen on the counter. I didn't want to go overboard, so all I wrote was:

I'm sorry, but I can't keep living this life. I'm going North to be with the man I should have stayed with. I'm only taking what I need for now. I'll send for the rest of my things later. Mama, take care of the kids until I send for them.

Love,

Daisy Mae

I felt so much better. I put the note on the kitchen table and set a saltshaker on top of it. I looked around the room and decided that it would be even more convincing if I packed the pillowcase with her stuff in it into a suitcase. I had seen three in her closet. I scurried back to the bedroom closet and was able to get all the clothes I'd snatched into the smallest suitcase. The only reason I didn't take one of the bigger ones was because they was so bulky and heavy, I'd have a hard time making it back to my house without stopping to rest three or four times along the way. Besides, the small one looked like a overnight case. I was glad that it was the same plain gray type that me and a lot of other folks owned. If I ran into somebody I knew and they got nosy, I would tell them I was on my way to spend the night with a sick friend.

Chapter 31

I WANTED TO RUN DOWN THE STREET BACK TO MY HOUSE, BUT THAT would have called attention to me, so I walked. I only passed a couple of folks I knew, but they didn't pay too much attention to me. When I got to my block, Mason Burris, the ornery old man who lived across the street, was sitting on his front porch steps. He didn't waste no time giving me the evil eye, which was what he usually did when he seen me. I waved to him anyway and he grumbled something I couldn't make out. Then he got up and stomped into the house he shared with his wife and a bunch of other relatives.

When I got inside, I took several deep breaths and locked the door before I set the suitcase down. My heart started racing when something dawned on me that I hadn't thought about yet. *What am I going to do with the suitcase?* My first thought was that I could take it to Mrs. Dowler's house and put it in her trash can. The garbage truck picked up trash on her street every Monday night, so it wouldn't be around for nobody to find it. Not that Mrs. Dowler would ever go through her trash. But she had them other folks who came to the house during the week to cook and clean. Not to mention that brother of hers. What if they noticed the suitcase? I considered taking it to the well, where I'd dumped Daisy, and tossing it on top of her. There was not much of a chance that anybody would go snooping in that old well, but I didn't want to take that chance neither.

I ended up burning her clothes in my backyard barbecue pit. Since the overnight case looked like one of the ones I already had, I wiped it off and put it in my bedroom closet.

All I had to do now was wait for somebody to discover that Daisy had left my son for another man.

I didn't have to wait long. Twenty minutes after six p.m., Claude called. I was in the living room leafing through a magazine. Hubert was standing at the kitchen sink, washing the turnip greens I was going to cook for supper. I had left him alone on purpose. I wanted him to be the one to answer the phone in case Claude called instead of coming over in person to tell us. I held my breath and stood close to the wall between the living room and kitchen with my ear up against it.

"What did you say? She done took off?" Hubert yelled. "Great day in the morning!"

I dashed into the kitchen and stood next to him with my mouth hanging open. "Who is that?" I mouthed.

Hubert stared at me with a dumbfounded expression on his face. "Son, your mama is standing right here. She got to hear this from you." He handed the phone to me.

"Mama, you ain't going to believe what happened," Claude told me. I was amazed how calm he sounded.

"What's the matter, sugar?" I gently asked. I couldn't make him or Hubert suspicious, so I couldn't get too frantic until he told me what was going on.

He answered in a voice so loud, you could have heard him across the room. "Mama, Daisy done packed up and left me for another man! I never would have guessed that something like this was going to happen—especially after all the hugging and kissing she done on me last night. Not to mention the plans we had already made for our wedding."

Now I could sound as frantic as he was. *"What did you say!"* I roared. "Do you know where she went and who she went with?"

"She left a note, but it didn't say much. Something about she was going up North to be with the man she should have stayed with, which could be just about anybody. She only took a few clothes and said she would send for the rest of her things, including her kids, later. I doubt if she'll claim them kids, though. They was part of the reason Daisy was so restless. Her mama always said she would end up dumping them kids off on her to raise, and she was right."

I wanted to sound sincere, so I put more emotion in my voice. With a sob, I said, "Son, I'm so sorry. I know how much you cared about her. Um . . . me and her was supposed to go pick blackberries this morning."

"Did y'all go?"

I had to think fast. Even though I hadn't seen nobody on the way to the patch, that didn't mean some looky-loo hadn't seen me with Daisy. "Well, we started to. Just before we got to the turnoff road to the patch, a man with a big mustache pulled up in a black car."

"Oh? Who was he and what did he say?"

"I don't know who he was, and I couldn't hear what they was talking about. She ran up to his car and poked her head in the window to talk to him. Next thing I knew, she told me to go on and she'd catch up with me in a few minutes. I didn't want to be in that patch by myself, so I told her we'd go another time. I think she was glad to hear that because she encouraged me to go on back home. So I did." I paused while my brain scrambled around for something else to add. "Um . . . as I was leaving, I seen her get in the car with that man."

"A man in a black car with a big mustache. That don't sound like nobody I know," Claude said. "When I mentioned that I was thinking about growing a mustache, so I'd look older, she told me she hated hair on a man's face!"

"Really? Well, maybe she found one she did like."

"I can't believe she done this to me, Mama!"

"Well, be glad she showed her true colors before y'all got married," I said gently. "What you going to do now?"

"Her mama just left here. She said she got a idea where Daisy went. She had a boyfriend that moved to Chicago last year. Her mama thinks it's him. I got a good mind to track her down!"

"What? Why would you want to do that? If the woman done left you, ain't that bad enough? If she really cared about you, she wouldn't have left. And, as wild as Daisy is, how easy do you think it would be for you to talk her into coming back home? And why would you want her back?"

"Let me speak to that boy again!" Hubert boomed. He snatched the phone out of my hand. "Son, you can't be that crazy. If you go running after that woman, somebody could get hurt real bad. For God's sake, Claude, the woman owns a gun!" Whatever Claude said must have been what Hubert wanted to hear because he started smiling. "Good. Get your stuff ready and I'll be there as fast as I can." Hubert hung up and let out a huge sigh of relief. He raised his hands and looked up toward the ceiling. "Thank you, Jesus!"

"What did he say?" I yelled as I tugged his sleeve.

Hubert let out another sigh and started grinning from ear to ear. "Well, sugar, we got what we wanted. Our son is moving back home." And then he gave me a thoughtful look before patting my shoulder. "What's even better is, he said that even if she come back, he ain't going to have nothing else to do with her. Let's just pray she stay wherever it is she went."

"I got a feeling she will," I said, sniffing. "You go on and get Claude. I'll finish getting supper ready."

Chapter 32

THE MINUTE HUBERT LEFT THE HOUSE, I DASHED INTO THE KITCHEN to call up my in-laws. I was so nervous and sweaty, I had to hold the telephone real tight to keep it from slipping out of my hand. Pa Wiggins answered.

"Good news! Daisy took off to be with another man, and Claude is moving back home. Hubert just left to go get him," I announced with a wall-to-wall grin on my face.

Pa Wiggins gasped so loud, it sounded like he was standing right next to me. "Daisy done left Claude for another man? Praise the Lord! I'm pleased to know the prayer chain worked. I didn't think it would solve the issue this fast, though. God is so good." My father-in-law was talking louder and faster than I was.

"He sure is," I said.

"Tell Maggie I said that the next time that boy acts a fool, I'm going to get a switch and whup his behind myself," my mother-in-law threatened in the background.

"Did you hear what Clarice said?" Pa Wiggins asked with a snicker.

"I sure did. And you tell her that when she stops whupping him, I'll pick up where she left off." I laughed so hard, my sides ached.

When I got off the telephone, I stood in the front window until Hubert pulled up in our driveway.

Claude looked so pitiful when he stumbled in the door with

his suitcase. Hubert was holding the box that contained the rest of his things. "Baby, go put your stuff back in your room. Supper will be ready directly," I said, giving him a warm smile.

"Okay, Mama," he muttered. "Thank you and Daddy for letting bygones be bygones."

"What do you mean, son?" Hubert asked.

"For y'all not being mad enough *not* to let me come back home."

"Claude, we don't care what you do. As long as me and your mama got a home, you got a home."

I was so proud of how firm and sincere Hubert sounded.

"I'm glad to hear that. I wish y'all had had other children. That way all of the focus wouldn't be on me. And it would have been nice to have some brothers and sisters to play with when I was growing up."

I was surprised I didn't see no tears in his eyes. I had plenty in mine and Hubert looked like he was about to squeeze out a few.

"I guess God had His reasons for only blessing y'all with one child."

"I guess He did," I mumbled. "Welcome home, baby." I kissed Claude on his cheek and patted him on the back.

Our supper was so pleasant, you never would have thought we'd just got out of such a unspeakable situation. I wondered if other mothers would have done what I did to make things right for their families again? One thing was for sure, if it happened again, I'd do the same thing to the next woman!

I slept like a baby when I went to bed. I woke up the next morning feeling like I had been reborn for the second time since I'd met Mrs. Dowler. I knew it was only my imagination, but everything in my house looked brand-new. Even my son.

When Claude and Hubert left to go to work Friday morning, I decided to do a few things around the house to keep my mind off what I had done to Daisy. I mopped all of my floors, washed a basket of clothes, and then I decided to go pick some blackberries to make a pie for supper. I went to a patch on the other side of town. The last thing I wanted to see right now was the well where Daisy was. The only way somebody would find out there was a body in it would be if they fell in. Also, if the city ever got around to filling it up, they wouldn't have no reason to snoop around to see what was at the bottom before they started dumping sand down into it.

When I got back home with my bucket of berries, which wasn't as plump and sweet as the ones in the patch near Sawburg Road, I got busy making a couple of pies and getting supper ready. Jessie let herself in just as I was seasoning the pig ears.

"Girl, everybody is talking about Daisy running off to be with another man!" she said, stumbling over to the table. She pulled out a chair and plopped down with a groan. "Lord, I wish some hussy would run off with Orville."

"Is he acting up again?"

"Every day. And it gets a little worse each time. Last night he went on a rampage and threw a ashtray at me and it missed my eye by just a few inches."

"I'm glad he missed," I said, sitting down in the chair facing Jessie. It was only then that I noticed she had a black eye again. "I guess I spoke too soon. When did that happen?" I asked, pointing at her eye.

"Yesterday evening. Right after I told him that Moline Thomas next door had told me about Daisy. That's how I found out." Jessie swallowed hard and looked around the room and lowered her voice. "I told him I been thinking about moving North myself. He said he'd hunt me down and cut my throat with a dull knife if I did."

"I know he's mean and all, but I don't think he'd really hurt you. I don't care how bad he behaves—I still believe he loves you to death."

"Humph! Let's pray he don't literally love me 'to death' someday."

"Don't even think about things like that. It'll only make you feel worse. Now that I don't have to worry about Claude so much, I feel so much better."

"Amen. I declare, you look rested and healthier than you've looked in . . . well . . . since Daisy entered the picture." Jessie paused and tilted her head to the side. "Do you think she is gone for good?"

"Uh-huh." I got up and went to stir the pig ears.

"I'm happy for you, girl. Now you ain't got nothing to worry about. Unless Claude takes up with another crazy woman."

"I think he got enough of that," I said, and we laughed. "It's going to be a while before he gets in another relationship."

"Oh, by the way, I been meaning to ask you something. Did that Dowler woman's brother come yet?"

I rolled my eyes and sat back down. "Uh-huh. He was there when I got to work on Tuesday. Mrs. Dowler done already warned me that he got some racist issues."

"Shoot. Tell me something I don't know. Most of the pecker-woods in the South got prejudice issues with colored folks. Thank God I don't run into none too often. I know some of the kindest, most wonderful white folks there is. Unfortunately, it's the bad ones we got to be wary of. All you need to do is mind Mrs. Dowler's brother and do everything you can to show him what a nice person you are. As long as we *behave* around racist crackers, they'll treat us good. Even some of the worst ones. Orville used to do yard work for a man who was a high-level muckety-muck in the Ku Klux Klan. He even kept his white hood and sheet hanging on the coatrack on the wall in his kitchen. But because Orville behaved and showed that sucker some respect, they got along real good. When he had to lay Orville off, he even gave him a twenty-dollar bonus and some of his old tools."

"I don't know if Mrs. Dowler's brother will be *that* nice to me, but I will still be nice to him. Anyway, I ain't too worried. I just seen him for a few minutes on Tuesday and I got a feeling he plans on staying out of my way too. He's in his sixties and so puny that I bet a mild breeze could blow him down."

"You probably right." Jessie rubbed her nose and glanced toward the stove. "Pig ears again, huh?"

I chuckled. "Other than my gumbo, that's the only other thing Hubert and Claude would eat every day if I cooked them."

"I would too. Speaking of gumbo, I hope you plan on cooking some more soon. It works like a tonic on Orville."

We laughed.

I couldn't believe how pleasant the next few days was. Daisy had already become a distant memory. Claude was in good spirits, but he did do a little complaining about a jealous colored coworker. This sucker had been giving him a hard time by reporting to the foreman every time Claude came in late, or when he didn't finish a job on time. When I asked him the name of this jackass so I could go give him a piece of my mind, he was horrified.

"Mama, the last thing I want is for you to start fighting my battles with people I work with, or anybody else. That episode with Daisy was pretty bad, but it worked itself out in the end. This thing at my job ain't nothing like that. It's something I can fix on my own, so don't you be concerned about it."

"I'm your mama. As long as there is a breath in my body, there will always be something for me to be concerned about when it comes to you," I said.

I wasn't going to bring up this subject with Claude no more. But if I heard any more complaints about the coworker, he was going to get what Daisy got!

Chapter 33

PEOPLE WAS STILL TALKING ABOUT DAISY'S SUDDEN DEPARTURE LAST Thursday, but not that much. Jessie told me that she'd heard Daisy's mama and sisters had cleaned out her house and put the rest of her things in their shed until she sent for them and her kids. Daisy's ex, who had moved to Chicago, still had a bunch of kinfolks in Lexington. When folks asked them if Daisy was with him, they said he swore he hadn't seen or heard from her since he left Alabama. Come to find out, that man was married to another woman and they had a baby on the way. So people started talking about how Daisy must have took off with one of her other used-to-be boyfriends. I didn't say much on the subject when it came up in my presence. I was concerned more about Mrs. Dowler's brother.

When I went back to work on Monday, Mr. Oswald must have been lying in wait for me. A few minutes after I started rinsing the laundry, which now included his shit-stained drawers and whiskey-puke-covered shirts, Mrs. Dowler left the house. She was going to pick up one of her friends so that they could do some shopping at the meat market and have lunch. I was amazed that Mrs. Dowler was still driving at the age of ninety. But she was as spry and sharp-minded as she was the day I met her. One minute after I heard her car drive off, I heard footsteps coming down the staircase. I was mortified when I looked up from the tub and seen Mr. Oswald standing in the kitchen doorway in his pajamas.

"Good morning, Mr. Oswald," I greeted, forcing myself to smile. I kept rinsing the laundry.

"Good morning to you. Where is Fern?"

"Mrs. Dowler went shopping with another lady. She said they was going to pick up some ribs and other stuff for the Fourth of July cookout they'll be throwing together next week. After they do that, they going to go have lunch. Mrs. Dowler said she wouldn't be gone too long, but she left you a plate in the oven in case you want to eat before she gets back."

His eyes was roaming over me just like they did the first time I met him.

"Shopping and lunch, huh? Then she'll be gone quite a spell."

"I don't know, sir. She never takes more than a hour and a half to shop and have lunch. She's already been gone . . . um . . . twenty minutes."

Mr. Oswald threw up his hands and gave me a doubtful look. "Pffftt! Ninety minutes, my foot. The way she drives and lollygags, I reckon it'll take her almost that long just to get across town to the market." He paused and inched closer to me. "She could be gone a right smart part of the day. Even several hours."

"I reckon she could, sir," I mumbled.

He blinked, slid his tongue across his bottom lip, and moved even closer to me. "I declare, you are right handsome for a colored gal. And way better-looking than those other backstreet frumps I used to pester before I moved to California. As a matter of fact, you look a lot like your mama." His last comment stunned me and disturbed me at the same time.

"Huh?" My whole body tensed up. "I didn't know you knew my mama. She died more than twenty years ago."

"I know that, but I knew Jeannette way before then. Who didn't? She was one of the sweetest pieces of tail working at that whorehouse out on Bandy Road. When she left there and starting working out of the honky-tonks, me and a slew of others followed her. Shoot. That old gal knew her stuff."

"Oh. Well, she stopped doing all that and got real jobs."

He snickered and waved his hand in the air like he was shooing a fly. "Aw balderdash! Once a whore, always a whore."

"I don't care what she done in her past, she was still a good mama," I said with my lips trembling. I prayed that he wouldn't see how flustered he was making me. Or that by me defending my mama, he wouldn't think I was being uppity.

"Jeannette sure was 'a good mama' to me, too. If you know what I mean." When he turned his head to the side and winked at me, my stomach turned.

"Well, I guess I should finish the laundry before Mrs. Dowler gets back home. She wants me to pull some weeds out of her garden before I leave today. She made a pot of coffee before she left. You want me to give you some?"

"You want to 'give me some'? That's an interesting choice of words, honey baby."

I started putting into the basket the laundry I'd rinsed and wrung out so I could go hang everything on the clothesline. I was scared to say anything else. I had a feeling that no matter what I said, Mr. Oswald was going to keep on talking nasty stuff. Or tell Mrs. Dowler that I "sassed" him again.

"Listen here. I'm going to be around for a while. Maybe permanently. I'll be needing a little physical pampering from time to time."

I froze and stared into his narrow, cloudy eyes. "You mean like them foot massages I do for Mrs. Dowler?" I glanced at his bare feet. The thought of putting my hands on them crusty dogs made me want to holler.

"That too. But I'm talking about something a little more intimate. If you know what I mean . . ."

"I don't know what you mean," I said dumbly.

"The hell you don't," he barked. I braced myself and waited to hear what he had to say next. I already knew it was going to be something I didn't want to hear. "I got mad as a hornet when I heard Jeannette had quit the business. My wife was too squeamish to do all the things I need a woman to do in the bedroom."

"I'm sorry to hear that, but you got the wrong idea about me.

I don't do none of them things to men that my mama done before she found Jesus and got married. Now, if you don't mind, I'd better get back to work. I'm going to go hang the clothes on the line." When I attempted to move toward the back door with the laundry basket, he lunged at me and grabbed my arm. He was squeezing it so tight, it was a wonder he didn't cut off my blood circulation. The smell of alcohol on his breath was so strong, it burned the insides of my nose.

"You like this job, huh?"

"Yes. I love working for Mrs. Dowler. She's the best boss I ever had, and I really need the money."

"Well, I'm going to make it even more profitable for you. You scratch my back, I'll scratch yours."

"Mr. Oswald, I just told you, I don't do what my mama used to do—"

"You sassing me again?" he growled.

"No, I ain't sassing you. I just don't want no trouble."

"Well, don't cause no trouble, won't be no trouble." Before he could go on, the front door creaked open and he let go of my arm. "We'll finish up this conversation later," he said in a raspy tone.

Mrs. Dowler skittered into the kitchen with a wild-eyed look on her face. "Would y'all believe that Lucille Hogan? She forgot all about our date and was still in bed when I got to her house. I'll have to go to the meat market later in the week, I guess!" she yelled. She blew out a breath and fanned her sweaty face with her hand. "Is there any of that coffee left I made?" She looked from me to her brother and back.

"Yes, ma'am," I muttered. I was so happy she was back, I could have kissed her.

"Oswald, did Maggie tell you I left your breakfast in the oven?"

"Yeah, she told me. And she took her time doing so," he sneered. "I'll eat it later. I'm going back to my room for now."

He spun around and strutted out of the kitchen. Mrs. Dowler came up to me and touched my arm. "How did you and him get along while I was gone?"

"Real good," I mumbled. "He seems like a nice man."

"See there. You're such a sweet and personable woman, Maggie. If you stay as you are, it won't be long before you have my brother as contented as you got me." She cocked her head to the side and gave me a warm smile. I smiled back.

I didn't see Mr. Oswald no more before I left to go home. When I walked out the door, I ran all the way to the bus stop.

Chapter 34

My bus ride home seemed to take forever. All I could think about was what Mr. Oswald had said to me and how he'd grabbed my arm. It was so hard to believe that after all I'd been through because of Daisy, I was about to have another nasty situation to deal with. One thing was for sure, I was going to do whatever I had to do to keep my job.

Despite how agitated I was, I enjoyed a very pleasant supper with my husband and our son. That was what kept me from thinking about Mr. Oswald too much.

Jessie helped keep him off my mind too. A few hours after I finished washing the supper dishes, she came to my house. We got comfortable in the living room with the tea I had just made. She was on the couch; I was in the chair facing her. Jessie was always the one to start up with a good gossip story, I didn't even need to prod her. But today she looked downright gloomy and hadn't said but a few words since she walked in the door ten minutes ago.

"What's the matter with you today? I ain't never seen you this quiet and long-faced," I said. I took a sip from my glass and gazed at her from the corner of my eye.

She hunched her shoulders before she said anything. "I declare, Maggie. I'm so blessed to have you as a friend. I tell everybody you got white folk sense."

I did a double take and gave Jessie a confused look. "What do you mean by that?"

"Most of the colored folks in this town, including me, wouldn't look at life the way you do. Like a smart white woman. We just accept everything as is and keep moving forward. You don't let *nothing* break you down—not being the daughter of the town drunk and a used-to-be-loose woman, that episode with Daisy, not to mention them kids that teased you all through school."

"How I handle bad situations ain't got nothing to do with me having 'white folk' sense. What I got is *common sense*, and that ain't got no color," I insisted.

"And you lucky as hell when it comes to love. I ain't never seen another man as sensitive, easygoing, devoted, and upstanding as Hubert. He got the kind of womanish qualities you rarely see in a man."

My stomach knotted up. "Jessie, I know firsthand, there ain't nothing 'womanish' about my husband . . ."

"That's for sure!" She lowered her voice to a whisper and added, "I seen the way he looks at your butt."

I threw up my hands. "Jessie, you nasty buzzard! You ought to be ashamed of yourself for saying something like that to the daughter-in-law of the most well-respected colored preacher in this town!" I scolded.

I sucked in a heap of air and gave her a sharp look. It was bad enough I'd had to listen to Mr. Oswald's sex-related comments today. I didn't want to listen to Jessie's too. "Now I don't want you to take this the wrong way, but I like to keep my personal life with my husband personal. Let's talk about something more impersonal and pleasant."

"Fine with me if you don't want to share." Jessie giggled and gave me a knowing look. "Whatever it is y'all do in the bedroom ain't none of my business. I wouldn't mind sharing with you, but I ain't having no action in that department no more. Orville ain't touched me in a year. And I don't miss him flopping around on top of me like a fish in a bucket of water." She giggled some more. And then she got a serious look on her face. "So, how you getting along with Mrs. Dowler's brother?"

"Um . . . okay. That pitiful old man. He is still so depressed about losing his wife, he stays in his room a lot. He drinks whiskey like it's going out of style and that's only making him more depressed. Mrs. Dowler told me he's even threatened to do away with hisself. He'd be the first man I knew who committed suicide."

"I wish Orville would get a notion to do that. All my troubles would be over," Jessie said.

There was a wistful look in her eyes. And then she inhaled with her mouth gaping open so wide, I could see her back teeth.

"Oh! I'm sorry. I don't know what made me say such a unholy thing! Especially knowing you want to discuss something more pleasant."

"It's all right if you want to talk about Orville. You know I'm always willing to listen for as long as you need me to."

"Girl, the man is driving me up the wall and back down. The older he gets, the meaner he gets."

"I didn't think he could get no meaner. What is he doing now that he ain't been doing for years?"

"Besides threatening to kill me if I leave him? He's also spending almost every penny he makes in the bootleggers' houses and juke joints buying drinks for all them hussies he hangs around with."

"He still don't help much with the bills?"

Jessie sucked on her teeth and rolled her eyes up so far, I thought they was going to disappear. "Naw. If that ain't bad enough, after he spends up all his own money, he takes almost every penny I got left. Our rent is current, but the rest of our bills done fell way behind. I bought Earl a pair of new shoes last week and Orville hit the roof. He made me take them back to the store to get a refund and give the money to him. Guess what he spent it on? A new wig-hat to give his girlfriend for her birthday! A lady I work with was at the bootlegger's house when he was there bragging about it."

"My Lord. Well, this late in the game, I doubt if you can make him straighten up and fly right. I think the best thing you can do for you and Earl is leave him. You got kinfolks in Ohio and Michigan. Can't you go stay with one of them for a spell?"

"Hiding out with one of my out-of-town kinfolks would be fine for me and Earl. But I can't take a chance on him doing harm to my mama, like he said he would do if I took off."

"Then what do you plan on doing? Keep taking his mess and be miserable the rest of your life?"

"I don't know what I'm going to do." Jessie stopped talking and a glazed look came over her face. She just sat there for a few seconds staring like she was in a trance. And then she narrowed her eyes and tucked in her bottom lip. "His heart is getting weaker and weaker because he don't get enough rest or eat right. No matter what his doctor tells him, it goes in one ear and out the other. Two weeks ago he had to stay in bed three whole days."

Jessie looked so miserable, I gave her the most sympathetic look I could come up with. "If Orville don't start taking better care of hisself, his heart is going to get worse. You can't even get him to be more concerned about his own health?"

She shook her head. "What makes you think I can do that if his doctor can't? That damn fool stopped listening to me a long time ago."

"Well, if he keeps on this way, he might get in that bed and never get back out."

Jessie leaned forward and whispered, "I know it ain't a nice thing to say, but I hope that happens soon."

I inhaled suddenly. I was surprised to hear something so ominous coming from a woman who wouldn't hurt a fly. "Then you'd have to take care of him for the rest of his life—bathing him, feeding him, dressing him. I know you don't want to end up like that. You might even have to give up your job."

"Let's change the subject again." Jessie cleared her throat and gave me a hopeful look. What she said next surprised me even more. "I wish I was you."

"Huh? Why?"

"Girl, you got it made in the shade. I don't know of a more fulfilled woman than you. You got the perfect family and the perfect job."

A big lump swelled up in my throat. "I declare, my life ain't exactly perfect. I'm glad you and so many other folks think it is. I'm going to do everything I can to keep it looking perfect . . ."

I wanted so bad to tell Jessie what Mr. Oswald had said the last time I seen him. But the more I thought about it, the more I didn't believe he was serious about me giving him some "physical pampering." For one thing, he'd been so drunk when he said it, he might not have even realized what he was saying. The other thing was, I was still willing to do whatever I had to do to keep my dream job.

Chapter 35

I DIDN'T SEE MR. OSWALD AT ALL WHEN I WENT TO WORK ON TUESday. I prayed that he would get in the habit of staying in his room every day until I left to go home.

I went shopping on Wednesday to pick up a few things I wanted to bring to the barbecue at my in-laws' house to celebrate the upcoming Fourth of July. Next to Thanksgiving and Christmas, this was my favorite holiday, so I was in a good mood, even though Mr. Oswald kept creeping into my head.

Me and Hubert and Claude went to church on Sunday. We hadn't been in weeks, but hadn't missed nothing. My father-in-law preached the same fire-and-brimstone sermons he preached almost every other week. After the evening service, we all went home with my in-laws to eat supper with them.

I helped my mother-in-law set the table. She had cooked enough black-eyed peas, hush puppies, macaroni and cheese, deep-fried chicken, and other fixings to feed a dozen folks. Despite all that, I had still brought along some of my flavorful gumbo in two different bowls. It was the first thing everybody reached for. The smaller bowl was for Hubert and Claude. I always remembered to separate theirs before I added the cayenne pepper just before it finished cooking. There was a few other folks who didn't like cayenne pepper in theirs neither. So, when they wanted some, I gave them theirs in separate bowls too.

Everybody was in such a good mood, especially Claude. He

apologized for the third or fourth time for the mess he'd put us through.

"Son, that's all behind us. We can stop discussing Daisy," I said. I was glad everybody at the table agreed with me. "You won't never see her again."

"Don't be so quick to jump the gun," Pa Wiggins said as he picked up several hush puppies at the same time. "Just like she changed her mind about Claude, she could change her mind about whoever she's with now and drag her tail back to Lexington. If she do, we'll treat her with respect and not harbor no hard feelings. Despite her behavior, she's still one of God's children. And, if she was to come back, I'd be the first one to start a prayer chain on her behalf."

"I don't care if she comes back here or not! I never want to see that heifer again!" Claude blasted.

"You remember them words if she do come back. You was pretty strung out on her," Hubert tossed in.

"By then, I hope you won't be available. There is a heap of single young women around here. I'm sure you'll meet one real soon," Ma Wiggins said with a twinkle in her eyes.

"When I do, the first time she starts talking off the wall, I'm going to run in the opposite direction," Claude said.

We all laughed.

After supper Pa Wiggins said a short prayer for Daisy to "straighten out the mess" she'd made. But I was the one who needed God's attention now. Ever since Tuesday I hadn't got much sleep because I dreaded going back to work on Monday. I had a inkling that Mr. Oswald's arm wasn't the only thing he had up his sleeve.

When me and Hubert and Claude got home, I went in the bedroom and got down on my knees and prayed. I thanked God for all my blessings and asked him to keep his eye on me and my loved ones. The last thing I prayed for was peace of mind, and for me not to lose my job.

I got a good night's sleep and was in a much better mood when I woke up Monday morning. Mr. Oswald was not at the house the whole time I was there. Mrs. Dowler told me that he'd gone out with some old friends the night before and had spent the night at their house.

Tuesday was the Fourth of July and Mrs. Dowler still wanted me to come to work. Me and Hubert wasn't going to the barbecue at his folks' house until later in the evening, so he didn't mind me going to work that morning.

While I was doing the ironing, Mr. Oswald came into the kitchen. He was holding a shot glass filled to the brim. His wiry gray hair was matted down on his head like a stocking cap and his face was as red as a tomato, especially his pointy nose. Dark shadows surrounded his glassy eyes.

"Hello, Mr. Oswald," I chirped. As hard as it was, I managed to smile as he walked over and stopped in front of me.

"Howdy do, Maggie-poo. Happy Fourth of July." He grinned and took a sip from his glass.

Mrs. Dowler was in the living room entertaining some of the folks who'd come to celebrate the holiday with her. She'd already served them the barbecue and all the fixings that she'd cooked the evening before.

Mr. Oswald moved closer to me. "Look-a-here. I'm going to drive you home today after you finish up. The buses run on a limited schedule today and I wouldn't want you to get home too late to celebrate the holiday with your family."

I threw up my hand so fast, I heard the joints in my elbow crack. "Oh no!" I said real quick. "That's all right. The bus I'm going to take today will get me home only a few minutes later than the regular one. Besides, I don't think you'll be in shape to drive by the time I get off." I chuckled. "You don't want to get arrested for drunk driving. That would be a big scandal for God-fearing folks like you and your sister."

"Me get arrested? That's never going to happen. I used to play checkers with Sheriff Yoakum. He wouldn't put me in jail if they paid him."

"I still don't think it's a good idea for you to be driving in your condition. You could wreck and hurt somebody."

"Pffftt! I've been drinking and driving all my life and I haven't wrecked yet. You can stop trying to use that excuse not to let me take you home. You're not taking that goddamned bus today. Stop being such a crybaby and let nature take its course, gal. I got something for you to do, that can't be put off no longer . . ."

"Mr. Oswald, your sister is the one I work for. I take all my orders from her."

"Hush up!" he snarled, shaking his fist in my face. "As long as I'm on the premises, you'll take orders from me too. Why are you being so uncooperative? I know I'm not the first white man to pay attention to you."

"All I'm here to do is the laundry and garden work when it's necessary. I ain't doing nothing . . . um . . . unnatural with you, so I wish you would leave me alone," I said through clenched teeth.

I couldn't believe I was standing up to Mr. Oswald in such a bold way. If he thought I'd sassed him before, there was no telling what he was going to think now. I just prayed that he didn't blab to his sister.

I was stunned at how fast his tone got so gentle. "Come on now, honey sugar. Be nice to me. I know Fern has told you how I've been hurting. The least you can do is try and help cheer me up. You're a woman and I'm a man. All I want is for us to do what men and women have been doing since God created us." He snorted and stared at me so long, I got even more uncomfortable. And then he started talking in a lower tone. "Listen, uh, once you get past all this resistance foolishness, you will enjoy as much pleasure as I'm going to."

"Mr. Oswald, I love my husband and I wouldn't never do nothing to disrespect him. My marriage means a lot to me."

His tone turned nasty again. "Hell's bells, gal! My marriage meant a lot to me and look what it got me." He waved his hands in the air and laughed. "I ain't asking you to run off with me! All I want is to have a little fun now and then. Nobody except you and me would ever know. Besides, I'll give you some pocket change each time, and I ain't paid for poontang in years. The whole time I lived in California, I got it for free. You ought to feel privileged knowing I'm fixing to start up that again with somebody like you." He stopped talking and looked me up and down, shaking his head. "You ain't bad-looking, but you ain't no spring chicken neither. How many other white men do you think would pay for a piece of black tail from a woman your age? Why can't you be nicer to me?" He had the nerve to stand there with a pout on his face like I'd hurt his feelings.

"Mr. Oswald, I don't want your money!"

"All right, then. I'll keep it. If you want to pleasure me for free, that's fine with me. I'll spend my money elsewhere. But don't say I didn't give you a chance first!"

"I told you—"

Mr. Oswald stopped me from finishing my sentence by slapping me hard across the face. I couldn't believe what was happening. Other than my daddy and Mr. Royster, no other man had ever struck me before. The sting of his cold calloused hand made me flinch.

"You've sassed me before and got away with it. From now on, when you do it, I'm going to put you back in your place." He glanced over his shoulder toward the doorway. When he turned back around, there was a scowl on his face that was so extreme, it looked like he had put on a mask. "If I was to tell Fern I caught you rifling through my wallet, what do you think she'll do? I'll tell you. She'll fire you lickety-split."

"She won't believe you. I don't steal from nobody," I said through clenched teeth.

"Okay. When her company leaves, I'll tell her how I caught you stealing from me. Do you think she'll take a nigger's word over mine? The daughter of a nigger whore at that."

"You wouldn't stoop that low!"

"Girl, I'd stoop as low as a snake's belly to have my way with you." He snickered and smacked his lips. They was so stained from all his drinking, they looked like raw liver. "I've been thinking about it since I saw how you looked at me that first day. And don't play innocent. I know you want me, and that's another thing I'll tell my sister. I'll tell her you've been coming on to me from day one."

"Please don't tell your sister all that. I really like my job and I need the money," I whined.

"Then what's it going to be? Are you going to let me have my way or not?"

I nodded. "Yes, sir."

"All right, then. Get your juicy tail out to the toolshed and wait for me. I'll go check and see how much longer Fern is going to be tied up with those old crows. We may only have a few minutes to have some fun, but that don't matter. It don't take long to content me. All I want is a quick tongue bath."

I couldn't risk losing my job. So that day I met Mr. Oswald in the toolshed and let him have his way with me.

Chapter 36

BEFORE I LEFT MRS. DOWLER'S HOUSE TUESDAY EVENING, I WENT in the bathroom on the other side of the kitchen that her other servants used. Normally, I would have gone to the one across the hall from her bedroom, like she had told me to do the first day I came to work for her. This time I was in such a hurry, I went into the closest one and gargled with warm water for several minutes, but I could still taste Mr. Oswald's vile pecker in my mouth. After I took a few deep breaths, I grabbed a towel and wiped off my lips and the rest of my face. It didn't do much good because I felt as nasty as before.

This nightmare had turned out worse than I thought it would. I had heard about people using their mouths on one another during sex, but I never thought I'd be one of them. All Mr. Royster had ever made me do was have intercourse or get him off with my hand.

I was so beside myself, I didn't realize I'd got on the wrong bus to go home by mistake until fifteen minutes later. I got off at the next stop and waited for the right bus. I had calmed down by the time I got home, so Claude and Hubert didn't notice nothing different about my demeanor. And when we got to my in-laws house twenty minutes later to celebrate the rest of the holiday with them, I pushed Mr. Oswald to the back of my mind and actually had a good time.

By the grace of God, I was able to go on about my business like nothing was wrong. I acted even more cheerful and pleasant than usual. After supper I went in the bathroom and rinsed out my mouth some more. When I came out, Jessie was in the living room sharing her latest gossip with Claude and Hubert.

Hubert was always interested in hearing Jessie's gossip. She had just reported how Mr. Burris, the grumpy old man across the street from us, had accused his wife of fooling around with another man because of a dream he'd had. He'd attempted to slap her, but had fell flat on his face and busted his lip. I laughed about that, along with everybody else. Even Earl.

When Claude and Hubert left to go outside to fiddle around under the hood of our car, Earl went in the kitchen and flopped down in a chair with a comic book. Jessie moved over to the couch where I was and gave me a hug.

"Girl, getting your son back home done really lifted your spirits. I wish life was as good to me as it is to you," she said with her voice cracking. "I wish I was in your shoes."

"Be careful what you wish for," I warned. "My shoes don't fit like they used to."

She reared back and gazed at me from the corner of her eye with a confused look on her face. "What's that supposed to mean?"

"Nothing. You need a ride to work tonight?" As much as I avoided driving, I still didn't mind taking Jessie to work. Besides, the round-trip took only ten minutes.

"Yeah. That's why I came over. Claude, with his sweet self, said he would look after Earl until you get back. Make sure he empties his bowels and bladder before he go to sleep."

It was Claude's idea for me and him and Hubert to go out to supper as a family on Saturday, something we didn't do too often. Hubert and I had been to a few places in town in the last few months, but it had been almost six months since Claude had come with us.

"Where do y'all want to go?" I asked. I was glad to do something different on a weekend for a change. Last Saturday evening I had helped Ma Wiggins clean some chitlins that she was going to cook for Sunday supper. The Saturday before that, me and Jessie had attended a funeral.

"Let's go see a movie after we eat supper," Claude suggested.

I shuddered. Going to the movies rarely crossed my mind. Lexington had only one theater. I hadn't been to it since I was in my twenties. Like everything else, the theaters in the South was segregated. White folks got to sit wherever they wanted, but we had to sit in the balcony. And we wasn't allowed to buy none of the snacks on the main floor. We had to bring our own.

"I don't think going to the movie theater is such a good idea. I feel so unwelcome there."

"Come on, Mama. I went with a couple of my friends last week," Claude said. "It ain't that bad, so long as we stay in our place. Besides, we ain't welcome no place where the white folks hang out. I thought you was used to that."

"Uh-uh. Forget about going to a movie. By the time we eat, it'll be too late to go to the theater," Hubert said. "We'll go see a movie some other time. There's a real nice barbecue restaurant on the outskirts of Mobile that we can go to this evening."

Just hearing him mention that city gave me a jolt. It brought back memories of my adventure with Claude's birth daddy. Every now and then, I still thought about Randolph. It was hard not to, because the older Claude got, the more he favored him.

"That's a long drive," I said with hesitation. "I wouldn't mind if we went to eat at a restaurant in Lexington. That place on Arch Street cooks chicken every way possible. Their chicken gizzard casserole is one of the best things on the menu."

"Come on, Mama! You need to let your hair down more often. Stop acting like a old lady. You better enjoy life more, while you still can. It'd be nice to go somewhere outside of this dull little town for a change!" Claude yelled. "We can be here today and gone tomorrow."

Claude's last words sent a shiver up my spine. Ever since the deaths of my parents and Uncle Roscoe, anything related to death distressed me. Being married to a undertaker, the subject was always on the table. Still, I avoided it as much as I could. Especially now that I was the reason somebody was dead. I still believed that killing Daisy had been the only way to keep my family intact. There was times when I wondered if Claude would have actually gone through with the marriage. I also wondered if Daisy would have eventually dropped him for another man anyway. I shook them thoughts out of my head when Hubert agreed with Claude.

"The boy's right, Maggie. Don't let life pass you by." He snorted right after he stopped talking. For a minute our eyes locked. I was glad I couldn't read minds because I didn't want to know what all was on his. I had a pretty good idea, though. I couldn't imagine what it was like to be what he was and having to hide it. Not only did I love Hubert—like a brother—I felt so sorry for him because of all the confusion and spiritual torture he had to endure.

I didn't think it would do me no good to keep protesting. "Okay," I mumbled. "But I don't want to stay over there too long. There is a lot of crime in Mobile."

We went to a cute little restaurant sitting between a flower shop and a notions store. It was owned by colored folks, but half of the customers tonight was white. Another thing I couldn't understand was how easy it was for them to come to our restaurants and other businesses, and still not allow us to patronize theirs without a hassle. I never spent much time thinking about such things, because all it did was give me a headache. Lately I had enough on my plate doing that already.

Our rib dinners was so good, we ordered some to go. On the way home, when we stopped to get gas, I got out to go use the toilet. There was three toilets at this station: one for white women, one for white men, and both was inside. There was a smelly little outhouse in the back of the building that colored folks had to use. I got in line behind two men and a woman. I'd been standing there less than a minute when I heard footsteps coming up behind me. When I turned around, I seen the last person in the world I ever expected—or wanted—to see again: Claude's birth daddy.

Chapter 37

UNTIL THIS EVENING, IT HAD BEEN A FEW MONTHS SINCE I'D thought about Claude's birth daddy. Seeing him after more than twenty years was like seeing a ghost. It must have been the opposite for Randolph. The way he started grinning with his eyes stretched open as wide as they could go, you would have thought I was his fairy godmother.

"Louise?" He moved closer and squinted. "Oh, my God! Louise, is it really you? Ain't you a sight for sore eyes!"

Nobody had ever looked so happy to see me.

"Huh? Do I know you?" I asked dumbly. I was so nervous, I almost peed on myself. Except for about twenty more pounds, deep lines on his forehead, and a few strands of gray hair, he still looked about the same.

"It's me! Randolph Webb. I know you ain't forgot me! My God! I declare, I never thought I'd see you again! Something told me to come over here tonight. Where you been? Do you know how often I dream about you since the last time we was together?"

He was talking so loud and fast, it made me even more nervous. The last thing I needed was for Claude or Hubert to walk up and witness this awkward encounter.

I stumbled and moved a few feet away from him. "I'm sorry, sir. But you got me mixed up with somebody else."

"Come on now. I ain't forgot what you look or sound like. We met in a bar. You came to my house, and everything, that same night. I really enjoyed your company and I thought you enjoyed mine. We got close real quick. I'll never forget that week you came to my house, three nights in a row." He stopped talking and looked around. "Oh! You here with somebody?"

"Yes, I'm here with somebody and my name ain't Louise. I'm from Huntsville and this is the first time I ever came to Mobile."

His face suddenly froze. And then he started talking real slow in a much lower tone. "Well, if you with somebody, I ain't going to cause no trouble. I'm just glad to see you. When you stopped coming to my house all of a sudden, I thought maybe something bad had happened to you. I . . . I had planned to ask you to marry me the next time I seen you."

"Look, Mr. whatever-you-said-your-name-is. I don't go to no bars or honky-tonks. Never have and never will."

I attempted to leave, but he grabbed my arm.

"Turn me loose!" I hollered.

The people in front of us turned around.

"Is this joker bothering you, ma'am?" one of the men asked.

"I'm fine," I insisted in a shaky voice.

Randolph let my arm go and gave me such a woeful look, I almost broke down and told him I was who he thought I was.

"I'm getting the message loud and clear. But in case you change your mind, I still live in the same house, if you ever want to come visit me again. I . . . I hope you enjoy the rest of your evening."

Before I could respond, he whirled around and took off so fast, you would have thought a mad dog was chasing him.

I took a deep breath and turned around to leave. My chest was so tight, it felt like a bear was hugging me. I got another shock when I seen Hubert walking toward me. "This line ain't moved since I got here. Let's go." I laughed to hide my panic.

"But I got to pee, sugar," Hubert whined.

"If I can hold it, you can too. Now, let's get up out of here and go home."

I didn't wait for Hubert to respond. I ran all the way back to the car. He looked puzzled when he got in the driver's seat, so I had to throw him off.

"One of the folks in front of me said he just seen a rat go in the colored folks' toilet."

"Rats!" Hubert and Claude yelled at the same time.

"Uh-huh. And y'all know they carry all kinds of germs and whatnot." I sniffed and rubbed my nose. "Hubert, when we get to some woods, stop the car so we can go behind a tree and do our business."

"All right. I just hope we don't get too close to none of the poison plants and end up with a rash."

I was glad Hubert laughed. So did me and Claude.

Other than a few comments about how much I had enjoyed the food we'd ate, I didn't do much talking on the way home. Hubert made a few remarks about some mundane things going on at the turpentine mill, but Claude did most of the talking.

The only thing he said that grabbed my attention was "I met this new girl the other day. Her family moved here from Birmingham two years ago. She helps clean up and tend to the worms at that bait store on Canal Street."

"Uh-oh. Don't tell us you done already fell in love again. Me and your mama better brace ourselves for a new storm," Hubert teased. He laughed and gave me a wink, but I knew he was serious.

"I ain't said nothing about being in love again. But I'm glad I'm still single, because I ain't never met a girl like Maybelle Gardner."

It was time for me to get in the conversation now. "What's so special about this one?"

"For one thing, she is the same age as me and ain't got no babies. Like me, she ain't got no brothers or sisters, so she knows what it's like being a only child. She is perfect," Claude announced with a twinkle in his eye I hadn't seen since he was a baby.

"She was lucky to get a job at that bait store. It's real hard for colored folks to get hired there. I tried three different times and they didn't hire me," I whined.

"Well, they didn't waste no time hiring Maybelle. She been there six months now. Her uncle works there too. I'm sure he helped her get hired."

"She lives with her uncle?" I asked.

"Nope. She lives with her mama and daddy. They are real nice people too. They both teach school. And the whole family belongs to the New Hope Baptist Church on Heggy Street. Maybelle and her mama sing in the choir, and her daddy is the choir director."

Schoolteachers and Christians! That got my attention even more. I didn't think of myself as a snob. But to have my son involved with folks in the education profession and in the Church was a great big step up from the sharecropping and other low-end work Daisy's folks did.

"This girl sounds like a real good choice," I gushed.

"Well, now. It sounds like you done really hit on something good this time, son," Hubert said, beaming with pride.

I had a feeling he was just as impressed as I was, maybe even more.

Claude chuckled. "Hold on now. Don't y'all go jumping the gun. I ain't even kissed her yet."

I wanted to hide the fact that I was excited, so I forced myself not to sound too eager. "Well, she sounds like a nice girl."

As much as I wanted to hold on to my son, I still wanted him to be in a relationship with somebody who was going to enhance his life, not destroy it.

"You mean she sounds like the kind of girl y'all want me to be with." Claude snickered. "Boy, oh boy! It's a good thing Daisy took off. Otherwise, I would never have been able to get with Maybelle. Mama, Daddy, she said she can't wait to meet y'all."

"Bring her to church this Sunday so we can check her out. If we like her, we'll have her go home after service with us and eat supper," Hubert suggested.

"Why don't we go by her house tonight? I told her if it wasn't too late when we got home, we might do that," Claude said.

"I don't feel like meeting nobody new tonight. I'm tired and I want to get to bed early," I said, yawning for good measure.

"Okay, Mama. I probably won't go to church this coming Sunday. I'll check with her and see if she can come eat supper with us one day next week." Claude paused, and then, out of nowhere, he asked me, "By the way, how are you getting along with the Dowler woman's brother?"

"Huh? Oh! Um . . . me and Mr. Oswald get along just fine. He's a nice man," I replied. Just hearing that devil's name made my blood boil. I promised myself that I'd stay as cool as I could whenever somebody brought him up.

"I'm glad to hear that. If there was more nice white folks like him and his sister, life for colored folks wouldn't be so abysmal," Hubert said with a weary sigh.

The only good thing about running into Claude's daddy was that it took my mind off Mr. Oswald for a little while. But not for long.

Monday morning, when I got to Mrs. Dowler's house, I seen him peeping at me from his bedroom window as I shuffled up the walkway. He didn't have a shot glass in his hand, like he usually did. This time he was holding a bottle. Before I looked away, he took a long pull and gave me a salute.

When I got inside, Mrs. Dowler was standing in front of the huge oval-shaped wall mirror in her living room, checking her makeup. Despite her age, she was as vain as she could be. She had on a pink tweed skirt and a white silk blouse. I stopped next to her and whistled.

"You look better than a film star today, Mrs. Dowler."

"Thank you, Maggie. I hate to rush off, but I promised Lorna Evans we'd go to the beauty parlor together today and then on to lunch. We won't be gone but two or three hours, I hope. But I never can tell with that long-winded Lorna. She can't get through a shampoo and set without giving me a detailed account of what's going on in her life, as well as everybody else's. I declare, they should add gossip to the list of deadly sins." Mrs. Dowler laughed. "It should be pretty quiet while I'm gone. The telephone might ring a few times, but you don't have to answer it. If anybody knocks on the door, don't open it. I've been dodging one of those pesky Rawleigh vitamin peddlers for days."

"Yes, ma'am."

"One more thing! Last night Oswald got drunker than he usually does. He's still in bed and I doubt if he'll wake up before I return. If he does, please handle him with care. He's what our dear old colored mammy used to call a cracked plate when he was a little boy, and he's still one today. Poor thing. He was so down in the dumps last night, he said he wished he could go to sleep and never wake up. Lord, it scared the bejesus out of me." Mrs. Dowler was talking so fast, she had to stop and catch her breath. "Just look at me rattling on and on without even asking you how you're doing!"

"Oh, I'm doing just fine, ma'am. Thank you for asking."

"Well, you look fine. Much better than you looked with those dark circles around your eyes the day you told me about the difficulty your son was causing. I'm sure you're tickled to death to have him back home!"

"I declare, I am. My baby is glad to be back home." I shook my head and waved my hands in the air. "And guess what? The boy done already got his eye on another girl." I smiled, but it was forced. "She's got a good job handling worms at the bait store, and she's from a good family. Both of her parents teach school and are in the Church."

"Do say! I truly believe that God looks out for His people. I can't think of anybody half as worthy to be blessed more than a sweet woman like you. Associating with wholesome folks like this girl's family will enrich your life tremendously." Just as Mrs. Dowler was about to speak again, somebody outside blew a horn. "That's Lorna! I hate to run, but I must. That old gal gets real impatient if I hold her up. Now, there's plenty of food left over from yesterday's supper, crab cakes, dumplings, turnip greens. Help yourself."

Mrs. Dowler wasn't gone five minutes before Mr. Oswald peeped into the kitchen while I was preparing the wash.

"You don't know how happy I am to see you," he growled as he strutted toward me, rubbing his palms together.

I threw up my hand. "Mr. Oswald, please don't ask me to do nothing nasty today," I pleaded.

"I ain't asking. I'm telling. Now give me some sugar!"

I held my breath and gave him a quick peck on his cheek.

"Come on now, honey. You can do better than that."

The next thing I knew, he wrapped his arms around me and hauled off and gave me a long, sloppy kiss on the lips. It was too disgusting for words.

"Now squat down on your knees," he ordered as he unzipped his pants.

When I crouched down, he grabbed me by my hair, stuck his limp pecker in my mouth, and started moving. He moaned and groaned and held my head in place until he was satisfied. Thank God it was less than a minute.

A hour later, he came at me again. I had just sprinkled arsenic in the garden and was in the pantry putting the can back on the shelf when he walked in with a grin on his face.

"Please, Mr. Oswald, I'm tired and—"

He cut me off by wagging his finger in my face. "Horsefeathers! Didn't I tell you to stop being such a crybaby? If anybody should be boo-hooing, it's me. You were right clumsy with me a little while ago. Gal, you've got a heap to learn about giving mouth service properly. That's why I am not going to waste my time on that procedure again. Shoot. We going to make love this time. Lift up your skirt!"

He didn't give me time to react. He pushed me up against the wall, lifted up my skirt, and slid my panties to the side.

"Spread your legs! If you move right and don't make me do all the work, it'll be more fun for you!"

He separated my legs with his knee and plunged into me so hard my head hit the wall with a thud.

I never felt so violated before in my life. Them times with Mr. Royster seemed like a tea party compared to what I was going through now.

Chapter 38

I DIDN'T THINK MY SITUATION COULD GET NO WORSE, BUT IT DID.

While I was in the upstairs linen closet on Tuesday putting away some of the items I had ironed, Mr. Oswald stormed in and made me do the same thing he'd made me do yesterday. Mrs. Dowler was just a few yards away in her bedroom.

I had no idea what I would do or say if she'd walked in before he finished. Mr. Oswald was so low-down, he would blame everything on me. I could just hear him spinning a tale about how I'd thrown myself at him while he was too drunk and weak to resist. He'd probably say that I'd asked him for money, and give more strength to his claim by saying that I was the daughter of a used-to-be prostitute, so my behavior was natural.

As much as I adored Mrs. Dowler, I reminded myself that she was still a white woman, and she doted on her baby brother. She would never take my word over his. Not only would I lose her as a friend, I'd be out of a job!

When Mr. Oswald finished with me, he pulled me into his arms and nuzzled my hair as he filled my ear with gibberish. I had to hold my breath to keep the bile creeping up my throat from oozing out of my mouth and splashing all over the place. He had already squirted a slimy mess onto the floor for me to clean up.

"Mmmm mmmm! That was much better. I got a good mind to ask Fern to start having you come twice as many days. I'm sure she could find a few more chores for you to do. Otherwise, I might have to be weaned so I can make it through the days you don't come."

"Why don't you pester the lady who comes on the days I ain't here?" I asked in a voice that sounded like it was coming from somebody at death's door.

"Pffftt! What makes you think I don't? And she enjoys it as much as I do. But that sow is three times your size. So maneuvering all that blubber is a real challenge." Mr. Oswald shrugged and then gave me a serious look. "But at the end of the day, tail is tail." After a mighty belch he slapped my behind and snarled, "I'm tired of gabbing. Go yonder to that shelf and get a towel and clean up that mess on the floor."

I did as I was told and then I scurried away from him like a scared squirrel. One thing I knew for sure was that after today Mr. Oswald would never touch me again.

When I got off work, there was only one thing on my mind: killing Mr. Oswald. I had no idea how or when I was going to do it, but it had to be done before he came at me again. That meant I had to kill him before next Monday. I knew I couldn't lure him off somewhere, like I'd done with Daisy, so I would have to do the deed in Mrs. Dowler's house.

I came up with a plan the next day. Mrs. Dowler told me that she went to church every Sunday morning around nine and stayed there until after four p.m. She never locked her doors, so I wouldn't have no trouble getting into her house while Mr. Oswald was alone. He got so drunk every evening, he slept like a log all night and rarely got out of bed before noon. I had to get there right after Mrs. Dowler left, in case she decided to come back home early.

The only problem I had was that the buses didn't run on Sunday, so I'd have to drive. Once I got there, I'd get the arsenic container out of the pantry and pour enough into the whiskey bottle Mrs. Dowler told me he kept on the nightstand in his bedroom. The way them critters in the garden writhed when they ate the arsenic, I knew it was a painful way to die. But it was quick. I'd make sure to put enough in the whiskey so Mr. Oswald would die in a hour or so, plenty of time before Mrs. Dowler got home from church to check on him.

It was so hard to get through the days leading up to Sunday. Mr. Oswald was on my mind all the time, but I didn't care. He'd be out of the picture soon enough.

I spent Wednesday and Thursday doing chores around my house and visiting some of my neighbors. One reason I liked to spend time with the folks on my block was because I enjoyed hearing them tell me how pleased they was to have me as a friend. My generous nature had a lot to do with it. When folks needed to borrow something, even money, I didn't hesitate to give it to them.

Claude told me and Hubert on Friday morning that he was bringing his new girlfriend to have supper with us on Saturday. I got as giddy as a child on Christmas morning. Hubert seemed just as happy. When Claude mentioned that white was Maybelle's favorite color, I went out Friday afternoon and bought a white cotton dress just for the occasion—even though it was my least favorite color.

I couldn't wait for Saturday to roll around. Claude surprised us and showed up with Maybelle on Friday evening.

"It is so nice to finally meet you," Hubert greeted as soon as Claude and Maybelle walked through the door a few minutes after six p.m.

"I'm glad to meet y'all too. I been really looking forward to this," she gushed.

She was a little on the heavy side, but I could tell from the way she carried herself that she was comfortable in her skin. The thin white dress she had on looked good next to her smooth bronze skin. With her short curly-styled black hair, big brown eyes, and buttonlike nose, I could see why Claude liked her. And the fact that she was from such a good family helped.

"My mama told me I should have baked a pie or something to go with supper, but I didn't have time. Claude had told me he was bringing me over here tomorrow."

"I couldn't wait another day," Claude piped in. He glanced from me to Hubert and added, "I'm sorry I didn't give y'all more notice that I was bringing Maybelle today."

"That's all right, son," I said, giving him my warmest smile.

He grabbed Maybelle by the hand and led her to the living-room couch. They plopped down so close together, their knees touched.

Hubert sat down in the chair facing them, but I was too antsy to sit. I was happy for Claude. Maybelle had made such a good impression, and I should have been concentrating more on that. But my mind was racing back and forth about the killing I was planning to do on Sunday. It was hard to believe that I was fixing to kill another person already. But what else could I do?

"Maggie, don't you want to sit down?" Hubert asked. He nodded toward the chair next to him.

"Oh, I'm fine. I spent enough time sitting on my tail today when Ma Wiggins was doing my hair. My behind stayed numb for the longest," I explained. Everybody laughed.

"Miss Maggie, Claude told me about that dream job you got working for Mrs. Dowler. She owns the house my cousin Melvin lives in. She ain't raised his rent since he moved in ten years ago," Maybelle said.

She had such a beautiful voice. It was like listening to birds chirping. Compared to her, Daisy had sounded like a frog.

"Oh, Mrs. Dowler is the most wonderful and generous lady I ever worked for," I said proudly. "Some days I have less than a dozen pieces to wash and iron and she still pays me the same amount she pays me when I have two or three loads."

"I would love to work for a lady like her someday," Maybelle said with a dreamy-eyed expression on her face.

"Don't you like your job?" Hubert asked. "I would think that with all the folks who like to fish in Lexington, business at the only bait store in town would be real good."

"Business is good. Handling them slimy worms is messy, but it took me four months to find a job, so I ain't complaining. I just got my first raise last week," Maybelle announced. "But someday I would like to do something more pleasant. My cousin is the maid for a lady who lives on Mrs. Dowler's street. She loves working in that area so she can see up close what rich white folks really live like."

"They don't live like us, that's for sure," I said, rolling my eyes. "And another thing, you'd be surprised how many white folks don't believe in all this doggone segregation and racism. Most of Mrs. Dowler's friends are as nice to me as she is." I looked directly at Maybelle. "I'll ask Mrs. Dowler if I can bring you to her house so you can meet her someday. She loves to entertain company."

"Ooh, I'd like that," Maybelle squealed. "If she likes me, maybe she'll let me take over if you ever quit. I really like living in Lexington and I hope to spend the rest of my life here."

"Maybelle just moved into her own house two days ago," Claude said. "So"—he paused and a smug look crossed his face—"I want y'all to know right now that I'm going to be spending a lot of time over there." A sheepish grin accompanied his words.

We spent another few minutes talking about a bunch of different mundane things before we ate supper. As much as I liked Maybelle, the way she was gobbling up the pinto beans, baked chicken, and rice I'd cooked, I knew she was going to end up with a more serious weight problem than she already had. But that didn't bother me one bit, for I'd never seen Claude so happy—and that was all that mattered.

After they finished eating, Claude and Maybelle left to go to the movies. He'd dropped a hint that he might spend the night at her house, so I didn't expect to see him until tomorrow.

"I like that girl," I told Hubert as we stood looking out the window as they strolled down the street holding hands. Actually, it looked more like they was gliding. When they got to the corner to let a truck pass, they kissed. "My goodness. It sure seems like our son is in love again already."

"And that's a fact. The good thing is, this time it's with the right gal." Hubert exhaled, puffed out his chest, and backed away from the window. "Baby, things are going so well for us. But you seem a little skittish lately. I noticed it the other day. Is something bothering you?"

"No, I'm fine. Um . . . it's just that I been having some female issues lately."

"Oh? Nothing serious, I hope."

"No. It's just menopause . . ."

Hubert gasped so hard, he hiccupped. "Already? You ain't but thirty-nine years old!"

"So? That's old enough for it to get started. And it could drag on for years and years."

"Tell me about it. Mama is in her seventies and she still complains about having hot flashes, night sweats, and strange mood swings."

"I think I'll drink some ginger tea and turn in early tonight. I'm feeling kind of under the weather too."

"I had planned on visiting a friend tonight. But if you ain't feeling well, maybe I should stay home with you in case you need me. I'd hate for you to get sick enough to miss work on Monday."

"You ain't got to worry about me missing work. I'm sure I'll be feeling fine by then. I took a pill Jessie gave me and she said they always work for her." I exhaled and gave Hubert one of my biggest smiles. "Thank you for being so concerned, sugar. Look, this has been a long, busy day. I'm going to do some sewing and a few other things before I get ready for bed. Why don't you get ready and go visit your friend?"

There was a blank expression on Hubert's face for a few moments. And then his eyebrows shot up. "You don't mind?"

I gave him the most incredulous look I could manage. "Hubert, why should I mind you going to visit your boyfriend? After all these years we been playing our roles, it's way too late in the game for me to say anything about what you do in your personal life."

He sniffed and rubbed his head. "All right, then. Um, it'll probably be very late when I get back, so don't wait up for me."

Chapter 39

HUBERT HADN'T COME HOME BY MIDNIGHT. I HAD PLANNED TO use the car to drive to Mrs. Dowler's house Sunday morning, but he had it. If he didn't get home early enough in the morning, I had to find another way to get over there. That was a problem I hadn't considered. I couldn't call up nobody to give me a ride. I had only one other choice: I had to drive over there in his hearse.

Just thinking about being in that scary thing alone chilled me to the bone.

I had a story ready in case somebody tried to reach me at home and wanted to know where I'd gone so early in the morning. I planned to tell them that Mrs. Dowler had asked me to come over and scrub her kitchen floor because she had guests coming for supper after church and she hadn't been able to get in touch with her usual cleaning woman to ask her to come in on her off day.

When Hubert had took over Uncle Roscoe's business, I told him that it made me nervous having the hearse sitting in front of our house. He immediately started parking it at the funeral home, which was only four blocks from our house. He'd either walk to and from there or get a ride with one of the men who worked for him. Some days I would take him and pick him up in our car. This would be the first time I rode in the hearse by myself and it was nerve-wracking. But once I got rid of Mr. Oswald,

I could focus on more important things. With Claude in a good place now, I could devote most of my time and energy to Hubert. Keeping him happy was still very important.

Hubert was concerned because things had been slow at the funeral home for a while. For some reason, people wasn't dying as fast as they used to. And most of the ones that was, their families was giving their business to the Fuller Brothers, the only other colored funeral home in Lexington. Hubert had recently started complaining about it: "Business done got so bad, I'm going to go back full-time at the turpentine mill until things pick up."

"Baby, business is just in a slump. With me working, you can still work at the mill part-time. Just last week, Mrs. Dowler mentioned giving me another big raise next month."

"I hope she keeps her word."

"Oh, I know she will. She ain't never let me down and I don't think she ever will."

When Hubert still hadn't come home with the car by nine a.m., on Sunday morning, I started walking toward the funeral home. When I got there, I went inside and wrapped the same scarf around my head that I had wore when I took care of Daisy. I had misplaced the sunglasses, but I wasn't that concerned about none of Mrs. Dowler's neighbors seeing me go in her house while she was at church. Most of them knew how fond Mrs. Dowler was of me, so they wouldn't have no reason to get suspicious. But I already had a story ready if it ever came up. I'd claim that I had accidentally left my wedding ring on the kitchen windowsill when I took it off to do the hand-washing the previous Monday and had come to pick it up. Because of the harsh soap Mrs. Dowler had me use, I always took it off. If somebody asked why I couldn't wait to get it on Monday, especially after it had been left behind a week ago, I would tell them that I hadn't noticed it was missing until Sunday. And that I couldn't take a chance on my husband finding out how careless I'd been.

The minute I got in the hearse, I got a strange feeling. Just sitting in the same space that so many dead bodies had occupied made me nervous. But not for long. I convinced myself that having to drive a death-related vehicle to go kill somebody was a sign that it was meant to be.

I drove slow and avoided streets where people I knew lived. I didn't want to attract any more attention than I already would. It wasn't common to see a woman cruising down the street behind the wheel of something as ominous as a hearse. Just seeing one gave most people the heebie-jeebies. When Hubert used to park it in our driveway, some of our neighbors complained about having it so close. That was another reason why he parked it at the funeral home.

When I was about a mile from Mrs. Dowler's house, something else crossed my mind that I hadn't thought about. Mrs. Dowler had some pretty superstitious neighbors too. If they seen a hearse sitting in her driveway, or in front of her house, there was no telling what they'd think. What would be even worse was if Mr. Oswald happened to be awake and looked out the window and seen it. There would be no way that I could go through with my plan if that happened. The only logical thing I could do was leave the hearse somewhere and walk the rest of the way. I drove around until I spotted a furniture warehouse that was closed on Sunday. I parked behind it and trotted back out to the street.

I didn't see Mr. Oswald peeping out his bedroom window. But when I got in the house, I tiptoed from room to room downstairs, just in case he had decided to get out of bed today and was lurking somewhere else in the house. I'd never known him to do that on the days I came, but there was a first time for everything.

When I seen that the coast was clear, I rushed to the pantry and grabbed one of the cans of arsenic. I was glad Mrs. Dowler had bought two of the real big ones this time. There'd be more than enough for me to get the job done, and leave enough for the next time I had to sprinkle her garden. I had on one of my drab dusters with pockets deep enough to hide the big can. Before I left the pantry, I closed my eyes and took a bunch of deep breaths. And then I told myself again that I was doing the only thing I could do if I wanted to keep my job and get Mr. Oswald off my back.

Before I made it to the end of the long hallway, where his room was, I could hear him snoring, even with his door shut. I gently opened the door, eased in, and crept over to his bed. He looked like the devil laying there on his stomach. Mrs. Dowler had told me that as soon as he woke up every morning, he finished whatever was left in the bottle he kept on his nightstand. When they found him dead, his fingerprints would be the only ones on his bottle because I'd brought a pair of socks to cover my hands with when I picked it up. On top of that detail, I'd leave the arsenic can on the nightstand, so when they found it, they'd believe he'd committed suicide. Once he was dead, I'd wrap his fingers around the arsenic can so his fingerprints would be on that too. I didn't see no reason for my plan not to work.

I held my breath for a few seconds, and then I let it out in a whoosh. I didn't want to take no longer than I had to. I put the socks on my hands and turned around to get his whiskey bottle so I could stir in a hefty dose. My mouth dropped open and my eyes got big when I seen that the whiskey bottle was completely empty! I panicked when he suddenly started moaning and grinding his teeth. When he got quiet, I backed out of the room.

For the next fifteen minutes, I searched high and low upstairs and downstairs for another bottle of whiskey and couldn't find one. I seen several bottles of the red wine in the pantry that Mrs. Dowler liked, but she'd made it clear that her bother never touched anything except whiskey. My mind was in a frenzy and I didn't know what to do. If I didn't get rid of him today, there was no telling when I'd get up enough nerve again.

One thing was for sure, I was not about to let that sucker take advantage of me again, so I couldn't leave him alive. Without giving it much thought, I picked up a pillow that had slid to the floor. Smothering him was the only reasonable choice that wouldn't look suspicious. Since he was already half facedown, I took the pillow and covered the rest of his face. He must have been drunker than usual because he didn't struggle or holler. I held the pillow in place until he stopped moving.

When I was convinced that he was dead, I lifted the pillow and stood over him for a few more minutes. I shook my head and cussed under my breath because Mr. Oswald was the ugliest and most disgusting beast I'd ever laid eyes on. He had on a pair of long gray underwear that looked three sizes too big. He was skinny the first time I seen him, but he'd lost even more weight since then. And I'd had to pleasure this nasty bag of bones! Well, not no more. I sighed and rolled his frail body over so that his face was completely mashed up against the mattress. I waited another few minutes before I felt his pulse and his chest. I didn't feel nothing. I turned his head just enough to get close to his mouth to see if I could feel any breath coming out. I didn't feel nothing, so I was sure I'd completed my mission. Being the wife of a undertaker, I knew death when I seen it.

I left the house as fast as I could. I didn't realize I still had the arsenic in my pocket until I was halfway home. I couldn't take a chance and go back and return it to the pantry in case Mrs. Dowler decided to come home early.

If any of her neighbors seen me in her house earlier, it might look suspicious if they seen me there again. I wasn't worried about her discovering that one of the containers was missing. If she went in the pantry before I got back, she had no reason to be checking on the arsenic.

I didn't want to be in the hearse no longer than I had to be. So the only thing I could do was put the arsenic back in the pantry on Monday.

Chapter 40

It was a strange ride home. When I passed a police car, I panicked and almost lost control of the hearse. I held my breath, thinking the peacemaker would turn around and follow me. If he pulled me over, I had no idea what I would tell him if he asked me why I was driving through a white neighborhood in a hearse. The police didn't pay no attention to me, but I didn't breathe easy again until I reached the colored part of town and had only a few more blocks to go.

During that time I couldn't stop thinking about some of the things Mr. Oswald had said and done to me, and what it had felt like to kill him. I was scared and nervous, but at the same time I was glad I had done what I did. I didn't feel guilty because he'd had it coming. Just like Daisy.

I truly believed that if I hadn't done what Mr. Oswald wanted me to do, he would have carried out his threat and Mrs. Dowler would have fired me. Whether she believed me or not, she would have done it to save face with the other white folks. I knew that Mr. Oswald would have run his mouth all over town to the white folks about me "stealing" from him. And if he did, I would never get another domestic job in Lexington. I didn't want to lose the one I had now, so what else could I do but kill him? The answer to my question was easy: nothing.

The economy was still moving at a snail's pace, so jobs was just as scarce as they'd been for several years. Colored folks who couldn't find work was leaving in droves to go up North, where everybody said there was better opportunities for us and less racism. A few had even moved to California. I didn't have nowhere to run to. Even if I did have somewhere else to go, I knew Hubert would never move to another state. I was stuck in Alabama and I was going to make the best of it. Meanwhile, I was still confident that Hubert's undertaking business would pick up again soon. Plus, I was determined to keep my job with Mrs. Dowler for as long as I could.

It bothered me knowing how hard that sweet old lady was going to take her brother's passing. But I was glad I hadn't had to make it look like he'd committed suicide. One suicide in her family was bad enough. I'd comfort her and weep and wail as much as I could. I was sure that my emotional support would help her get through the bereavement period a little sooner. It was the least I could do.

I returned the hearse to the funeral home and walked to my house.

Our car was in the driveway. When I walked into the living room with a smile on my face, Hubert was stretched out on the couch. He sat up fast and gave me a curious look. "Where you been, Maggie?"

"Huh? Oh, I went to get some washing powder. I need to do our laundry this week," I answered. I dropped my purse on the coffee table and sat at the other end of the couch.

"Where is the washing powder at?" he asked as he gawked at my empty hands.

"Huh? Oh, the store was closed," I said with a sheepish grin. "I stopped by Jessie's house to see if she had some I could borrow, but she wasn't home."

"Maggie, you know all the stores in Lexington is closed on Sunday."

"I guess I got so much on my mind, I got my days mixed up. I got up this morning, thinking today was Saturday." I didn't like the way he was looking at me, so I turned the tables. "Where was you since Friday night?"

He gave me a impatient look. "Where do you think?"

"Of course," I sneered. "What you do with your boyfriend is your business. It's too late for me to be sticking my nose in it. Just keep being careful so nobody we know will ever find you out. If they do, our lives won't be worth a plugged nickel."

"You ain't got to worry about me getting caught and wrecking our happy home. And I know I ain't got to worry about you doing nothing that'll turn folks against us." The huge grin on Hubert's face now was making me uncomfortable.

"Why you looking at me like I'm something good to eat?" I asked.

"Maggie, I feel so blessed to have a saintly wife like you. Perfect in every way! No wonder that old Dowler woman is so pleased. Her brother is probably just as happy with your services, huh?"

"Um, yeah." He was, but he won't be no more, I said to myself. I had to hold my breath to keep from grinning too.

I glanced toward the hallway. "Did Claude come home yet?"

"Nope. He called a few minutes ago and said he'd be home later today."

I rolled my eyes and sighed. "The boy's in love for sure," I said, waving my hands in the air. "At least we ain't got to worry about Maybelle hurting him, or making him act like a fool."

"That's for sure," Hubert agreed with a chuckle.

"Guess what? I got a itching to make gumbo for supper. I better get in the kitchen and get started. You know how I like to let it simmer for about two hours." I put Mr. Oswald out of my mind and practically glided into the kitchen, with Hubert right behind me.

"That's a good idea. Just make sure you set aside some for me before you dump in all that cayenne pepper. Also, in case Claude comes home in time for supper, set aside enough for him too. That pepper makes him sneeze and burns his gullet."

"Pffftt!" I rolled my eyes. "Don't you think I know by now how you and Claude like your gumbo?"

"You just said you got so much on your mind. If you can forget what day it is, you can forgot to set aside some—"

"Hush up!" I teased as I waved my hand in Hubert's face. As mundane as this conversation was, it took my mind off the crime I'd committed this morning. For a while, at least.

"Put a little more sausage and a pinch of sugar in my portion too," Hubert suggested.

"I will, and I'm going to make a extra big pot. Half-a-dozen folks in the neighborhood done asked me when I was going to make some more."

When the gumbo finished simmering, I called up several neighbors to let them know. They didn't waste no time storming our house. My in-laws happened to drop by, so they ate some too. By the time Jessie and her son arrived, it was almost all gone.

"Girl, I'm glad I got here in time to get some and to fix a bowl to take home to Orville," she said as she dipped the ladle into the pot until it was empty. She and Earl had just finished eating and would have finished it off if they hadn't had to consider Orville.

"Daddy say that's the only thing he likes about you," Earl said in a low tone.

This was the first time I'd heard him say something this month. I loved it when something I did brought him out of his shell.

"When you going to make gumbo again, Miss Maggie?"

"Oh, you ain't got to worry. I'll start making it more often, and when I do, y'all will be the first ones I tell," I said, beaming like a flashlight.

Me and Hubert had a very pleasant evening. When Claude and Maybelle showed up, the evening got even more pleasant. He looked so content, I didn't have the nerve to scold him about staying out two nights in a row and not calling until this morning.

"Mama, I wish you had told me you was making gumbo. We would have come over in time to get some," he told me.

"Baby, I'll make another pot tomorrow. Just for you and Maybelle," I promised.

"Miss Maggie, you are so good to Claude," Maybelle commented. "But you don't have to keep going out of your way to do things just for him. I don't want you to think I can't take care of my womanly business."

"Sweetie, I would never think that of you. I don't mind doing extra things for Claude," I assured her.

"There ain't nothing Maggie wouldn't do to keep Claude happy," Hubert threw in. "Or herself."

I smiled and nodded. They had no idea what I would do, or had done, for Claude and myself to stay happy.

Chapter 41

I HEADED TO WORK LIKE IT WAS JUST ANOTHER ORDINARY MONDAY morning. I was a little nervous because I had no idea what to expect when I got there. I prayed that it would look like Orville had accidentally smothered hisself, and not committed suicide like Mrs. Dowler had been afraid he'd do.

When I got to her house, I was not surprised to see several cars and trucks lined up in front and in the driveway. I took my time walking up on the porch to knock. A tall man, who looked like a younger male version of Mrs. Dowler, opened the front door. He had on a navy blue suit with a white shirt and a red tie. For the first few moments, he just stood there and stared at me with his lips pressed together.

"Who might you be?" he finally asked as he raked his fingers through his limp gray-and-brown hair.

Before I could answer, a long-faced redheaded woman strutted over to the door. She had on a hat that looked like a flowerpot; fake long-stemmed carnations was sticking up like antlers. With a gasp, she gave me the fisheye and boomed, "Gal, after all we've taught you people, don't you know the proper decorum when you come to a white woman's house? You hightail yourself around to the back door like you're supposed to!"

"I'm sorry. Mrs. Dowler always had me come in through the front door," I explained. "I'll go around to the back."

"That won't be necessary," the man said. Then he looked at

the redheaded woman. "It's all right, Josephine. Let me handle this."

She narrowed her eyes, mumbled a few cuss words, and moved back across the room. There was more than a dozen folks milling about. Some was moaning and groaning, but a few was laughing like they was at a party. I didn't know what to think.

"How can I help you?" the man asked. He smelled like beer, cigars, and sweat. My legs was shaking like leaves, and my heart was beating like a drum.

I cleared my throat and forced myself to smile. "I'm Maggie Wiggins, sir. I do Mrs. Dowler's laundry every week," I muttered. I made sure I sounded and acted humble—like the white folks wanted us to be.

He caressed his chin and gave me a cautious look. "Maggie. Oh yes! Mama calls and regales us with stories about you quite often. I declare, she's right fond of you. If folks didn't know any better, they'd think you were family. Your father-in-law is a preacher and you're married to a undertaker, right? Y'all live in that green house on Pike Street? She pointed it out to me when we drove past it one day, a couple of years ago."

"Yes, sir." I was surprised Mrs. Dowler had told anybody in her family so much about me.

"I'm her eldest son, Hammond. My wife and our youngest daughter got here from Atlanta shortly after one a.m."

"Oh. Well, I didn't know Mrs. Dowler was expecting company this week." I cleared my throat again and glanced around the room.

All of them other folks was staring at me. A woman in a blue dress and a wide-brimmed hat was crying, honking into a white handkerchief, and moaning like a dying mule. The woman with the red hair was standing in the middle of the floor with her arms folded across her chest and a scowl on her face.

"She wasn't expecting company. We've got a family issue that we need to sort out. There is no necessity for you to do any washing today."

"Oh? Did something happen to Mrs. Dowler? I hope she's all right."

Mr. Hammond shook his head and held up his hand. "No, she's fine for now. You see, her brother expired this past weekend. I told Mama weeks ago, I saw something like this coming. Uncle Oswald's been the family fool as far back as I can remember. That old fart!" Mr. Hammond must have drunk a lot of beer to be talking so freely and making them unkind remarks about his uncle to a colored cleaning woman.

"Uh, I'm so sorry to hear about Mr. Oswald's passing," I said. "I hope he didn't suffer . . ."

"Oh, he'd been suffering for quite some time now. He's been a wreck since his wife kicked him out. We always thought he'd just drink himself to death. But I'll say one thing, the way he did die was a heap more dignified."

"Uh . . . how did he die?"

"Apparently, he was so drunk, he rolled over in his sleep onto his face and smothered himself."

Them words was music to my ears. My plan had worked!

"My goodness. What a odd way to die!" I exclaimed. I sniffled and fished my handkerchief out of my purse and dabbed at the few tears I managed to squeeze out. "He . . . he was a nice man."

"Humph. Maybe he was to you, but very few folks could stand him. No wonder his wife got rid of him. I won't be surprised if she doesn't come to pay her respects. The only reason I came is because Mama begged me to."

"Can I see Mrs. Dowler? I'd like to hug her."

"I don't think that's a good idea right now. As a matter of fact, you can go on back home right now. There is no need for you to hang around. I'll let her know you came by."

"Okay. When should I come back? I don't mind doing the washing and ironing later in the week, or even doubling up on it next week."

"I don't know when you should come back. We haven't even made the funeral arrangements yet. But don't plan on coming back this week. I'll make sure you get paid for today and tomorrow anyway. Now, if you'll excuse me."

"Okay. It was nice meeting you," I said, sobbing.

Hammond nodded and shut the door.

It suddenly dawned on me that with all the relatives Mrs. Dowler had, another nasty devil could show up and pick up where Mr. Oswald left off. I scolded myself for even letting that thought enter my mind. And then I promised myself that I wouldn't spend any more time fretting about something that might happen and might not.

On Tuesday morning I was mortified to find out my plan had backfired. Hubert and Claude was at work. Jessie was in the kitchen gobbling up the biscuits left over from the breakfast I'd cooked. Somebody knocked on the front door at nine a.m. When I peeped out the window and seen Mr. Hammond standing there in a black suit, looking like a undertaker hisself, I was surprised but pleased. I figured he had come to tell me when to return to work.

"Mr. Hammond, come on in!" I squealed, opening the door as wide as I could. "This is such a nice surprise. Is your mama doing better now?"

He answered my question by shaking his head and letting out a long, drawn-out sigh. "I can't stay. I need to get to the funeral home. I just came to give you your pay for this week, like I said I would." He pulled several dollar bills out of his pocket. "I included a extra ten."

"Uh, when should I come back to work?"

He shook his head again. "There won't be any need to. My mama is in pretty bad shape. She had to be admitted to the hospital last night. It appears she's had a complete nervous breakdown. Uncle Oswald was the only sibling she had left. She doted on him, so she's taking his passing harder than we expected. I'm taking her back to Atlanta as soon as they release her."

I was so flabbergasted—you could have knocked me over with a spoon. I didn't want to believe my ears.

"I'm so sorry to hear that. How long do you plan on keeping her?"

"This will be a permanent arrangement. I should have

stepped in long before now. She's way too old to be living on her own. We've already started closing up the house. Our lawyers will start sorting out her other affairs momentarily."

I wanted to scream. "I sure would like to see her one more time before y'all leave," I whimpered.

"I don't think that's a good idea. When she's doing better, I will be sure and let her know how thoughtful you were. If she's up to seeing you, I'll bring her back for a visit. Or you can come visit her. Now, you have a pleasant rest of the day. So long, ma'am."

He tipped his hat and spun around so fast, I didn't have time to say nothing else.

Just like that, my life had been turned upside down again anyway. I couldn't believe it. I was still standing in the doorway when Jessie walked up and stood next to me with a pitiful look on her face.

"I heard what he told you. So you ain't got a job no more?"

"No, I ain't."

Chapter 42

I WAS GLAD WHEN HUBERT GOT HOME SO I COULD TELL HIM ABOUT Mr. Hammond's visit and that I'd lost my job. I didn't even give him time to sit down before I blurted it all out.

He sighed and stood in the middle of the living-room floor, looking as hopeless as I felt.

"I hope it don't take too long for you to find something else. And I hope whatever it is, it pays as good as what Mrs. Dowler was giving you," Hubert said in a tired voice. "Business at the funeral home is getting slower and slower. Paying rent on the facilities, maintaining the hearse, and all our other bills is really putting us in a bind."

"I'm sure I'll find something else soon. I'm going to go out every day this week."

I didn't waste no time. I started looking for another job the next day.

The only thing that kept me from going crazy was the news that Claude and Maybelle had suddenly decided to get married next Saturday afternoon. I was concerned because Claude had only known her for a few weeks. But I had promised Hubert and myself that I would not interfere and try and talk him into waiting a while to make sure she was the right one this time. Just from what I knew about her, I was convinced she was.

One thing I was really proud of was that fact that him and Maybelle had decided (or claimed, I should say) that they would wait until they got married to have sex. When they told me that a hour before Pa Wiggins married them in the same living room where he had married me and Hubert, I knew she was the right girl for my baby. So it was a good thing he'd snatched her up before some other young man did. Virtuous girls like her didn't stay single long.

At the reception everybody raved about the feast me, Jessie, and my mother-in-law had prepared. On top of the cake I'd baked, I'd also cooked four big pots of gumbo and had to give rain checks to the folks who hadn't come in time to get some. Everybody was having a good time, especially me. When Maybelle's daddy danced with her, I got downright slaphappy and actually drunk some of the champagne her family had provided. I didn't drink but one glass, though, so I only got slightly tipsy.

One thing I had learned about alcohol was that it could loosen lips. It would have been a disaster for everybody involved if I'd let something slip out about Daisy's "disappearance" and Mr. Oswald's sudden departure thirteen days ago. I told myself that if I could go on with my life and act normal after killing Daisy, I could do the same thing in Mr. Oswald's case.

Just as things was winding down, Jessie took me aside. She had a frantic look on her face, so I knew she had some disturbing news to give me. We stood in a corner in the back of the room, several feet away from everybody.

"Orville is getting worse and worse. He didn't want me to leave him in the house by hisself today, so he hid all of my shoes," she told me with her teeth clenched.

I looked down at Jessie's feet. She had on a pair of black pumps.

"How did you get your shoes back?" I asked.

"I didn't. I borrowed a pair from Carlene next door."

"My God. Why didn't Orville come to the wedding? He was invited."

"You'd have to ask him that. But he's been moaning and groaning for two or three days now about not feeling good. I'm sure it's got something to do with his heart because he keeps wrapping ice in a towel and laying it on his chest." Jessie blinked hard, but not fast enough to stop a huge tear from sliding down her face. She sniffled and rooted around in her purse until she found her handkerchief.

"Maggie, I know the man got health issues, but if I thought I could kill him and get away with it, I would," she whispered as she dabbed at her eyes and the tears rolling down her cheeks.

I gasped and turned around to make sure nobody was listening. "Girl, don't say things like that. You would never even hurt a fly," I whispered back. Just a few weeks ago, I could have said the same thing about myself. "You wouldn't hurt your own husband, would you?"

Jessie sighed. "No, I guess not. But sometimes I feel so hopeless and trapped, I can't help myself."

"I have a couple of extra pairs of shoes you can have. Hide them in a place where he can't find them."

"Thank you, Maggie. I don't know what I'd do without you."

The tears had stopped oozing from her eyes, but she dabbed at them again anyway. And then she honked into her handkerchief.

"Have you heard from anybody in Mrs. Dowler's family yet? When they say she's well enough for you to come visit, I hope I'll be able to go with you. I got a uncle in Atlanta and we can stay with him."

"I ain't heard a peep out of nobody in that family. Me and Hubert drove past her house the other day and the windows is all boarded up. I don't think I'll ever see her again." I sighed. "For now, I need to concentrate on getting a job."

"I been asking around for you. So far, I ain't been able to get no leads on nothing."

"Thanks, girl. I appreciate all the help I can get. I was going to come apply at the nursing home where you work."

"Don't even bother. They done started laying folks off, left and right, and I'm on pins and needles, praying they don't let me go. If they do, Orville will blame me for that too, and there is no telling what he'll do to me. He depends on my paycheck."

I shook my head and gave Jessie a quick hug. "Let's try not to worry too much about our problems. I got a feeling everything will be all right for both of us."

The minute me and Hubert got home, he went straight to bed, even though it wasn't even dark outside. I figured he was tired from all the socializing we'd done at the reception. When I got in the bed, three hours later, he was still wide-awake and he looked worried. The lamp on the nightstand next to his side was on and his Bible was laying next to it. He often read a few scriptures in bed, so I didn't think much about it.

"This sure was a long and hectic day. I'm so glad it's over," I said. "Don't forget to pick up my pots from your mama's house tomorrow. I'll be making more gumbo in the next day or so."

Instead of his eyes sparkling the way they usually did when I told him I was going to cook his favorite meal again, he looked even more worried.

"Hubert, what is the matter?" I finally asked.

He cleared his throat and let out a loud sigh. "Maggie, we might have to move in with Mama and Daddy and rent out our house."

My jaw dropped. "Say what? Why?"

"We can't go on too much longer without the money you was bringing in. I ain't had a body in a month."

"Well, sugar, folks is healthier than ever these days. They ain't dying as fast as they used to." I didn't know how my comments sounded to Hubert, but I regretted the words as soon as they slid out of my mouth. "Lord, forgive me! I hope that didn't sound too uncaring!"

"Baby, I feel the same way. The Fuller Brothers got the last two bodies."

"That's because they was close to the families of them two men. Most of the bodies you get is people close to us. Them Fuller Brothers can be so . . . so *mercenary*. Every time I turn around, they visiting the families of folks on their deathbeds, waiting like spiders to collect the bodies!"

"Yeah, I realize that. And there ain't nothing I can do about it.

Uncle Roscoe warned me about them years ago. That's why he made me promise I would always do a good job and go out of my way to make things easier on the families of the deceased, so they'd continue to do business with me." Hubert bit his bottom lip and blinked. "But if folks ain't dying, I ain't getting paid. I sure would hate to give up this nice house. I love Mama and Daddy to death, but living with them wouldn't be no picnic. They'd be all up in my business when I went off to . . ."

I finished Hubert's sentence for him. "Go visit one of your friends?"

"Yeah." He gave me a tight smile. "Let's try and get some sleep. I got a headache from all this worrying. Our son got married today and we should be happy."

"I'm happy. But I think it's too soon for us to be worrying so much about our finances and having to move. We'll be okay."

"How can you be so confident?"

I gave Hubert a thoughtful look and patted his shoulder. "Well, sooner or later, somebody is going to offer me a job. And . . . uh . . . we know a whole lot of old, sickly people. I just know that your business will pick up soon, and Pa Wiggins might have to preach funerals back-to-back . . ."

On Monday morning Jessie barged in ten minutes after Hubert left to go work at the turpentine mill. She was still in her housecoat and nightgown as she stumbled to the kitchen and plopped down at the table across from me.

"Girl, Orville tried to choke me just now when I told him to tell his girlfriend not to come to my house no more!"

She undid the two top buttons on her nightgown so I could see her neck. There was so many black-and-purple bruises on it, it looked like she had on a collar.

"Jessie, how much longer are you going to put up with that man's behavior?"

"I don't know. Earl tried to stop him today and he socked him so hard, he busted his lip."

"Where is Earl at now?"

"Still at the house. Orville told me I could go, but his son was staying with him. Can you believe that? He rarely pays any attention to the boy, and now all of a sudden he's trying to act like a daddy. He knows how important Earl is to me, so I'm scared to death he'll eventually use him to get back at me."

"Oh, Lord. I sure hope it don't come to that. Why don't you and Earl go stay with your mama for a few days? Or come stay with us? I'd love the company. Hubert's been in such a dark mood lately, I need something to cheer me up."

"What good would it do for me and Earl to take off? Orville done already said he'd hurt my mama if I ever left him. I'm sure he wouldn't hesitate to chastise you and Hubert if y'all tried to help me."

I looked at the floor for a few seconds. Jessie was breathing through her mouth and fidgeting around in her chair.

"I better get back home before he do something bad to my child. I . . . I just came over here to let you know what was going on. If I don't come back for you to drive me to work tonight, you know it'll be because he done something to me. Please promise me you'll call the police then."

"I will, Jessie. I know I keep saying this, but I really do think everything is going to be all right."

"I sure hope so." She gave me a hopeful look as she wobbled up out of her seat.

"I'll do all I can to help ease your pain. Please let Orville know I'm cooking gumbo again this evening. Ask him if he wants me to bring him a bowl."

That made Jessie perk up a little. "I'm sure he will want some. Your gumbo always puts a smile on his face. But you don't have to cook it again so soon, on my account."

"I was going to cook some again, today, for the folks who got left out at the reception anyway."

I opened the door, and before Jessie walked out, I gave her a big hug. I was going to do all I could to help Jessie, and bring Hubert out of the dumps.

* * *

One of the ladies I had approached about work called me up yesterday and said she was seriously thinking about offering me a job in the next few days. She used to visit Mrs. Dowler, and the colored woman who had been working for her for years died two days ago. When Hubert found out that the Fuller Brothers would be handling her funeral arrangements, he took it real hard.

Despite the facts, I didn't think of myself as a murderer, at least not like the people who killed for stupid reasons like robbery, love, and whatnot. What I'd done to Daisy and Mr. Oswald had been "self-defense," in my book. I'd had to get them before they got me. There was even justification in the Bible for what I'd done: a eye for a eye.

And now I had another idea brewing in my head that would help my husband and Jessie at the same time: I had to kill Orville. She'd be free and Hubert would finally get some business.

I still had the arsenic I'd took from Mrs. Dowler's pantry. I was glad I had more than enough to put a big lummox like Orville down. I had everything ready to get my gumbo started when Hubert got home Monday evening with the pots I'd left at my in-laws' house.

The minute the gumbo finished simmering, I took a big bowl of it to Jessie's house. She was sitting on her living-room couch with a wet towel on a black eye she hadn't had when she left my house.

"You all right?" I asked dumbly, walking over to her.

She shrugged. "He won't do nothing else tonight. His heart started racing real fast, right after he gave me this shiner. He said he was sorry."

"I'm sure he is. Did you tell him I was bringing him some gumbo this evening?"

"Yeah. I'm glad you came now, because he was getting impatient. I was going to come back to your house in a few minutes to see if you was still going to come through." Jessie stood up. "If you don't mind, could you put some in a bowl and leave it in the icebox for me and Earl, so we can eat it later. Orville's been whining for his since I told him you was making it, so can you take it to him? I don't want to see his face no time soon. You know where I keep the spoons."

"No problem." I started moving toward the kitchen. "You sit there and get your rest. I'm sure Orville will feel better after he eats."

"I sure hope so. That medicine they gave him at the clinic don't seem to be doing much good for his heart. I know the gumbo ain't medicine, but at least it'll put him in a better mood." Jessie paused and rubbed her black eye. "I won't be going to work tonight. I don't want my coworkers to see me looking like this."

"Can't you tell them you fell or walked into a wall?"

"No, Maggie, I can't. That's what I told them the last time."

Chapter 43

I WAS GLAD HUBERT WAS WITH ME WHEN JESSIE CAME RUNNING INTO the house on Tuesday morning, ten minutes past eight, barefoot and still in her bathrobe and hair curlers. We was still eating breakfast.

"Y'all ain't going to believe it! Orville done died!" she yelled. Her eyes had bugged out and sweat was all over her face.

"Who killed him?" Hubert blurted out. That question made my chest tighten.

"Ain't nobody killed him. It was his heart. He died in his sleep," Jessie told him with a sniffle.

"My Lord. May he rest in peace," Hubert said in a gentle tone. He walked up to Jessie and gave her a big hug. "He is the only person I know that lived this long with a heart as feeble as his was." Hubert choked on a sob and gave Jessie a pitiful look. "I remember how he would have to miss school and stay home in bed for days at a time because of his bad heart. Every year he missed almost every holiday party. He was kind of mean, especially to me, but we all felt sorry for him."

I got up and hugged Jessie too. "Poor Orville. I don't like to speak ill of the dead, but he was so hardheaded. If he had done what the doctor kept telling him to do, he might have lived another twenty or thirty years," I said.

From the corner of my eye, I seen Jessie cringe. I would have too—if I'd been in her shoes. The thought of spending that many more years with a brute like Orville was almost unbearable.

"As big a devil as he was, I still hope he's at peace," Jessie mumbled, leaning against the counter.

I would have offered her a seat, but she was too jittery to sit down. Me and Hubert stood side by side in front of her.

"The last few years was bad, but I have to give him credit for the early years when he was good to me."

I was hoping she wouldn't get too sentimental. One thing I didn't need was for her to say something that would make me feel bad about what I'd done. I loved Jessie like a sister so I couldn't have watched Orville abuse her too much longer. At the rate he'd been going, it would have been just a matter of time before he went through with his threat to kill her.

I had stirred a great big dose of arsenic into Orville's gumbo. When I'd gone into his bedroom to give him his "last supper," he'd glared at me and said, "It's about time you got here."

He hadn't thanked me or said nothing else, but I'd still told him with a smile, "I hope it'll make you feel better."

He'd sucked on his teeth and dismissed me with a sharp wave. I started backing out of the room as soon as he started eating. One spoonful was enough to kill him, but I had to ask anyway. "Jessie, you sure Orville is dead?"

"Oh, he's dead as a doornail, all right. It happened during the night. He had been acting so cranky last night, I decided to sleep on the couch. When I went to wake him up this morning, he was as cold and stiff as ice. He had vomited blood all over my new pillowcase. Just like my granddaddy when he had his heart attack." Jessie blew out a loud breath and shook her head real slow. "Hubert, I done already talked to his mama and daddy about his arrangements. They said to let you know they would cover all the funeral expenses. I told them I would chip in as much as I could. I declare, they wasn't the least bit surprised when I went over to their house this morning to let them know. He was mean to them too, but I know they'll miss him."

"It ain't no secret how mean he was to his own mama and

daddy. But no matter how he treated them, he was still their son. I know grief is going all through them right about now," Hubert said gently.

"I will miss him too," Jessie admitted. She sniffled and wiped a few tears from her eyes with the back of her hand. "But I guess it was his time to go." All of a sudden she sounded real perky. "And I ain't one to question the mysterious ways of God."

"Amen to that," Hubert tossed in. "Well, I won't be going to work at the mill today. Maggie, it looks like it's fixing to rain, and I don't want to get caught in it. I'll need for you to drive me over to the funeral home to pick up the hearse so I can collect Orville's body." Hubert took Jessie's hands in his and told her, "I'll need for you to being me his burial outfit no later than day after tomorrow."

"Okay. His sister gave him a new blue suit for his birthday last week. She made him promise he'd only wear it on special occasions. It's a doggone shame he hadn't had no special occasion to wear it to yet," Jessie whimpered.

Me and Hubert looked at each other, then at Jessie.

"Well, he got a special occasion now," I said in the most compassionate tone I could.

The funeral was on Saturday. A lot of folks came, but I had a feeling some had come just to make sure Orville was dead. His parents, his latest girlfriend, and his kids by other women was the only ones that actually shed a few tears. The sister who had bought him the blue suit got so overcome with grief, she fainted on her way into the church and was out cold until after the service. I heard a few people whispering about how "calm and collected" Jessie and Earl was acting. But while we was eating in the dining area, I heard them same folks make comments about how relieved Jessie must be to have "that beast" out of her life.

When me and Hubert got back home after the burial and was resting on the couch, he told me, "I hate to say this, but Orville's passing couldn't have come at a better time. We sure do need the money. His folks was real forgiving about how bad he had treated them. When his daddy came to pick out the casket, he told me Orville was going to a much better place, so the family really wanted to send him off in style. That's why they bought one of the most expensive caskets I got in stock."

"See there, Hubert. I knew business would pick up soon, and it's going to keep picking up. Jessie told me that Sister Baxter is dying. She could go any day now."

Hubert raised his eyebrows. "You mean the old lady who used to mind me when I was a little boy?"

"Uh-huh. Her family will definitely have you handle her funeral. And it'll be a doozy of a service. They own a feed store and two of Sister Baxter's sons is big-time bootleggers. So they'll spend a heap of money."

"I ain't going to get my hopes up too high yet, Maggie. Sister Baxter has been 'dying' since last year. That's one tough old lady. She done survived two heart attacks and a stroke. She could outlive me and you. In the meantime, you need to keep looking hard for a job. There ain't no telling when I'll get the next body."

I nodded. "I know. I'm waiting to hear back from that last lady I went to see about a job. If she don't hire me, I know somebody else will, sooner or later."

"Well, just pray it's sooner rather than later."

The economy was still in a slump and some of the folks who had been doing all right before the Great Depression hit was having all kinds of financial problems now. Some of the used-to-be rich families I had worked for a few years ago was looking for work themselves now. We listened to President Roosevelt's speeches on the radio. He kept telling everybody that things would get better soon. Well, it probably would for the white folks. But like it had always been, we still had to fend for ourselves the best way we could.

A few of the young men I knew didn't have much faith left in finding a long-term job, so they joined the military. Some bragged about how they would get to eat free food and have a roof over their heads. To me, that was a foolish reason to leave home, especially since some of the men who had been discharged from the army complained about how bad the colored servicemen was being treated. I didn't know anything about how the military decided who to draft. But I didn't know of any men older than thirty who had got selected, so me and Hubert had stopped worrying about him getting drafted. Unfortunately, like a lot of the younger men I knew, my son had registered so that was a new worry. I prayed every night that he would be as lucky as his daddy.

"If I didn't have my job, I'd join up myself instead of waiting for them to draft me. At least I could send a few bucks home to help you and Daddy out," Claude told us on his last visit to the house.

Hubert gasped and almost fell off the couch we was sharing that day. I almost fainted.

"Why y'all getting all upset?" Claude asked. He had turned a chair backward and was straddling it, facing us.

"You ain't going nowhere, boy—unless they make you! Shut your mouth before I shut it for you! You got a wife now!" I had to stop talking for a few seconds so I could catch my breath.

When I was able to speak again, I added, "Me and your daddy don't need you to make such a sacrifice just so you can send us money. We have always been able to find ways to stay afloat. All colored folks need to do is sit tight and keep living like good Christians," I said in the most serious tone I could manage without getting emotional.

"Your mama is right, son. If we wait long enough, things will get better. God promised us that and His Word carries a lot more weight than President Roosevelt's."

Hubert sounded so confident, it made me relax. But I didn't know for how long.

Chapter 44

IT HAD BEEN TWO MONTHS SINCE MRS. DOWLER HAD GONE TO LIVE with her son. Looking for another job was a job itself. To save money on gas and bus fare, I walked to as many interviews as I could. One day I went to a white neighborhood and knocked on the doors of eight houses and nobody needed help. One nice lady told me that if I had come the day before, she would have hired me to do her washing and ironing and some light cleaning.

Some folks put ads in the newspaper and tacked up notes on the board in the post office when they needed help. If the jobs was for maids, mammies, or somebody to do laundry, more than two dozen women—colored and white—applied for the same job. We couldn't compete with white women for work. No matter how much experience a colored woman had for a particular job, a white woman with little or no experience always got hired over her.

Going to the employment office was a bad joke. When white folks was in line, we had to wait until they all got waited on first. The last time I was there, I stood in line a whole hour. When I was the next one to talk to the person behind the counter, a scowling white woman waltzed into the office and got in front of me. She took the last job they had available that day. I left that place almost in tears.

"Any luck?" Hubert asked when he got home today.

I joined him on the couch, flopping down like I was about to run out of energy.

"No," I mumbled. "One lady wanted somebody to cook three meals a day, do the laundry, take care of her elderly grandmother, tend to five young kids, and clean the whole house for five days a week." I shook my head. "All she was offering to pay was two dollars a day."

"Well, that's better than nothing," Hubert said, giving me a hot look. "You ain't in no position to be choosey right now."

I gave him a hot look back. "Hubert, would you do that much work for ten dollars a week? Sister Cranston down the street takes care of a grandfather and a grandmother—nothing else—and that family pays her twelve dollars a week."

"As long as you looking, there is hope. You just need to look harder, I guess."

"Hubert, I'm looking as hard as I can," I hollered. "What else do you want me to do?"

"Well, don't stop looking. We done used up most of the money we'd saved, and my check from the turpentine mill is gone before I even get it."

"I know, sugar." I groaned as I slid off my shoes and reared back on the couch. I was aching from the head on down, but I was still able to swing my feet up onto the coffee table. "Just be a little more patient."

"If I was any more patient, I'd have to change my name to Job."

"Now, don't you bring the Bible into this," I scolded. I laughed, but Hubert didn't.

"I'm as patient as I can be. But if you don't get a job soon, we ain't going to be able to keep helping Claude pay some of his bills, like we been doing. We can't even fall back on my undertaking business." Hubert gave me a thoughtful look and scratched his head. "Folks *still ain't* dying as often as they used to. I ain't had no more bodies since Orville died last month. I remember the days when the undertakers was making more money than the colored bootleggers, lawyers, and doctors put together. When Uncle Roscoe was still alive, he was collecting bodies left and right."

"And you will be too!" I insisted. "With all the elderly colored folks in this town, business has to pick up soon."

"I hope you know what you talking about. The last thing I want us to do is move in with Mama and Daddy. Like I already told you, me going out would be a problem with them. They'd be in my business like flies on horse manure. And God knows what they would say if I stayed out all night."

"And while you off with one of your friends, they'd grill me like a slab of ribs, trying to get more information out of me."

"Sure enough. I ain't got to worry about you telling them nothing, right?"

I glared at Hubert. "What's wrong with you? I'm just as deep into our lies as you. So, why would I let the cat out of the bag?"

"I'm sorry, Maggie. I need to think more before I speak."

"Every day," I sneered.

Another week went by and I still hadn't heard from the last lady I'd interviewed with. So I took it upon myself to give her a call. I was very disappointed when her son told me she had already hired another woman. When I told Hubert, he looked like he wanted to cry. I couldn't stand to see him that way, so I left him slumped on the living-room couch and I went to sit on our front porch.

I was sitting on the steps, minding my own business, when a big rock whizzed past my head and hit the wall by the door with a loud thud. I looked around and didn't see none of the unruly neighborhood kids lurking near my house. They was known for tossing rocks at each other, usually hitting some innocent person who happened to be nearby.

When I heard somebody cough and then laugh, I looked across the street. Elderly Mr. Burris was standing in his front yard with a smug look on his long, high-yellow face. He glared at me and then hawked out a big glob of chewing tobacco spit. I stood up and walked out to the sidewalk.

"Did you just throw a rock at me, Mr. Burris?" I hollered.

"What if I did? You going to do something about it?"

"What's wrong with you, old man?"

"You been trampling on my grass! I seen you with my own eyes!"

I had no idea what he was talking about, but I went along with his accusation anyway. "Well, you should have come and talked to me instead of throwing a rock at me!"

"As long as I'm on my own property, I will do whatever I want!"

I shook my head and turned around to go back inside. Neighbors had been complaining about Mr. Burris for years. He was in his late eighties, so people gave him the benefit of the doubt and blamed his behavior on his age. On top of cussing at people and spitting chewing tobacco on them, he was doing more dangerous things now. He had recently started throwing rocks at cars and chasing folks down the street and clobbering them with his cane.

Two days ago he'd took his shotgun and blasted out the window in the neighbors' house next door because they'd been playing their music too loud. This was the sixth or seventh time he'd done that since we moved to the neighborhood. He had been a problem for a long time.

I went to the living room, where Hubert was still sitting on the couch, leafing through a magazine. I was glad to see that he didn't look so gloomy now. "That Mr. Burris is really getting out of control," I said.

Hubert snorted and raised his eyebrows. I told him about the rock-throwing incident. Hubert shook his head and set the magazine on the coffee table.

"He's getting harder to tolerate. I bumped into his wife yesterday. She said she's at her wit's end. That old goat is driving her and everybody else in that house crazy."

I was glad we had something else to talk about to take Hubert's mind off our finances. "I'm sure he is. Too bad they can't find a old folks' home to put him in."

"Now, Maggie, you know that ain't something colored folks like to do. We always take care of our own. Besides, there ain't no facility in Lexington that takes in colored people. The nearest one is in Mobile."

Whenever somebody mentioned Mobile, my heart skipped a beat. I hadn't been back over there since that night I seen Claude's daddy at the gas station. If I could help it, I would never set foot in that city again.

"Well, that'd be a long way for his wife and family to have to go to visit him." I cleared my throat, hoping Hubert wouldn't mention nothing about Mobile again.

"Mobile ain't that far," he pointed out.

I rolled my eyes. As far as I could know, Hubert was still involved with a man who lived in that city. Maybe a new one, or more than one. It never mattered before and it didn't matter now. I decided to steer the conversation in a slightly different direction.

"Uh . . . I hope Mr. Burris never hits anybody with all them shotgun blasts." Before Hubert could respond to my comment, somebody knocked on the front door. I answered and was surprised to see the old man's wife, Berniece, standing there.

"Hello, Sister Burris. Come on in." I waved her in as graciously as I could. But she was so jumpy, she almost fell coming through the door.

"Maggie, I'm sorry to bother you. My grandson just told me that Mason chucked a rock at you."

"He got a bad aim, so no harm was done," I said, forcing myself to laugh. "Come on in and have a seat. I'm pleased to see that you done recovered from the grippe."

"Thank you kindly. But now I'm having trouble with my back, and my eyesight is getting worse by the day. Anyway, I didn't come over here to discuss my health. I just wanted to come over here and apologize to you."

I waved my hand in the air. "Pffftt! It wasn't no big deal, so let's forget about it."

"I chastised him and he promised me he would apologize to

you. He's becoming so hard to control, I'm about to lose my mind."

"He ain't got to apologize to me. I know his mind ain't what it used to be. And I know it's getting worse over time."

"No, he's going to tell you how sorry he is. I can't let him get away with what he done. It was bad enough I couldn't get him to apologize to the Lewis family next door for shooting out their window again."

"Okay. You want me to come over there, or do you want to bring him here?"

"His eighty-ninth birthday is this Saturday. Me and the kids thought it'd be nice to have a little celebration for him. We'd sure love to have you and Hubert join us. If your boy and his wife can make it, tell them to come too. Jessie's still grieving Orville's passing, but she said she'll come anyway."

Mrs. Burris heaved out a loud sigh. There was such a woeful expression on her face, I gave her a hug.

"Mason is such a handful these days. Believe it or not, there was a time when he was as righteous as Hubert. He didn't start acting crazy until the Klan lynched our firstborn son. What a hellish thing that was. I still have nightmares about it myself."

"I had just started school when that happened, but I still remember it."

"Poor Mason. He'll never be the same." Mrs. Burris gave me a woebegone look. "I'm scared to death he's going to sass or attack a white person. If he do, we'll have to plan his funeral the same day."

"I hope it never comes to that. I'm so sorry for you and your family. At your husband's age, he's got to slow down eventually. It's a good thing you got folks living with you to help keep him under control."

"I couldn't deal with him on my own. But even with various relatives living with us over the years, and my youngest son and his wife and their three teenagers living in the house with us now, it's still a mess. Mason don't like so many folks underfoot. That, and my son threatening to get rid of his shotgun, made him so mad, he said he's going to burn down the house with us in it, the first chance he gets."

I gasped. "Oh, my God. Do you think he'd really do something like that?"

"As many times as he done shot out the window next door and could have killed somebody, why would I not believe he'd burn us all up?"

Mrs. Burris was twenty years younger than her husband, but she looked as old as he was.

"Me and the kids take turns sitting up all night to keep a eye on him. I ain't been to sleep in two days, so I'm going to go on home now and take a long snooze."

"Well, you take care of yourself, Sister Burris. If there is anything me and Hubert can do, just let us know."

"Thank you, Maggie. I do hope y'all will come to the celebration."

"Unless something serious comes up, we'll be there for sure. What time?"

"Two o'clock sharp. Mason's usually on his best behavior earlier in the day."

"We'll even come a little early in case you need my help getting everything ready."

"I'd like that. You can help cut up the ribs. Just one thing, though. We done invited more folks than we bought enough food for, so we asking everybody to bring something. If it ain't too much trouble, can you bless us with some of your delicious gumbo?"

"It won't be no trouble at all."

"Remember that Mason got some issues with his stomach, so he can't eat nothing too spicy no more. I hope you don't mind me asking you not to be too heavy-handed with the spices."

"I don't mind at all. My husband and son won't eat nothing too spicy neither. I always have to set some aside for them before I add the cayenne pepper."

"Okay, then. Mason would like that. It'll make him feel special."

I had put Mr. Burris out of my mind by the time me and Hubert finished eating supper.

"I'm going to go outside and get some fresh air," I told him right after I finished washing the dishes.

"I'll be in the bedroom listening to the radio some more. I'd like to hear what lies President Roosevelt got to tell us this time."

We laughed.

I hadn't been sitting on the front porch steps again for five minutes before I seen Mr. Burris peeping from around the black walnut tree in his front yard. It was dark and their porch light was dim, but I could still see that he had his shotgun in his hand. I yelped when he jumped from behind the tree and aimed it directly at me. I scrambled up off the steps and ran into the house. I didn't stop until I got to the bedroom.

"What's wrong with you? You look like Satan's nipping at your heels."

"Mr. Burris just pointed his shotgun at me!" I panted. I checked the windows to make sure they was locked before I flopped down on the bed. "I ought to call the police. *If* they come over here and do what they supposed to do, a few nights in jail might do that old man a world of good."

"Pffftt! What good would that do? The last thing we need in this neighborhood is them prejudiced peckerwood cops getting in our business. You know that already."

"Yeah," I said in a tired tone. "But if somebody don't do something, that old man really is going to hurt somebody. I just hope it won't be me or you. Do you think we should go over there and let his wife know what he just did?"

"For what? Maggie, that old fool ain't responsible. If we was to go over there in the next ten minutes, he'll probably have forgot even seeing you this evening, let alone throwing a rock at you and pointing a shotgun."

I sighed. "You're probably right. Maybe we should skip that birthday get-together they having for him this Saturday."

"We don't have to go if you don't want to. But Sister Burris will sure enough be disappointed—especially since she's counting on you to bring that gumbo. Sleep on it. If you still feel nervous about it in the morning, let her know we changed our minds."

"It'd be a shame to miss out on all them ribs and socializing with some of our neighbors," I admitted.

"And that's another thing. With a mob there, Old Man Burris won't have time to focus on you. I'm sure he'll be more interested in tormenting somebody else by then."

I kicked off my shoes and started unbuttoning my dress. "All right. But it'll be a while before I relax on our front porch steps again."

Chapter 45

TWO GOOD THINGS HAPPENED ON TUESDAY THAT MADE ME FEEL so much better. One, I finally got a new job! One of the ladies who had interviewed me called me right after I got out of bed. Her name was Mrs. Finley. She wanted me to start at ten a.m. today to do her laundry. I told her I couldn't come that soon because I had to attend a funeral in a few hours. *That* was the other good thing.

"All right," Mrs. Finley said.

She was a few years older than me, but she sounded almost as young as a teenager. She'd been so cheerful and friendly when she interviewed me, I knew we would get along just fine. Even though she was only willing to pay me half of what I had earned working for Mrs. Dowler, at least she didn't have no brothers or other male relatives living in her house that might pester me to do sexual chores.

"Can you start tomorrow?"

"Yes, ma'am. I'll be there with bells on," I chirped. Then I remembered I'd just told her I was going to a funeral. I cleared my throat and said in a real sad tone, "I haven't been to a funeral in quite a while."

"Nor have I. And I hope I won't have to go to one anytime soon. Now, if you don't mind me asking, whose funeral are you going to?"

"A real nice man named Mason Burris. He's a neighbor of mine."

"My Lord! Is he a light-skinned, bowlegged buck up in age?"

"Un-huh. Did you know him?"

"What a small world it is we live in. Years ago he used to drive the sugarcane wagon for a friend of mine. He was a good man. Bless his soul."

"Yes, he was a good man. My husband is handling the arrangements."

I hoped that none of my other friends or neighbors told me they was having serious problems with their husbands. Or that somebody else came into my life and posed a threat to my well-being. By now, I didn't have no problem eliminating threats. The more I did it, the easier it got. But from a moral standpoint, I knew that killing was wrong. I prayed to God and asked Him to help me control my actions. The last thing I ever wanted to do again was take another life—even if it meant putting a stop to a lunatic's violence, and more business for Hubert.

"You're married to an undertaker?"

"Yes, ma'am. Over twenty years now."

"I see. Well, the whole business of death scares me, so I don't even like to talk about it unless I have to. Anyway, give my condolences to Mason's family. I hope he didn't suffer long. Did he die of natural causes?"

"He didn't suffer long, and his death was accidental. He got real drunk on his birthday celebration on Saturday. He could barely stand up on his own, and whacked folks with his cane when they tried to help him. So everybody stayed out of his way. On his way to the bathroom, he fell and hit his head on the edge of the living-room coffee table. A few moments later, he had a spasm and started vomiting blood and messing in his pants." I was talking so fast I had to pause and catch my breath.

"Poor Mason. That must have been some fall," Mrs. Finley muttered.

"It was. When they got him to his bed, his wife cleaned him up and then he just laid there moaning for a little while before he went to sleep. Somebody checked on him every few minutes and he was still sleeping. But a couple of hours after the accident when his wife went to check on him again, poor Mason had died because of that fall . . ."

That's what everybody believed. But I knew that the arsenic in his gumbo is what really made him have his "accident."

From the relieved-looking expressions on some of Mr. Burris's relatives' faces (especially Mrs. Burris) when they heard he was dead, I knew that they was glad he was gone. The woman who lived in the house that he kept shooting the window out of had actually smiled when she heard the news. When she'd seen me looking at her, she suddenly put on a poker face and started dabbing at her eyes with the same napkin she'd had wrapped around the bottle of beer in her hand.

I was glad Hubert had been on the premises, because Mrs. Burris told him before Mr. Burris had even get cold, that she wanted him to handle the funeral arrangements.

When colored folks in a one-horse country town like Lexington died in a accident or of natural causes, nobody even called the police to come out and take a report. One of our doctors would decide what killed that person, give the information to the coroner, and then have a undertaker come get the body and haul it to the mortuary to be embalmed and prepared for funeral and burial. Even without verifying the cause of death, the coroner issued a death certificate to the undertaker to give the family.

The white folks running the show couldn't have cared less about us. The only time the police got involved was when a colored person murdered another colored person, which hadn't happened since I was in my early thirties. When a colored man was the victim of a race-related lynching or beating, or when a colored woman got raped by a white man, the police came to our neighborhood, scribbled on a notepad, and usually never came back. If they did, they jotted a few more notes, told the family to let them handle everything, and that was about it.

It was no secret that almost all of the white men in Lexington in positions of power was members of the Ku Klux Klan. That included our sheriff, his three deputies, and even our mayor. Unlike a lot of colored folks, I refused to believe all white people were devils. Mrs. Dowler was proof of that. And I'd known a heap of other nice white folks too.

Daisy was the only one I felt a little bit sorry about killing, since she'd been a mother. But her murder had been a blessing in disguise for her kids. Jessie had told me that the same day folks found out Daisy had "run off with another man," her mama moved the kids in with her and that they was doing so much better.

I didn't feel too much pity for my other three victims. If I hadn't killed Orville when I did, his bad heart would have done it eventually. Mr. Oswald was a drunk and probably had ruined his liver. That could've killed him, or his depression might have. And old men like Mason Burris couldn't have lived too much longer anyway. At the end of the day, each one had got what they had coming.

Even after lacing Mason's gumbo with a mighty big dose of the arsenic, the container was still almost half full. I had noticed a few bugs in our backyard, so that would be a good place to use the rest of it.

Besides, I didn't like the way I felt knowing I had a can of deadly poison in my house. I was starting to wonder if maybe the easy access was making all this a little *too* easy.

Now that I had a new job, I didn't have to fake my smile. Mrs. Finley wanted me to do her laundry and a few other weekly household chores. This week she wanted me to start on Friday instead of Wednesday, and my regular days would be Monday, Tuesday, and Friday. I was really looking forward to getting into the swing of things, so I showed up at her house a hour early on Friday.

She was very nice to me, but she wasn't half as personable as Mrs. Dowler. She was hog-heavy fat and plain and wore clothes drabber than what I wore to work. But I made her feel good about herself by making a fuss about her pretty red hair and dainty hands, her sweet voice, and a few other things. Each time she blushed like a new bride.

The first couple of weeks was very pleasant. Mrs. Finley's family, which included her elderly mother and two slouchy teenage daughters, was rarely in the house when I was there. And when they was, they only spoke to me when they wanted me to do something for them.

Every time I was at the Finley house—where I had to come and go through the back door—I couldn't help thinking about how good I'd had it with Mrs. Dowler. I hadn't heard from her son again, so I had no idea what was going on with her. She could have passed away, for all I knew. Every time I thought about that, I got sad. But I would always wonder if she really would have flipped the switch and fired me if Mr. Oswald had told her I'd stole from him.

I gave thanks to God every day because I had other blessings that was even more important to me than work.

Claude and Maybelle was doing so well, and Jessie was too. She was looking better than she had in years. She'd gained a few pounds and bought herself and her son a few new clothes, which was something she hadn't done in a long time. Jessie was anxious to find another man and get on with her life, and I encouraged her to do so as often as I could. I was so pleased that the people I cared about was so happy. Life was good again.

The last week in October, I noticed a change in Hubert's behavior. He'd gone to visit one of his friends three nights in a row the week before. But each time when he came home, he looked miserable. He wouldn't talk or eat much, and he plodded around the house with a puppy-dog look on his face. All the other times when he visited one of his boyfriends, he'd come home acting as giddy as a schoolboy. After more than twenty years, him suddenly changing his tune was a big concern for me.

I knew that whatever was bothering him didn't have nothing to do with money. Sister Baxter, the lady who used to watch him as a child, had finally died last week. Her family had spent a fortune on her funeral. Three elderly members of our church had passed this week, and Hubert had got two of the bodies. Four more was on their deathbeds and expected to leave this world at any moment. Folks was suddenly dying so fast now, Hubert and the other funeral home could barely keep up.

I didn't want to bring up nothing too soon; I thought Hubert was just going through a phase brought on by middle age. But after almost a month, with him looking gloomier by the day, I had to say something. It was Wednesday night, the week before Thanksgiving. We had just finished discussing our plans to have Thanksgiving supper with Claude, Maybelle, and Ma and Pa Wiggins. We was sitting up in bed. I was darning a pair of his favorite socks and he was flipping through a Sears, Roebuck and Company catalog. But there was a glazed look on his face that I couldn't ignore.

I set my darning items on the nightstand and leaned closer to Hubert and asked, "What's the matter with you?"

He sighed and gave me a blank look. I was mortified when I noticed he had tears in his eyes. That told me it was something seriously bothering him.

"Why do you ask?"

"You just seem different lately. Our money situation is in good shape now, so we ain't got nothing to worry about for a while."

"There is way more serious things besides money to worry about, Maggie."

I gave him a thoughtful look and patted his shoulder. "Well, I hope it don't have nothing to do with Claude. Things couldn't be going better for him. His marriage is going well and that coworker who had been giving him a hard time got fired."

"It ain't Claude. I got other things on my mind, though."

"Well, you know you can always talk to me about anything. Lord knows we ain't got no secrets."

He blinked and scrunched up his lips, but he wouldn't look at me now. "What you getting at?"

I cleared my throat and said something that made him look at me and gasp: "Well, I need to come clean about something that's been eating at me for a while."

"What did you do, Maggie?"

I geared up and took a couple of deep breaths so I could say what was on my mind and be done with it. "Claude and Maybelle keep asking me when we could all have supper at a restaurant in Mobile, and I keep giving them lame excuses."

Hubert hunched his shoulders and gave me a confused look. "How come you don't want to go back to Mobile, Maggie? If it's because you didn't like the restaurant we went to—even though you claimed you did—we could eat at a different one."

"I ain't never setting foot in that town again if I can help it!"

"Oh. Then is it because I spend so much time over there with my friends?"

"No, it ain't got nothing to do with your boyfriends." I had to stop talking for a few seconds so I could organize the words better that I wanted to let out. "Remember when on the way home from that restaurant in Mobile, you stopped at that gas station for me to use the toilet?" I had to pause and take another deep breath before I could get it all out. "I bumped into Claude's daddy. He looks like Claude's twin and he even got the same voice."

Hubert's eyebrows shot up so fast, it made my head swim. And the way he flinched! You would have thought I'd asked him to have sex with me.

"Say what? How come you just now telling me?"

"I didn't think it was that important."

"Maggie, the man is our son's daddy. Just knowing you bumped into him after all these years is unsettling to me. I pray to God he never figures out he got another child!" Hubert was talking so fast, I could barely understand what he was saying. "Did he know who you was? Did you talk to him?"

"Randolph recognized me right off the bat, but I told him he got me mixed up with some other woman. But that man ain't stupid. He didn't believe me for a minute. That was the real reason I was in such a rush to leave."

"Dammit! You could have told me before now!" he blasted. His tone was so harsh, I was the one flinching now.

"I know I should have, and it's been on my mind ever since." I couldn't believe how meek my voice sounded.

"Oh? Then how come you telling me now?" he asked, giving me a suspicious look. "Maggie, are you up to something I need to know about?"

I sighed. "Well, to tell you the truth, I'm telling you I seen Randolph, because I *don't like* being deceitful."

Hubert's eyebrows shot up again. "Ain't it a little late for that?"

"It is. But what I mean is, I don't like being deceitful *to you.* I don't care about fooling everybody else. I don't see no reason why anybody needs to know our marriage ain't for real. Don't you feel the same way?"

He was taking too long to answer and that made me nervous. I got even more nervous when he rose up off the bed and stood by the side with a distressed look on his face. I was not prepared for what he said next and it had nothing to do with the question I'd just asked.

"Maggie, I . . . I . . . um . . . see." He stopped stammering and then he blurted it out in one quick breath. "I'm glad you told me about seeing Randolph. And I'm glad you don't want to be deceitful with me, because I don't want to be deceitful to you neither . . ."

"Where you going with this, Hubert?" I asked, gazing at him from the corner of my eye.

"I declare, I been trying to decide the best time and way to tell you." He stopped talking and looked up at the ceiling. When he looked back at me, his lips was trembling so hard, I was surprised he was able to get another sentence out. And when he did, it was a bombshell.

"Maggie, this marriage ain't working for me no more."

Chapter 46

HUBERT'S WORDS SLAMMED INTO MY EARS LIKE BRICKS. I WAS IN such a state of shock, you could have knocked me to the floor with a leaf.

"What did you just say?"

"You heard me."

I tumbled out of bed and ran around to his side. I got so close to him, my face almost touched his.

"I heard you all right!" I screamed. "What you just said don't make no sense! I think them dead folks and the fumes from that embalming fluid is finally getting to you. That's the only reason I can think of for you to be talking out of your head all of a sudden."

Hubert moved back a few steps. I put my hands on my hips and got even closer to him. This time he stayed in the same spot, gazing at me like I was talking out of my head too.

"I ain't talking out of my head and them dead folks ain't got nothing to do with how I been feeling."

"Hubert, I know you inside out. This ain't—wait a minute. Is this a joke?"

"I ain't joking. I'm going to come clean to my folks about why we got married in the first place."

My jaw dropped so low, my cheeks ached. I wanted to grab Hubert and shake some sense into him, then wring his neck. But I was feeling so much rage, my body felt paralyzed. At that moment the only thing I could move was my mouth.

"W-Why do you want to 'come clean' about our marriage?"

"Maggie, this marriage ain't helping me be the man I want to be. I thought it would, but it ain't. If I don't do something to fix this mess I got myself in, I'll go crazy."

If he had slapped my face, I couldn't have been more stunned.

I gasped. "In the first place, this was *your* idea. And in the second place, you didn't say nothing about getting married so it would help you be the man you want to be. You gave me the impression that you wanted to get married and have a family so you could keep everybody from knowing you like men! After all this time you telling me *now* that you want a divorce?"

Hubert shook his head. "I do want a divorce eventually. I can't keep living such a unholy lie." He let out a low moan and then looked me straight in the eyes with a look of hopelessness on his face I'd never seen. "My mama and daddy ain't going to be around too much longer. All their lives they been proud of me and praise me all the time for being such a good husband and daddy."

"Well, you have been a good husband and daddy. All these years we been together, have *I* ever complained?"

"No. Not yet," he muttered, waving his hand and blinking about a mile a minute. So much blood had drained from his face, he looked a shade lighter.

"What do you mean 'not yet'? Are you telling me you been expecting me to complain?" I waved my finger in his face and would have slapped him if I had been the violent type.

"Don't twist my words, Maggie. The point is, I feel bad enough about being so deceitful. I can't let my folks go to their graves never knowing the real me. Once they get to heaven, they'll be looking down and seeing everything I do anyway. I don't want them to have to wait that long to find out they had a sissy for a son. They'd never rest in peace after that."

I swallowed hard. "Uh-uh! You are going to shock and upset your mama and daddy if . . ." I had to stop because it was hard for me to finish my sentence. Hubert finished it for me.

"Tell them *everything*? Yes, I am. I ain't leaving no stone unturned."

"You can't be serious!" I hollered. I stomped my foot so hard, a sharp pain shot up from the sole to the top of my ankle. "Hearing something like that would kill them!"

"Keeping up this masquerade is about to kill me!" he yelled. "Besides, my partner is going to tell his wife and the rest of his family about me and him."

"Hubert, your mama and daddy might be able to get through this. But once the word gets out, how long do you think it'd be before everybody in Lexington hears about you? Do you know what that would mean? Not only would your parents and everybody else look down on you, they'd look down on me. I'm the one that came from such a lowly background, so they'll probably put most of the blame on me for what we done. I'd be lucky if they didn't stone me like they did them unholy women in the Bible! And what about Claude? Don't you think you should really think this through before you do it? Once you confess, you'll never be able to take it back."

"I done thought this through and through. I ain't going to let that stop me, though. My mind is made up. My partner is giving up everything for me. As a Christian, I'm duty-bound to do the same thing for him. It's the least I can do for the man I love. Our family and friends have all been good to me and you. They deserve to know the truth about us. And it's high time."

"Maybe that's what you think, but I sure don't! Do you think family and them good friends will let you live in peace with a *man*?"

"They'll have a hard time dealing with it at first. But they'll get used to it. If they love me as much as I think they do, they'll be a little more understanding and forgiving, I hope. Doing what I do is a crime, so I don't think I have to worry about them telling the wrong people—if they tell anybody else at all. They know that the trouble I'd be in with the law would cause them even more pain. I know I'm taking a big risk by coming clean, but the pressure of hiding my true self done really took a toll on me and

I can't take too much more." He rubbed the back of his head, took a long deep breath, and went on. "Now you need to get some sleep because we both need to get up early in the morning to go to work."

"*Sleep?* After what you just told me, do you expect me to go to sleep like this is just another regular day?"

"Well, things will get messy, so it would benefit us both to be well-rested and clear-headed. We can't let this jeopardize our health."

"Too late. Everything on my body is about to shut down."

Hubert threw up his hands and looked at me with so much exasperation, I shuddered.

"You ain't got to get all dramatic. We need to be able to keep working because no matter what the outcome is, we'll still need money to pay our bills, Maggie."

"You just told me you're about to ruin all our lives. But have you thought about your daddy's position in the Church? What do you think his congregation will do? That is, if he still has a congregation when they hear this news?"

"I ain't worried about them. They'll have to deal with it in their own way. Now this conversation is over."

Hubert got back in the bed, pulled the covers up to his neck, and didn't say nothing else.

When I got in the bed, he was so close to the edge on his side, it was a wonder he didn't roll off. It didn't take long for him to start snoring like a mule. I was too angry and stunned to go to sleep. I got up and went to the living-room couch and sat there staring at the wall.

All kinds of thoughts was whirling around in my head. I was even reevaluating my feelings about sex. I knew other women who had been molested when they was kids. They still got married and had normal relationships. I was convinced that if me and Hubert hadn't got married, I probably would have met a man who would have made me forget about the things Mr. Royster had done to me. There was a good chance that that man could have given me the children I wanted.

And it could have even been Randolph Webb. Men didn't come no better than him, and they didn't stay single for too long. There was times over the years when I actually regretted tricking him into getting me pregnant. I blamed it mostly on the fact that me and Hubert had been so young and desperate to understand what we was doing. I truly believed that if we had been older, we wouldn't have done it.

While I was recollecting, I also thought about what I'd done to Daisy, Mr. Oswald, Orville, and Mason Burris. I couldn't blame what I did to them on me being too young to understand what I was doing. But I still felt that they'd got what they deserved. I wasn't proud of the fact that I was a murderer, but I truly believed that God would give me some mercy for all the good I'd done.

My thoughts was giving me a headache, but I managed to push them aside for the time being. The main thing on my mind now was what Hubert was about to do. I couldn't imagine what would become of Claude when everybody knew the truth about his daddy. They would probably think he was funny too! I couldn't stand the thought of my baby being teased and taunted the way I had been when I was young.

What would folks say when they found out Hubert wasn't Claude's daddy, and that we had found a stranger to get me pregnant? Good God! Hubert hadn't mentioned that. A chill ran up my spine. I leaped off the couch and trotted back into the bedroom and shook him until he woke up.

"Hubert, we need to talk about one more thing."

"Can't you tell I don't want to talk about this no more?" he said with a yawn. He didn't move until I mauled the side of his head with my fist. That made him yelp and sit bolt upright. "What the hell—"

"There is something else we need to discuss and I ain't letting you go back to sleep until we do."

"What?"

"If you tell everybody me and you never had relations, they'll know you ain't Claude's daddy."

"I done already told you, I was going to tell everything."

The pain of hearing them words was so bad, I got dizzy. I could feel my blood pressure rising. Everything from my chest to my throat tightened and I had to breathe through my mouth.

"So you're going to tell the world how we hunted up a man to get me pregnant?"

"What's the point of leaving that part out? Look, I done gave this a whole lot of thought and I know it's the Christian thing to do. You'll have to live with that. Shoot. I hope that by now you done got over them problems you had about having sex with a man. All you need to do is find the right one. You still got a few good years left on you, so you could still have more children."

"I ain't never getting married again," I said in a raspy tone.

Hubert hunched his shoulders and gave me the last kind of look I wanted to see: pity.

"Well, it's your life and you can do whatever you want. When I leave, as long as you stay single, I'll help you out with money as much as I can. Now get in this bed and go to sleep."

"I just need to know one more thing. Then I'll leave you alone."

"What?"

"You was one of the things that helped me get through the rough time I had growing up with the kind of parents I had. No matter what happens, I will always be grateful to you for being my friend back then. So, for old times' sake, is there anything I can say or do to make you change your mind?"

"Nope."

That one word sealed his fate.

Chapter 47

I SPENT THE NIGHT ON THE COUCH AND GOT UP AT THE CRACK OF dawn. When I went back into the bedroom, Hubert was in the bathroom. Everything felt so normal, I tried to convince myself that I had dreamed what he'd told me last night. I knew I hadn't, though, because I'd only slept a few minutes at a time the whole night.

When he came into the bedroom, I was sitting on my side of the bed. He flopped down on his side and started putting on his shoes. "Maggie, you doing all right?" He didn't even turn around to look at me.

"Hell no, I ain't doing 'all right.'" I couldn't believe he had the nerve to ask me such a dumb question. "Are you?"

"I'm at peace, Maggie. It's been a long time coming. I'm sorry I didn't make this decision five or ten years ago."

I gasped. "Do you mean to tell me that you been *unhappy* with me for that many years?"

"I didn't say I'd been 'unhappy.' I was happy with you, but I could have been happier . . . with somebody I really did love. I just can't do this no more. A smart woman like you ought to be able to understand where I'm coming from."

"I wish I'd been smart enough not to marry your 'happy' black ass!"

Hubert had finished putting on his shoes, but he still hadn't turned around to face me. I was glad he hadn't, because if he had seen the evil look on my face, he would have run out of the room like a scared rat.

"So you really going to go through with what you told me last night?"

He let out a disgusted sigh and whirled around to face me. "Ain't I made everything clear enough? How many more times do I have to tell you? Look, Maggie, this is just as hard on me as it is on you." He rubbed his head and started talking in a low, raspy tone. "Remember that time when I was a little boy and got that splinter stuck in the sole of my foot?"

"I remember. What's that got to do with anything?"

"It was stuck in so deep, even Mama couldn't get it out. I walked around in pain for days. It had stopped hurting so much, but it hurt enough to let me know it was still there. Anyway, Mama finally took me to the clinic and the doctor told her that if she hadn't brought me in when she did, that splinter might have caused a infection and they might have had to cut off my whole foot. I could have even died if gangrene had set in." Hubert paused and gave me a hopeless look. "Maggie, our marriage done become a splinter . . ."

It felt like he had rammed a knife in my back. "Being married to me made you feel that bad? You just said you'd been happy?" I sniffled as I wiped a few tears off my face. It was a wonder I hadn't already cried up a storm.

"I was, but . . ."

"But nothing. You used me!"

His mouth dropped open. "You used me too."

"I know I did. But I really was happy, up until last night. Do you really hate being married to me now?"

"Maggie, stop torturing yourself and me. Accept the fact that I'm going to end this marriage. Don't make me feel no worse than I already do."

I nodded. "It ain't easy, Hubert. But I want you to know now that I don't regret marrying you. I don't know what I would have done if we hadn't got married."

"You would have done just fine. Now, please promise me you'll be all right."

"I'll be as 'all right' as I'm going to be for somebody whose life is about to be turned upside down!" I boomed. "How soon do you plan on telling your folks?"

"I was planning to tell them tomorrow. I'll go over there after I get off work at the mill."

My head felt like it was about to explode. "What's the matter with you, Hubert?" I roared. My voice was so loud, my ears was aching. As thin as the walls in our house was, I decided to lower my tone. But now I was rasping like somebody in great pain. And I was.

"I declare, I can't believe what I'm hearing. Why do you want to rush and tell your mama and daddy something this serious the week before Thanksgiving? Can't you wait until after all the holidays?"

"You talking about several more weeks. I can't wait that long. I done put this off as long as I can," he grumbled.

"If you tell them tomorrow, it'll ruin Thanksgiving for them. I'm sure they won't have recovered by Christmas, so that'll be ruined too. Do you really want to do that? They're going to be hurt enough, so have some compassion and let them spend the rest of the year in harmony."

"Well, I'm sorry about that. But no matter what day I tell them, they'll be upset." He stood up and brushed off the sleeves of his shirt. "Claude is going to ride to Toxey with Maybelle and her cousin to visit some of their folks when he gets off work tomorrow. They'll be gone until Sunday night. By the time I see him again, the dust will have settled, and he might not take the news so hard."

"He already told me he would be too busy to visit us this weekend. I'm glad he'll be with his wife. That poor boy will need her more than ever. Praise the Lord he won't pop up at your folks' place while you telling them." I exhaled and stood up. "And I sure won't. I can't imagine how disappointed Ma Wiggins is going to be with me, knowing that I went along with your scheme. I don't know how and when I'll be able to face her and your daddy again."

"I can't help that," Hubert whined with a puppy-dog look on

his face. "But it might look better if you was there when I told them. Not just for my sake, but for yours too."

"Not a chance in hell. I don't want to see the hurt on their faces. I'll see it soon enough—if they ever speak to me again."

"Maggie, my folks love us both. For all we know, they might not take this as hard as we think. Oh, they will be upset. But at the end of the day, they will probably forgive and forget."

I nodded. "Okay, Hubert. You go tell them, but I ain't going with you. When do you plan on moving out?"

"I . . . I done already packed some of my clothes. I'll finish up this weekend."

"What about your work? You been at the turpentine mill for over twenty years! I doubt if the white folks you work for will let a man in your condition stay on there."

"My 'condition' ain't a disease. I'm funny, not afflicted. If it was catching, half of my coworkers would have turned sissy by now."

"And how many of the straitlaced Christian folks, do you think, will keep letting a sissy handle their loved ones' funerals? Have you thought about that?"

"I ain't worried about nary one of my jobs. I done already figured out what I'm going to do. I'm going to tell my boss at the turpentine mill that I quit. I promised Tyrone and Jerome years ago that if I ever wanted to quit undertaking, I'd turn the business over to them. I'll work out the details on paper when I can. It'll be a great opportunity for them. I done taught both of them everything Uncle Roscoe taught me, so they'll be good undertakers. Daryl . . . um . . . that's my friend's name, he's going to help me find work in Mobile."

"So you moving away too?"

Hubert gave me a stunned look. "What's wrong with you? Did you think I was going to stay on in this one-horse town with all these narrow-minded folks? I would never have a minute's peace."

"Poor Claude. He'll be devastated to know you ain't his birth daddy."

"I know. But I will always think of him as my son until the day

I die. Even if he chooses to have nothing to do with me after I drop the news."

I waved my hands in the air and shook my head. Then I rubbed my temples, but that didn't stop the throbbing pain I was feeling now. "I can't think straight right now. I just wish you had told me this sooner," I complained with my lips quivering and my jaws twitching. My body was breaking down, a part at a time. At the rate I was going, I'd be in a million little pieces before I knew it.

"Would it have made you feel any better?"

"No, but I would have had more time to digest it."

"Well, you still got until tomorrow. That ought to be enough time for you to digest everything and make plans for your future. One thing you might consider is having Jessie move in with you. She can help with the household bills and keep you company. Uh, I don't have much of a appetite, so I won't be eating breakfast with you this morning."

"I ain't got no appetite neither. But we got to eat something so we can keep up our strength. Something tells me we'll be needing a heap more of it for a while."

"I don't think it'll be that bad. Now that I've told you, I feel better already. Being as strong a woman as you are, I'm sure you will feel better in no time too. I declare, for the past few weeks, I been carrying around a load that was weighing so heavy on me, it's a wonder I ain't lost my mind." Hubert sighed with what sounded like relief. "I can already feel my appetite coming back, so I'm sure I'll want a nice big supper this evening. How about some pinto beans and rice?"

"That's what I had planned on cooking anyway. Um . . . I'm going to make a pot of gumbo again tomorrow. Do you think you'll have enough of a appetite then so we can have supper before you go to your parents' house? It will probably be our last meal together."

"If it'll make you feel better, I'd be glad to eat with you one more time—whether I have a appetite or not. And no matter what happens from this point on, I hope that when the shock wears off for you, we can still be friends."

"Yeah," I mumbled. "I think I'm going to go lay down for a little while."

"Good. You look like you need more rest."

I stretched out in the bed for a while and tossed, turned, and cried, until I got tired. When I got back up, Hubert was gone. Our car was in the driveway, so I assumed he'd walked to the mill or took the bus.

Somehow I managed to make it through the rest of the morning and afternoon without falling apart. The telephone rang at five p.m.; it was Hubert calling.

"I'll be home late. I'm going to go out for a while," he told me, sounding so distant he could have been calling from another country.

"Do you want me to leave a plate in the oven for you in case you come home after I go to bed?"

"Um . . . no, you don't have to worry about supper for me today. But I would still like some gumbo tomorrow evening before I go talk to Mama and Daddy."

"You can count on it," I said.

Chapter 48

EIGHT P.M. CAME AND WENT, AND HUBERT HADN'T COME HOME. I figured he'd been picked up after work to go to Mobile so he could celebrate his upcoming "freedom" with Daryl. Just thinking about the name of his current boyfriend made my skin crawl.

I didn't even bother to cook no supper. I couldn't have ate nothing if somebody had paid me. I wandered around the house, cussing under my breath one minute, praying the next. I was still hoping I was in a bad dream and would wake up any minute. I even pinched myself several times to make sure I wasn't asleep.

A few minutes before nine p.m., Jessie pounded on my front door, but I played possum and didn't let her in. I couldn't talk to her or anybody else at the moment. I wanted to spend my last days as a wife alone.

Hubert didn't come home at all Thursday night. When I got up Friday morning, I went to work as usual. While I was at Mrs. Finley's house doing the ironing, he called me up at ten a.m. He had never called me at work before, so I immediately thought something was wrong.

"What's the matter?" I asked with my heart racing.

"Nothing. I'm fine."

"Mrs. Finley don't like her help getting personal phone calls," I said in a low tone. Mrs. Finley was outside, but she could walk in any minute.

"Don't worry. I ain't going to talk long. This will be the first and last time I call you at work."

"Okay. But be quick."

I had never felt so awkward talking to Hubert before in my life. I was hoping he wouldn't say nothing that would make me go to pieces at work. The last thing I needed—especially now—was to lose another job. I decided to try and keep the conversation light.

"Where you at, Mobile?"

"Uh-huh. Daryl wanted me to be with him yesterday when he told his wife."

"Oh? How did she take it?" Holding my breath for a few seconds and rubbing my chest helped keep me calm.

"Not good. She lit into him like a wildcat. Daryl was so upset, he left with the clothes on his back and we checked into a motel. He called his house to talk to his kids last night. They told him they never wanted to see or talk to him again."

It didn't make me feel no better knowing that another woman was in the same boat I was in. I was so sorry for her, it felt like I was going to go to pieces sooner than I thought.

"Well, I ain't surprised. So, do you still want to have supper with me this evening?"

"Yes, I do. I meant what I said about having one more bowl of your gumbo."

"I'm glad to hear that."

"Please don't forget to set aside a bowl for me before you dump in the cayenne pepper."

"Hubert, I been separating your portion for over twenty years. You don't have to keep reminding me."

"I know. But a few times you did forget, and I had the runs for days. I just need to make sure you don't forget this time. Anyway, I'm pleased to hear you sounding so much better. I don't feel so bad now."

I took my time responding. I wasn't quite sure if I really wanted to say what was on my mind. But since I didn't have nothing else to lose, I bit the bullet and let the words spurt out.

"Hubert, did you mean what you said about us still being friends?"

"I sure did. They say that time heals all wounds. If you still want to be in my life, I want you in it. I hope that eventually Claude will want the same thing in time."

"I'm glad you feel that way. I'll see you when you get home."

"I'm going to spend a few more hours in Mobile, but I'll be at the funeral home this afternoon around three. I spoke to Tyrone a few minutes ago. He told me him and Jerome picked up Brother Porter's body this morning. He had a massive stroke last night. He was the nicest usher that ever worked for Daddy, and I'd like to be the one to get him situated for his home-going. I don't plan on hanging around for the funeral, though. Something tells me that Daddy and Mama won't like me being present at the service on Monday no how." Hubert sucked on his teeth and moaned. "I declare, Brother Porter is one body I wish the Fuller Brothers had got. Oh, well. Anyway, I'll probably be home no later than four or five. I . . . I'm planning to go over and talk to Mama and Daddy around seven."

"All right, then. I'll see you this evening."

I knew I'd eventually get over Hubert's betrayal. But I wasn't sure about my son. Claude was the most important person in my life, and I would *always* do what I had to do to keep him safe and happy. I knew that he was going to be mad at Hubert and might never speak to him again. My worst nightmare was that he'd be mad at me too for being part of the deception. All I could do at this point was hope for the best.

When I got home at three p.m., I went directly to the kitchen and got the gumbo started. Then I went to the bedroom closet. I had put the arsenic in a paper bag and set it on the shelf behind several bottles of my smell-goods. I hadn't used any since Mason Burris's birthday dose, so there was more than enough left for me to do what I had to do.

While the gumbo was simmering, I called the funeral home to talk to Hubert. My heart was beating like a drum. If he had decided to go to his parents' house before he came home for supper, it would be too late. I had to get to him in time. I almost passed out with relief when he answered the phone.

"Something's come up." I didn't give him time to ask what. "A lady I met when I was working for Mrs. Dowler called me up a few minutes ago. She asked if I could come help her serve at a party she's throwing this evening. Her name is Mrs. Blake. One of her servants got sick and had to go home early. She was so desperate, I felt sorry for her. I told her I'd come. Um . . . I don't know how long the party is going to go on, so there is no telling what time I'll get home. Probably not before nine. I hope you won't be needing the car tonight."

"I won't. Daryl is going to meet me somewhere and pick me up after I leave Mama and Daddy's house tonight. Me and him will go back to that motel, I guess." There was a awkward moment of silence. "Well, if you got to go work a party tonight, I guess me and you won't be having supper together tonight, huh? I was counting on having that gumbo."

"You can still have some. It's almost done. I started cooking it as soon as I got home this afternoon. I was at loose ends, and I needed to do something other than sit around listening to the radio or more of Jessie's gossip."

Hubert took his time responding. "Maggie, I hope you won't be at 'loose ends' too often. I feel bad enough—"

"Hubert, we don't need to discuss that subject no more. I done accepted it."

"Do you still not want to be with me when I go tell Mama and Daddy? If you do, I'll wait until you finish up with the Blake woman's party and do it then. I hope they don't go to bed before I get there."

"No. I don't want to be there when you tell them."

"Okay. By the way, I'm going to let you keep the car. Daryl's got a truck and we don't need two vehicles. And you can have the house too. I'll take my name off the deed and it'll be yours, free and clear."

"Thanks. I appreciate that. Okay. I have to get off this phone and get ready to go to Mrs. Blake's house. I'll leave your bowl in the icebox. All you'll have to do is heat it up."

I left the house half a hour after my conversation with Hubert. As much as I didn't like to drive, I drove up and down a few back roads for a while and then I drove all the way to the next county and back twice. That killed a little over two hours. That should have been more than enough time for Hubert to have made it to the house and ate his last supper. I prayed he had died with some dignity. I figured that when he'd started feeling sick, he'd stumbled to the bedroom or the couch. All I had to do now was go home and put on the performance of my life.

My butt was numb from sitting so long in the car. I had cramps in my legs by the time I got back to Lexington. When I turned onto my block, my eyes got big when I seen Jessie, Sister Burris, and a few other neighbors coming out my front door. I smiled because each one looked distressed.

As soon as I parked and piled out of the car, Jessie dashed off the porch and ran toward me, flapping her arms like she was fixing to take flight. "Praise the Lord you here!" she hollered.

"What in the world is going on?" I asked, freezing in my tracks. I looked up at Sister Burris. She and other folks on my porch suddenly started boo-hooing like they was at a funeral.

"Oh, Maggie! It's a mess!" Jessie boomed. She was wringing her hands and shifting her weight from one foot to the other. "Poor Hubert!"

The first thing that came to my mind was that Jessie had entered my house and found Hubert dead. But I had to hear her tell me that.

"You better tell me what's going on and you better do it fast! I can take only so much! Is Hubert home?" I asked as we tramped up the porch steps.

"Yeah, he's all right. Sister Burris drove him to the clinic and back, but he's a wreck! I swear to God, I never thought something like this would happen."

I was in such a state of shock and confusion, I couldn't tell which way was up.

"What happened?"

My body felt like it had turned to mush. If Jessie hadn't put her arm around my shoulder when she did, I would have crumpled to the ground.

"Go to your husband, girl. We'll give y'all some privacy," Jessie answered, pushing me toward the door.

I opened it and darted inside. Hubert was sitting on the living-room couch, rocking back and forth, crying like a baby. My head was spinning like a top. I couldn't believe he was still alive if he'd eaten the tainted gumbo. I had put in twice as much arsenic as I'd given Orville, so he should have been dead! What I couldn't understand was if he'd been to the clinic, why hadn't they kept him? Nothing was making sense.

The only thing I could think of was that he hadn't eaten any of the gumbo. Because if he had swallowed one spoonful, he'd be dead. But then why would he go to the clinic and be back home now looking as healthy as I was? I didn't want to mention the gumbo until I knew exactly what was going on.

I was panting like a big dog as I leaned over and whispered in his ear, "Did you tell them folks on our porch about . . . you know?"

He shook his head so hard, sweat and tears splashed off his face onto mine. "I ain't told nobody nothing about us. And I ain't going to."

I stood up straight and reared back on my legs. "Then why is Jessie and all them neighbors outside so upset? She told me Sister Burris took you to the clinic! What for? And what do you mean you ain't going to tell folks nothing about us?"

"Like I just said, I didn't tell nobody nothing about me or our marriage, and I ain't going to."

"W-what . . . w-why did you go to the clinic? You sick?" I stuttered.

Hubert shook his head again. His lips was moving, but no words was coming out of his mouth.

I was so confused, I didn't know what to say next. The next thing I said came out in a croak: "Thank God you didn't tell nobody our business. Now poor Claude won't have to know—" I stopped talking when I seen the strange look on Hubert's face.

"Maggie, Claude is dead."

Chapter 49

When Hubert told me he was going to come clean about our marriage and every other lie we'd been living, I thought that was the worst thing I'd ever hear from him. But what he'd just said was a hundred times more devastating. His statement sent shock waves in every direction throughout my body.

I slapped the side of my head and narrowed my eyes. And then I rubbed my ears.

"What did you say?" It was my voice, but it was so hoarse and loud, I almost didn't recognize it.

"Claude is dead," Hubert repeated. "Sister Burris helped me get him to the clinic. But by the time we got there, it was too late."

I stared at him and shook my head so hard, I thought my brains was going to bust out of my skull.

"No. No. That can't be true," I whimpered.

"The folks at the clinic think it was a heart attack."

"W-what in the world are you talking about? Claude didn't have no bad heart! There was nothing wrong with his health!"

"It don't matter what it was. One of the doctors at the clinic said if it wasn't a heart attack, it could have been a couple of other things. Last year a young girl was brought to the clinic and she dropped dead out of the blue. She had been the picture of health until then. Her folks told the doctor how she'd had a couple of fits the day before. Another thing the doctor said was that Claude could have had a stroke. That's what I think it was, or something just as serious. He had wheezed, shuddered, and vomited blood all the way to the clinic. Before we could get him inside, he had a spasm. I don't think we'll ever know what really happened to our boy. Them quacks at that place don't know as much as they need to. It's a damn shame colored folks can't go to them real educated white doctors. I know they would find out what caused my son's death!"

Hubert stopped talking and shed some more tears. When he stopped, he looked up at me with the most desperate look I ever seen on a man's face.

"Maggie, we done lost him. I could have lived with him not wanting me in his life no more if he found out the truth about me. But I never thought I'd lose him this way."

I was in such a daze, the words was forming and coming out of my mouth on their own. It seemed like I wasn't in control of nothing.

"He was supposed to go with Maybelle and one of her cousins to visit her folks in Toxey this evening. That's where I thought he was."

"He was going to do just that, but one of his friends wanted him to go with him to help check out a car he wanted to buy. The man selling it told him he had to come this evening, or he would sell it to somebody else. Claude's friend told him he'd give him a ride to Maybelle's folks' house afterward. I told Claude to slide through here so he could get him some gumbo before it was all gone. The real reason I wanted to see him was because I thought it might be the last time I got to spend time with him. He came right away.

"While I was in the bathroom, he heated up part of what you'd put in the icebox for me. Not long after he finished eating, he said he didn't feel good. So he went to go lay down before his friend came to pick him up. Seeing him looking so innocent, I knew I couldn't hurt him the way Daryl had hurt his kids. I realized then that there was no way I could tell anybody about me and our marriage. As it turned out, it *was* the last time

I got to spend with my son." Hubert choked up again. "While he was laying on the couch, he suddenly started having some kind of fit. And then he was vomiting blood. Jessie said Orville had vomited blood when his heart gave out so at first I thought it was Claude's heart too. I was so beside myself, I didn't know which way was up. That's when I ran out on the front porch and hollered for Sister Burris to come help me. We didn't even take time to wash him off and change his shirt. Once we got him on the road and halfway to the clinic, he wet his pants and—."

I didn't want to hear no more details at the time, so I cut Hubert off. "W-where is he?" I asked, almost choking on my words.

Hubert sniffed and swallowed hard before he answered. "I had Jerome and Tyrone take the hearse over to the clinic to pick him up. Mama and Daddy went to Toxey to pick up Maybelle and they should be here any minute. And then we can all go to the mortuary together and . . ."

Hubert couldn't finish his sentence. He screwed up his face and started crying so hard, I couldn't stand to look at him any longer.

The light was on in the room, but all I could see in front of me now was darkness. *I have killed my child.* If Satan had reached up from hell and pulled me down there with him, I wouldn't have cared. That was where I belonged. I had murdered *five* people in less than five months! I didn't say nothing else. As overwrought as Hubert was now, he probably wouldn't have heard me anyway.

My in-laws arrived twenty minutes later. They stormed the house like gangbusters, with Jessie right behind them. She and Ma and Pa Wiggins stopped in the middle of the living-room floor, looking dazed and confused. Maybelle rushed over to the couch, where me and Hubert was huddled together.

"I . . . I don't know what I'm going to do now! Claude was my whole world!" she screamed as she fell to her knees.

Jessie was wringing her hands and shifting her weight from one foot to the other. Ma Wiggins flopped down in the chair facing us, crying and babbling. Pa Wiggins looked so rigid, it seemed like he was glued in place.

"I can't believe this! He was such a healthy boy! Other than the measles, Claude ain't never been sick a day in his life!" Pa Wiggins paused and lowered his tone. "Well, I guess it was his time to go," he said, giving me a sympathetic look.

"That's the truth," Ma Wiggins agreed with a nod. "But we ain't never questioned the Lord's motives and we ain't going to do that now."

We all whooped and hollered and prayed out loud for the next five minutes. When it got quiet enough, I muttered, "I want to go see my son."

"We'll go see him directly. Let's calm down first," Hubert told me.

"I want to see my baby now," I insisted. I gave Hubert a sharp look. "You don't have to take me to him, I'll drive myself." My legs felt like jelly, but I was able to stand up anyway.

"Maggie, you ain't in no shape to be driving or even leaving this house—especially to go gaze at that boy in the state he is in," Pa Wiggins said. He walked up to me and put his hands on my shoulders. "Why don't you go in the bedroom and lay down for a spell? You look like you might fall down any minute."

I swallowed a huge lump and shook my head. "I'll lay down for a little while, but I ain't going to sleep tonight until I go see my child."

I spun around and scurried out of the room. When I got to my bedroom, I threw myself facedown on the bed and cried some more.

Half a hour later, I stopped crying, but I felt even worse. When I pictured Claude's coffin being lowered into the ground, I stumbled back to the living room.

Jessie rushed up to me and caressed the side of my face. "Maggie, I was just saying that it's a good thing that you and Hubert still young enough to have another child," she mumbled.

I whirled around and gawked at Hubert with my mouth hanging open. He gave me a sheepish look and turned his head away real quick.

"We tried for years to have more children," he said with a heavy sigh. "I guess it wasn't meant to be . . ."

"And that's a shame," Jessie said with a sniff. She sat down next to Hubert and put her hand on his shoulder. "I declare, if God created a son better than Claude, he kept him for Hisself. Hubert, the boy was so much like you. Not only did he favor you from head to toe, he had the same upstanding, generous, loving personality. Brother, you done real good. It just goes to show that good stock breeds good stock."

"Y'all, let's all keep in mind that our bodies is only on loan to us. Maggie, you and Hubert should be thankful that God let y'all borrow Claude for twenty-one years," Pa Wiggins pointed out.

"Amen to that. Let's all be thankful that we'll see the boy again when our time is up," Ma Wiggins tossed in.

I sucked in a deep breath and blinked back a few more tears. "I'm going to go to the mortuary and spend a few minutes with my child," I announced in a firm tone. "And don't nobody try to stop me."

Everybody gasped.

Jessie leaped up off the couch. "I'll go with you," she said, giving me a hopeless look.

I shook my head. "You ain't going no place," I insisted. "As bad as you look, you need to sit yourself back down and just rest."

"Then I'll go with you," Hubert said, wobbling up off the couch.

"No! I want to be alone with him!" I hollered.

"But, Maggie, Claude was Hubert's son too!" Jessie yelled. "Let him go with you. You ain't in no shape to be driving no how."

Pa Wiggins stomped to the middle of the floor with his hands in the air. "We can all go see him tonight," he said.

"I don't want to see him until . . . until the wake," Ma Wiggins said, choking on a sob.

"Maggie, why don't you wait until tomorrow, when we'll all be feeling better? You can come to the house first and help me pick out what he'll be buried in," Maybelle suggested in a low weak tone.

"Okay," I mumbled.

I held my breath and looked from one face to the other. I wanted to run out of the room, but I was rooted in my spot like a oak tree. I couldn't believe how much misery I had caused. Especially to myself. And I didn't see no end to my pain. Every inch of my body was aching, and my head felt like somebody had stuck a time bomb in it that was about to go off any second.

"We got a lot of planning to do in the next few days. I guess we should leave and let y'all get some rest," Ma Wiggins said as she rubbed the side of her head. "Unless y'all want us to spend the night?"

Hubert waved his hand. "Y'all can go on home."

He hugged everybody and walked them out. When he came back in, he gave me a quick hug.

"Maggie, Sister Burris and everybody else done left the porch, but I know everybody will be back tomorrow. For now, we really need to go to bed and get some rest before we fall to the floor. You look like you about to keel over. If you still look this bad in the morning, I'm going to take you to the clinic."

"Don't worry about me," I said, waving him away. "I'm going to be just fine."

When me and Hubert finally went to bed a few minutes later, we was so exhausted, it didn't take long for us to go to sleep. I was pleased because that was one way to put everything on hold. I wasn't pleased for long because Claude came to me in a dream.

It looked like he was in a room with nothing but darkness surrounding him. He didn't say nothing, and I couldn't either. He was smiling and beckoning with both hands for me to join him! That was the straw that broke the camel's back.

When I abruptly woke up, the pain was so much more unbearable, I knew that there was no way I would be able to make it through my son's funeral without losing what was left of my mind. And I knew I'd never be able to look at him again period. So going to the funeral home in the morning with Hubert and everybody else was out of the question. Especially because I knew that I was the reason Claude was there.

Was I going to be able to live with myself now and watch the rest of the family suffer because of what I'd done? The answer was no.

I had been taught all my life that suicide was the worst form of murder. According to Pa Wiggins and every other preacher I knew, it was the only sin even God would never forgive. The only way I could make things easier for everybody was to make my death look natural too.

I eased out of bed and tiptoed to my bedroom closet to get the arsenic again. And then I shuffled into the kitchen. My hands was shaking when I dipped a cup of gumbo out of the pot and put it in a bowl. I didn't even bother to heat it before I dumped in what was left of the arsenic, which was the biggest dose of all.

I wrapped the empty container in a dishrag, took it outside, and hid it up under a pile of other garbage in the trash can. Nobody would have no reason to root around in the trash before it went to the dump on Monday. If everybody knew what I'd done to myself, they would probably get suspicious about Claude's death! The thought of anybody thinking I'd killed my son sent a sharp pain up my spine. Even in death I didn't want nobody to think I was a monster.

When I got back to the kitchen, I ate the gumbo as fast as I could, because I knew it would take only about a hour for it to end my pain. I had nothing else to live for and this was the quickest and only way out for me. I started to feel the effects of the arsenic right away. The inside of my throat felt like somebody had set it on fire. I covered my mouth with both hands to keep from screaming. The next thing I knew, I was vomiting blood and my head was spinning as I staggered to the living room and plopped down on the couch. I wanted to die in the same spot where my baby had last laid down in the house. Before I lost consciousness, I prayed that Claude would forgive me. Being the kind of man we'd raised him to be, I knew he would.

READING GROUP GUIDE

MRS. WIGGINS

Mary Monroe

ABOUT THIS GUIDE

The suggested questions that follow are included to enhance your group's reading of this book.

DISCUSSION QUESTIONS

1. Homosexuality was a taboo subject in small black Southern communities during the 1910s through 1930s. Did you think Hubert was being selfish for talking Maggie into a sham marriage to help him conceal his true sexuality? He convinced her that it would be a smart move for them both. Do you agree?

2. Maggie and Hubert were intelligent, hardworking, humble people who wanted everyone to believe they were a "normal" married couple. Because of all the lies they had to tell to keep everyone in the dark about their relationship, did you think they would be able to sustain a marriage that was based on deceit?

3. Hubert made it clear to Maggie before their marriage that he would never have sex with her. She didn't care because she had no interest in it anyway. But they desperately wanted to be parents. Did you think their plan to search for an unsuspecting stranger and set him up to father a child with Maggie was coldhearted and selfish?

4. Randolph Webb was a good man who didn't deserve to be used as Maggie's sperm donor. Was this upsetting to you?

5. Maggie and Hubert doted on their son, Claude. Did they go too far by interfering in twenty-one-year-old Claude's relationship with much older Daisy Compton?

6. If your answer to question #5 is yes, what would you do if a conniving woman like Daisy took advantage of your son?

7. When Maggie realized how dangerous Daisy was, she decided to take matters into her own hands. Were you surprised she resorted to murder?

8. When Maggie went to work for the charming and charitable Mrs. Dowler, it gave Maggie a new outlook on life. They became good friends and Maggie earned more money than ever. When Mrs. Dowler's lecherous brother, Oswald, moved into her home and forced Maggie to perform sex acts with him, she chose to murder again. Should she have told Mrs. Dowler what was going on, quit her job, or continued to submit to Oswald's demands just to hold on to her "dream" job?

9. Maggie felt justified in killing anyone who caused her grief. Did you predict more murders after the second one?

10. By the time Maggie killed her second, third, and fourth victims within five months after the first one, did you think she'd lost touch with reality?

11. Maggie was devastated when Hubert told her that not only was he going to end their marriage, he was also going to let everyone know it was a sham, reveal his homosexuality, and move in with his lover. Her main concern was the impact Hubert's actions would have on Claude, other relatives, friends, and the wholesome image she'd maintained in her church and community for so many years. Did you predict how she would stop Hubert from hurting so many people?

12. When Maggie's plan to murder Hubert with arsenic backfired and Claude accidentally became her next victim, it was more than she could stand. Were you surprised she committed suicide?

13. Because of all the traumatic events Maggie had endured in her lifetime, did you feel sorry for her in the end?